NO CORNERS FOR THE DEVIL

Although relative newcomers to the old round house, the Baxter family have been welcomed into the close-knit farming community on the Roseland Peninsula in Cornwall. In this idyllic setting, the body of a teenage girl is found on the beach by the Baxters' younger boy. Sally Baxter finds herself protecting one son and fighting for the other, while trying to get closer to her teenage daughter and fathom her husband's odd attitude to the murder. The investigating officer, DCI Channon, calm, capable and honest, finds himself drawn increasingly to the family at the round house, and especially Sally herself.

NO CORNERS FOR
THE DEVIL

No Corners For The Devil

by

Olive Etchells

Magna Large Print Books
Long Preston, North Yorkshire,
BD23 4ND, England.

British Library Cataloguing in Publication Data.

Etchells, Olive
    No corners for the devil.

    A catalogue record of this book is
    available from the British Library

    ISBN   0-7505-2550-9
    ISBN   978-0-7505-2550-3

First published in Great Britain 2005
by Constable & Robinson Ltd.

Cover illustration by arrangement with Constable & Robinson

Published in Large Print 2006 by arrangement with
Constable & Robinson Ltd.

Magna Large Print is an imprint of Library Magna Books Ltd.

Printed and bound in Great Britain by
T.J. (International) Ltd., Cornwall, PL28 8RW

For my sister and fellow writer,
Edith (Abigail) Gordon,
with my love

For their expertise, willingly shared, and their advice, gratefully accepted, my sincere thanks to:

David Robert Price,
Police Superintendent (retired)
Stephen Merritt, organic farming adviser
My son Daniel Etchells,
computer specialist

Chapter One

It was silent on the beach: no seabirds crying, no wind whistling through the grasses of the cliff top, not a soul to be seen. Even the water was quiet, the tide ebbing like silk across the glistening sand.

Two young boys ran down the track from a cluster of white houses set among trees. They climbed the low stone breakwater and looked out to sea, the older boy thrilled by the sight of the perfect little beach. Sometimes he wondered if one day he would get tired of it, but he never did. It always gave him what he thought of as 'the wobbly feeling' inside his chest, especially when everything was gold and silver and blue, like this morning. He concealed such feelings from his companion, who seemed to take such surroundings for granted.

Rolling up the legs of their jeans and tossing their trainers aside, they set off side by side on their daily inspection of the high-water line; two boys alike in interests but not in appearance: the eleven-year-old big for his age and very fair, the younger one dark, wiry and quick-moving.

Examining the beach was an activity of

which they never tired, the high spot of their day. They collected plastic bags and bottles and other washed-up rubbish and put it in the litter bin; everything else was examined with care and the best items kept in their secret den. Once in the winter they had found what they thought was a bottle of whisky, only to watch in dismay as the grown-ups sniffed at it and then poured it down the loo.

Today the tide had brought little of interest: merely an old tin can, a satin-smooth twist of driftwood, a red clothes peg and a baby's plastic duck. The younger boy eyed the meagre collection in disgust. 'Oh, come on,' he urged, 'let's explore the pools.'

They ran to the rocks at one end of the beach and clambered around, stamping on seaweed to pop the pods. The pools left by the tide were ice-cold and contained no crabs or fishes, so they fell to shying stones into the departing sea and then hiding behind rocks to have a pretend gun-fight. In his excitement the older boy slipped and almost went face down into a dark little pool. Laughing, he raised himself and then stared down into the shadows. 'Hey!' he shouted. 'Look!'

A hand lay in the water, curved fingers beckoning. The tips of the fingers were blue – dark blue, and dimpled. With the plastic duck in mind the boy told himself that this must be plastic as well. He touched the hand and found it very cold – heavy yet not quite solid, like rubber. Pushing aside a tangle of seaweed he saw that the hand was attached to an arm in a knitted white sleeve, with a fern-like drift of weed around the elbow. 'Look!' he cried again as the younger boy scrambled to his side. 'Look here!'

The other stared, then cleared the water with his hands, revealing more white sweater and the back of a blonde head with long hair wafting to the surface. Legs in blue jeans were under the water as well, bent at an angle around the far side of the rock. 'It's a girl!' he gasped. 'No – a woman!' Clutching at his head like a bad actor in a melodrama, he cried: 'It's a dead body!'

At that they both raised their eyes to the cliff face above them. It was yellow-grey, with tufts of grass growing from the rock and at the top a tangle of brambles and gorse spiking dark against the sky. They looked at each other, thrilled and yet repelled, then the younger one took charge. 'She's fallen over the edge,' he announced firmly. 'Let's turn her over. She might be from the village – we might know her.'

The older boy was telling himself not to be sick. The hand had been firm and very cold – not a child's hand, yet not as big as his mother's. 'Don't touch,' he muttered thickly. 'You're not supposed to touch dead bodies.'

Annoyed with himself, the younger one blinked defensively. 'I know *that*,' he protested, 'everybody knows *that*. We'll – we'll have to get the police. Let's go and tell your mum and dad.'

Climbing back over the rocks they raced across the sand and then ran barefoot and intent towards the white houses in the trees. Behind them the little beach basked in the morning sun, silent again except for the soft slap of the waves.

Chapter Two

Solitude ... solitude ... solitude. Did every woman who loved her family yearn to get away from them? Sally parked her car near St Mawes Castle and headed for the National Trust land overlooking the glistening waterway of the Carrick Roads.

Perhaps not *every* woman, she decided, but if they'd all had a year like she'd just had it would be ninety-nine per cent of them. There had been times when she would have liked to be a hermit, living in a remote shack on Bodmin Moor or an isolated little house back in Lancashire – maybe on a windswept hillside in the Pennines.

But not any longer. The upheaval of the

move was over, the long arguments half forgotten, the children reconciled to the move – or almost. The family was settled here in this wonderful, beautiful, tranquil place that could have been a million miles from Manchester.

She walked past the big houses facing the water, then on to the open fields, which were deserted. Of course it was early in the year for holidaymakers – early in the day, come to that. It was a Saturday, not yet 9 a.m., and she should have been doing a mammoth shop in Truro instead of indulging her craving for peace and quiet. She had driven miles out of her way just to come here, which was mad when she could have achieved solitude at home merely by walking in either direction along the coastal path.

It was odd that the last year should seem in retrospect an eternity, because wasn't time supposed to fly when you were rushed off your feet? Now, it felt as if she'd been living in another life the day Rob marched in and said to them all: 'Right. How would you like to move to Cornwall?'

It *had* been another life, of course, in the big, red-brick house on the outskirts of Manchester: the good state schools, Rob doing well at work while she adored her freelance job in the classier shops of the city – her own treasured, creative little earner... All that had been the good side. The bad was Ben's asthma, the chemical works half a mile away, the burglaries they'd suffered, and finally, the shooting at the end of their road. That, as Rob put it with an angry lack of originality, was the last straw.

They hadn't known the victim, he'd just been shot as he drove along the main road. 'A drugs killing,' the police told them with weary resignation. 'Sorry you've been upset. A lot of the big dealers are moving out of the more dodgy areas to places like this, but we're doing all we can to keep the situation under control.'

'Not wipe it out,' Rob had said grimly that night in bed. 'Not eradicate it. Oh, no, they're hoping to control it – big deal! Sal – we've got to get away from here. If I started up on my own I could work from anywhere in Britain.'

Anywhere in Britain had turned out to be the Roseland Peninsula in South Cornwall, and every day Sally told herself that they could have done much worse. Now, she sat on a bench at her favourite vantage point – rising ground with a view of both the open sea and the broad curve of the river.

Two yachts were scudding along in mid-channel, one with white sails, the other with yellow. She watched them, idly thinking that a wind must be getting up to enable them to move so fast. There had been neither wind nor breeze when she left home just after eight, not so much as a flutter among the new green foliage of the garden. The air had been soft and sweet, like honey in a bowl...

Now she could see clouds coming in from the south-west, distant but purposeful. Not rain on the way, she thought – not today, with the first tenants of the season due to arrive that afternoon ... their first holiday bookings, the cottages ready and waiting, equipped down to the last teaspoon. Half the groceries she was about to buy were what the visitors had asked for on their shopping lists.

For the hundredth time she wondered what it would feel like to help families enjoy their holidays, to have them living in the four little houses that had been up for sale along with their converted roundhouse. From the moment he first saw the place there had been no stopping Rob; he had swept her along on the tide of his enthusiasm, tempting her: 'A completely round house, love, built in the last century by a minister of the church. There are quite a few in that part of Cornwall, and there's four holiday cottages in the deal – if we can let them the income will almost cover the mortgage. They all need doing up so you can have a free hand with the decor – you know you'd like that. As for letting them – I'll advertise on the Web, and do it all direct...'

They sold the Manchester house with

surprising speed and ten months later here they were – ready for their first visitors, and if she hadn't worked like a dog she wouldn't have been able to sit here gazing across the Carrick Roads as if she hadn't a care in the world. She'd needed it though – needed a brief slowing down before they took this new direction in their lives. All at once light-hearted, she was smiling to herself as she walked back to the car; a plump, energetic figure, her dark hair ruffled by the rising wind.

The clouds were still far distant as she drove back through the little town of St Mawes.

Still in high good humour after a whizz round the Truro shops and a long session at the supermarket, Sally drove along between tall hedgerows fronting farmland. Ahead of her lay Curdower beach, and home.

When they first arrived she'd been petrified on the steep, single-track roads; red-faced and sweating when she'd needed to reverse in the face of a rare, oncoming car. But in time she'd adjusted, realizing that there was no need to do anything quickly: holidaymakers were usually good-humored and Cornish drivers far more relaxed than those in Lancashire. Within a matter of weeks she'd been using the maze of narrow roads around Curdower village with calm assurance.

She rounded the last bend and there below her lay the beach, gold against the blue-green of the sea and the vast pale bowl of the sky. It registered that there were what looked like long white streamers stretched across the cobbled slope down to the sand, and was that – yes, it was a police car! She was at the roundhouse before she could take another look and then she had to brake hard. A second police car was parked just inside the gates, next to Rob's Discovery. She heard a frightened squeal and realized that it was coming from her. 'Shut up,' she said out loud, and threw herself out of the car. It was Luke – he'd had an accident on his motorbike. They should never have let him have it, she'd said as much. Was it a pile-up on the main road? Cars, lorries, a bus?

Rob opened the front door before she reached it. He looked big and fair and capable the same as always, but she saw at once that his upper lip was tight against his teeth and that he was blinking rapidly behind his glasses. 'What is it?' she asked fearfully.

'Where the hell have you *been?*' he demanded. 'You never said you'd be away for hours!'

It was something awful! 'What's happened, Rob? Is somebody hurt?'

'No, somebody's dead!' he snapped. 'A dead body on the beach – our beach. Ben found it, Ben and Malachi. I've told you before that kid's a weirdo.'

She stared up at him. What had that to do with it? And if anybody was a weirdo in Malachi's family, it was his mother Zennie. But it seemed that Luke was all right, thank God. She wallowed in relief and at once was ashamed. Somebody was dead, for heaven's sake. 'Who is it?' she asked. 'Rob – whose body is it?'

'How should I know? I just had a quick look to make sure they weren't imagining it. It was a – a girl – a young woman. They've taken her away.'

Sally looked at the car. 'Are the police indoors?'

'They were here earlier, taking statements from Ben and Malachi and having a word with Tessa. They're all down on the beach now.'

'Where are the boys?'

'Ben's in his room. He's a bit upset. He's been sick and Tessa's sitting with him. Malachi's gone home with his mother. I rang her and told her to get down here for when the police talked to him.'

'Where's Luke?' she asked.

Rob shrugged irritably. His manner was hostile, to say the least, but why? Because she hadn't been here when he needed her? 'I don't know,' he said shortly. 'He went out just after you and Ben, and I haven't seen him since.'

20

She pushed past him into the big circular living room, telling herself there was no reason to feel guilty, except that she'd been in St Mawes yearning for solitude while the youngest and gentlest of her children was discovering a dead body less than a hundred yards from the house. Ben loved that beach, really loved it...

He was in bed, with his sister holding his hand, and Sally's heart lurched. He must be feeling awful or he would never have let Tessa do that ... and she would never have wanted to, in normal circumstances. Sally touched her on the shoulder to thank her and sat on the bed. 'Hello, Ben. What a terrible thing – I'm sorry I wasn't here. Are you feeling a bit better?'

Tessa answered for him as if he was a one-year-old infant. 'He's over the sickness, Mum, but he's been wheezing a bit.'

That was no surprise. The asthma had improved, but not as much as they'd hoped. It could still flare up, especially in times of stress, and finding a dead body might just possibly come under that heading. 'We'll keep an eye on him,' she said calmly.

Ben was shifting his shoulders against the piled-up pillows. 'I'm all right now,' he said abruptly. 'I think I'll get up, Mum.'

She wanted to talk to him on his own, and looked enquiringly at Tessa. Quick on the uptake as always, her daughter rolled her eyes but stood up and gave Ben a gentle thump in farewell, her long brown plait swinging as she closed the door behind her.

Sally still sat on the bed. 'Do you want to talk about it, love?'

'There's nothing much to tell,' Ben protested, 'except it was horrible.' He shot a look at the door. 'Dad was horrible, as well,' he whispered resentfully.

He still is, she thought, and I don't know why. Out loud she said, 'Horrible? I expect he was upset that it was you who found the body. He doesn't like it if anything unpleasant happens to any of you, love. Were the police nice to you? Did they write down what you told them?'

'They call it making a statement, Mum.'

'All right,' she agreed, 'so you made a statement.' It was clear that he didn't want to say more, but instinct urged her to get him to talk. 'Ben,' she said carefully, 'do you think she'd drowned?'

For the first time he looked her full in the face, his eyes just like Rob's, deep blue, but at that moment over-bright, as if he had a fever. 'Forensic are on the job,' he said flatly. He'd heard the police say that, and other things as well, but he was trying to forget them. His mum usually made it easier to forget horrible things, but now she was trying to make him talk about it.

He could tell she was worried, though; she

was twisting her hands together ... long hands they were, very smooth and pale, because she always wore gloves for dirty jobs. He chewed his lips and said: 'Her fingers were purply-blue, Mum, and all dimpled with being in the water. They felt like rubber, but hard and sort of heavy. Malachi said we might know her.'

Sally longed to hold him close, but made herself wait. 'And did you?' she asked gently.

'I don't know,' he said hoarsely. 'I wouldn't let him turn her over. Nobody's supposed to touch dead bodies except the police.' All at once his lower lip started to tremble and he couldn't make it keep still. His face was hot and his throat felt as if there was a lump inside it.

He was nearly twelve years old but when Sally opened her arms he put his head against her breast and cried like a baby.

A fine rain was blowing in from the sea as they unloaded the groceries. Tessa was there under duress, telling herself that she'd been looking forward to today and the visitors arriving, but now everything was awful. That PC Plod had been pathetic with his stilted little questions ... no wonder television detectives were so popular if that was what real ones were like. 'Are we going to tell them about the body, Mum?' she asked. 'The visitors, I mean.'

23

Sally lifted plastic bags from the boot and eyed her daughter closely. What was this? First she'd been good with Ben and now she was thinking about the visitors... At fifteen Tessa was frighteningly self-absorbed, self-centred, call it what you liked. She was on edge now, of course, like the rest of them. 'We can't do any other than tell them, love. If the beach is still cordoned off when they arrive they'll see for themselves that something's wrong.'

Tessa stood there clutching a cool-bag against her stomach. 'It's not a very good start to their holiday,' she said gloomily.

The understatement of the year. 'No,' agreed Sally, 'it's awful, but the children who are coming are too young to be upset, and there are other beaches nearby if they can't go on this one. Come on, love, some of this food's for them. I want the perishable stuff in their fridges and everything else sorted out for when they arrive.'

'I'll do it,' offered Tessa. She was bored rigid, she told herself, in spite of all the fuss with the police. 'Just give me their lists.'

Sally concealed her amazement. 'Thanks, that'll be a help. Let's get it indoors first.'

A voice behind them said, 'Mrs Baxter?' They turned to find a man standing there; tall and thin with sandy hair and pale eyelashes. He flashed a card. 'Detective Sergeant Bowles.'

He was in plain clothes. CID, she thought, and at once felt melodramatic and unreal. 'I'm Sally Baxter,' she said. 'Can I help you?'

'Detective Chief Inspector Channon would like to see all the family in an hour's time, if that's convenient, ma'am. Five of you, isn't it?'

'But you've already spoken to my son Ben, and my daughter here.'

'Yes, ma'am. Just another word, though. Could we say one thirty?' He watched her under his lashes. This was the mother, then. No chicken, but a type he liked, not too tall and well-upholstered.

Sally was observing him just as closely and, seeing the glint in his eyes, misread it completely. Was it excitement? Anticipation? Was there something going on that the family didn't know about? She found herself taking hold of Tessa's unwilling hand. 'Our younger son is a bit upset, so I don't particularly want him involved again,' she said firmly. 'My other son should be back before one thirty, though, so yes, it'll be convenient. Do you know any more about the – the death? Was it an accident?'

He didn't answer. 'One thirty,' he repeated, and turned to go. He'd been up half the night on a GBH and now he was having questions fired at him before he was allowed to give anything away.

At any other time Sally would have shrugged and dismissed him as ill-mannered, but it was only five minutes since Ben had wept in her arms. 'I asked you a question, sergeant,' she said coolly. 'Perhaps you didn't hear?'

'Nice one,' muttered Tessa.

'I heard,' said Bowles coolly, 'but I can't answer. We don't know – for certain – ma'am.' With that he turned away and headed back to the beach.

Sally released Tessa's hand and smiled grimly. 'Charm personified! Come on, Tess, let's get moving. We'd better have an early lunch.'

Carrying the bags indoors, Tessa decided that there were times when she was quite proud of her mother.

'What do you mean, uptight?' Rob was swinging back and forth in his computer chair, his eyes still on the screen.

'Oh, come on,' said Sally. 'You're being as awkward as hell and I want to know why.'

He jumped up to give her a squeeze, and for an instant she relaxed against the familiar warmth of his chest. 'I'm sorry, love,' he said. 'I suppose it's just that I feel a bit of an idiot. One of the reasons I wanted to come here was to protect the kids from anything unpleasant and now Ben – Ben, of all people – goes and finds a dead body on the day our first visitors are due. I just lost my cool, that's all.'

She pushed herself out of his arms. He might be upset about Ben but he hadn't exactly fallen over himself to give the child comfort and support. 'Well,' she said drily, 'you'd better find your cool and what's more hang on to it. A chief inspector is coming at half past one to talk to us all. Not Ben, though, if I can help it.'

She saw him stiffen. 'What about?'

'What do you think? The sergeant wasn't very forthcoming, but clearly he expected us to agree to "just another word". That's how he put it.' It was disconcerting to find no closeness between her and Rob. They'd always tuned in to each other's reactions, sometimes even to each other's thoughts: a look, a twitch of the lips, a touch of the hands but not now. She felt unpleasantly bereft and gave herself a mental shake. They were feeling the strain, that was all.

Rob's mind appeared to be on the tenants. 'We'll have to tell them as soon as they arrive,' he muttered. 'Not that there's much they can do about it, except keep off the beach if the cops are still there.'

The sound of a motorbike came from the front of the roundhouse. 'That's Luke,' she said in relief. 'I wonder if he's heard whether anybody's been reported missing?'

Rob turned away and sat in front of the

screen again. 'There's one way to find out,' he said.

Sally looked at the back of his head. He wasn't uptight? He'd just lost his cool for a minute? Pull the other one. 'Snack lunch,' she told him briskly. 'Come down whenever you want, as long as it's no later than one.'

'So who's in charge? Somebody from Truro?' Luke was at the kitchen table, demolishing his favourite snack of a whole ciabatta crammed with cheese and mustard pickle. Having heard about the body on the rural grapevine, he seemed a trifle put out at having missed all the excitement.

Sally didn't reply. Part of her mind was on Ben, who was still in his room, and on Rob, now in the garden after swallowing a ham sandwich and a mug of tea without uttering more than a couple of sentences.

Luke chewed with concentration and pushed a few wavy brown locks in the general direction of his pony-tail. 'Mum, about Ben ... is he, you know, is he all right?'

Sally gave him her full attention. There was a bond between the brothers, despite the difference in their ages and person-alities. Luke was the extrovert, the charmer, who had been reconciled to leaving Man-chester and all his friends as soon as he heard that the new school allowed long hair for boys. But Ben; shy, gentle, oversized Ben had been devastated by the move, finding solace only on the beach or in the fields until one day he stood up to a couple of bullies on behalf of Malachi Gribble, and became friends with the local boy...

'He's upset,' she said. 'He touched the dead girl's hand, Luke. Don't let on, but he cried when he told me. I think he'll be all right as long as this inspector doesn't say anything stupid.'

Luke surveyed her with his intelligent hazel eyes. 'Surely Ben's told them all he knows? Why should he have to answer any more questions?'

'I'm hoping he won't have to.'

'What does Dad say?'

Not much that helps, she thought grimly. 'Oh, he thinks the same as me,' she said lightly. 'We'll see how it goes, love. I don't expect they'll be here for long.'

Luke helped himself to a bowl of Shreddies. 'The men on the beach are wearing white overalls and boots,' he announced, crunching thoughtfully.

Sally had watched them from the bedroom window. She had also watched the occasional thriller on the box, and read several whodunits. She looked up from stacking the dishwasher. 'I think they wear special gear to prevent contamination of evidence and so forth,' she said.

Luke was eating his cereal with dedication, but paused to give a scornful bark of a laugh. 'Somebody ought to tell them that the tide won't only contaminate evidence, it'll wash it away for ever,' he said.

He was on his second bowl of Shreddies when the doorbell rang.

In contrast to his sergeant, Chief Inspector Channon was broad and swarthy, his thick black hair streaked with grey. He spoke softly, with the Cornish intonation, scrupulously polite with his 'sir' and his 'madam'. Sally detected steel beneath the gentle tones and decided with relief that he wasn't going to waste time.

Introductions over, he said: 'Just a brief chat, for now, and we won't trouble your youngest son again at the moment. I want to know the family's movements last evening, from, say, eight o'clock onwards.'

'But the girl,' protested Sally. 'Do you know who she is?'

'Yes,' replied Channon, 'we do. First though, your movements for last evening, if you please. Perhaps you'd begin, sir?'

Rob was quite calm. 'We finished our evening meal about – about what, Sal? Seven thirty? Then I had a spell in the garden and after that I went to my computer room.'

'Is that a hobby, sir?'

'No, it's my job. I work from home. I'm a database specialist for finance houses, banks and so forth. Oh – I help out with A level Computer Studies at the local school on a voluntary basis, as well – two half-days a week. I take them for finance, as that's my subject, and environmental studies.'

Channon surveyed him with calm dark eyes. 'I see. And after being in your computer room, sir?'

'I watched News at Ten, then went up again for a spell on the Internet. I didn't linger and I went to bed about eleven – maybe a bit later, I'm not really sure.'

'You heard and saw nothing unusual from outside the house – from the direction of the coastal path?'

Rob shrugged. 'No.'

'The four small dwellings on your property here – they're let as holiday cottages, I believe?'

Irritated, Rob tucked in a corner of his mouth. 'Our very first tenants are due this afternoon,' he said shortly, 'at two of the cottages, that is. All four of them are booked solid from the end of May onwards.'

Channon nodded and turned to Sally. 'And you, madam?'

Sally told herself that she felt like a character in an Agatha Christie novel. Channon, though, was no Hercule Poirot ... dapper he was not, nor did he have an egg-shaped head and a magnificent moustache. His mouth was clearly visible, wide and firm and shapely; dark eyes stared into hers expectantly. 'I cleared up after the meal,' she told him, 'then looked at Ben's English homework with him for a bit. Then I finished some sewing. I watched the news with my husband and went to bed soon afterwards. I didn't hear anything.' There was a weight inside her chest, she told herself, as if something heavy was pressing against her lower ribs. Was it anxiety? Was it—

'Thank you,' murmured Channon briskly. 'And now – it's Luke, isn't it? You were out last evening, I believe?'

'Yes. We had our weekly disco in the gym at school – sixth formers only, though it's not exactly a rave. I was there until ten o'clock.' He wriggled his shoulders, embarrassed at having to admit to leaving at such a juvenile hour. 'Events on school property have to finish early, you see.'

'You attend the Community School in Pencannon?'

'Yes. So do my brother and sister.'

'And did you come straight home, Luke?'

'No – I gave somebody a lift.'

'Who was that?'

Luke smiled slightly. 'A girl from my form, Samantha Trudgeon – but everybody calls her Sammy. She works in her auntie's pub in the next bay at weekends – serving coffee and ice-cream and stuff in the annexe when they're busy.'

'And they're busy now, with the season barely under way?'

'Not really, apart from last night. No, at present she's helping to finish some painting and decorating, so she sleeps there on Friday and Saturday nights. I lent her my spare helmet and took her on my bike. Her parents were away for the day, but they knew she might ask for a lift – they said it was OK.'

'And you arrived at what time?'

'Oh, ten thirty, maybe a bit after.' Luke hesitated and nibbled his lip. 'We – we talked a bit and then I had a ride along the coast road for a few miles and came home.'

'I heard him come in,' interrupted Sally. 'It was just on eleven.' She always heard him come in, it was force of habit to listen for his bike.

Channon nodded again. 'Did you see her go inside the Martennis, Luke?'

'Not really. She just went round the back of the pub. I'm not sure where she sleeps, or anything.' Luke was speaking slowly and clearly, with the air of one humouring a person who is fussing about nothing, but Channon didn't seem to notice. Sally eyed her son in bewilderment. He was bright – very bright, but he didn't seem to see where the questions might be leading ... he wasn't even uneasy.

All at once his eyes widened, as if the possible significance of the questions was dawning at last. He leaned forward in his chair and wrapped his arms across his midriff. 'Who's the girl, inspector? Has she been identified?'

But Channon was turning to Tessa, who had pulled her plait on to her chest and was fiddling with the end of it. Sally nodded at her encouragingly, but received a hard stare in return. 'I told the constable earlier,' Tessa said haughtily. 'I was in all evening. Homework and television, Mum can confirm it.'

Channon exchanged a look with the lanky Bowles, who had been making notes. Both men rose to go and stood side by side with their backs to the door. 'Thank you,' said Channon gravely. 'Now, as to the body of the young woman. I'm sorry to tell you that we're treating it as a case of murder.'

Sally saw the eyes of both detectives swivelling from one to the other of them, gauging their reaction. The ache beneath her ribs intensified, and all at once she recognized it as dread. She'd known – no, not known – she'd sensed that something terrible was happening. Her eyes sought Rob's, but he was staring at Channon, his teeth tight against his upper lip. Was he thinking like her, that they'd left Manchester with its clubs and drugs and shootings, for this? Unconsciously she massaged her rib-cage. There was more to come, she was sure of it.

'We'll probably have to take signed statements from all of you later today,' Channon continued. 'Men will be on the beach for some time yet, and a constable is on duty at your gate, so please don't leave the house without telling him where you're going. And perhaps you'd review what you've told us so far, to make sure there are no,' he paused, 'no errors.'

They all stared at him as if transfixed. 'But who's the girl?' asked Tessa hoarsely.

The inspector gazed around him at the beautiful, circular room. Either he hadn't heard or he didn't want to answer. 'No corners for the devil in a roundhouse,' he murmured, 'nor for witches' broomsticks. That's what they say, isn't it, madam?'

He was giving them all a breathing space, thought Sally. 'Yes,' she agreed stiffly, 'the locals say it all the time.' She remembered Rob himself repeating it with amusement the day he first asked them how they'd like to move to Cornwall.

At the door now, Channon sighed audibly, and Sally could have sworn she saw pity in his eyes. 'The young woman has been formally identified by her parents as Samantha Trudgeon,' he said gently. 'You'll appreciate that Luke here must have been one of the last to see her alive.'

Chapter Three

'Well, what do you think of him?' asked Channon as they went back to the car. 'The lad, I mean.' He didn't much like Bowles as an individual, but the younger man had a keen instinct for detection.

'If he's lying he's the best I've seen,' declared Bowles. 'He should be treading the boards in London. He's what? Seventeen – eighteen? Full of testosterone at that age, aren't they? It could have been thwarted lust, I suppose, if she wouldn't let him.' He started the engine. 'Where to?'

'Pathology for the post-mortem. They said two thirty, so we'll have to move... I want to see what they come up with and get the time of death settled. After that you can go and see the head of Pencannon School – he'll expect an official visit, though he'll have heard the news by now. Then it'll be routine stuff – talking to staff and fellow students and everybody who was at the Martennis for the darts game. Extra men are being drafted in for that starting at four today, but we can't begin on the door-to-door until I've decided what line of questioning to take.'

Bowles sped along the narrow roads. He liked working with Channon, who was said to be a difficult sod but had the habit of airing his views out loud and asking the opinions of underlings. Some CID inspectors played everything close to their chest and thought they were God Almighty, but not this one. When he himself got his promotion he'd make some of the lower ranks jump to it – he'd done enough jumping himself... 'The Baxter father might know the girl,' he told the senior man. 'He might have taught her on his two half-days a week.'

Channon nodded, but was wondering what was going on in the room they'd just left. Was the mother giving her son the third degree? Probably not, she seemed the protective type. The father, then? Mmm ... maybe... 'About the boy,' he said now, 'are you suggesting that Samantha walked over from the next bay for a midnight get-together only an hour or so after he dropped her at the aunt's, and that he killed her practically on his own doorstep?'

Bowles narrowed his eyes at the road ahead. 'She'd had a shower and changed her bra, her pants and her sweater, so she must have intended meeting somebody. Luke wouldn't have planned it, after all, if it was simply thwarted sex.'

Channon was dubious. 'Forensic will clarify things,' he said thoughtfully. 'It's our hard luck that the aunt didn't look to see she was safely tucked up in bed and then next morning took it she was having her usual lie-in. No wonder the poor woman was half demented.'

'It was a busy night in the pub,' pointed out Bowles. 'The area darts championship!' He rolled his pale eyes mockingly. 'I ask you – two coachloads of locals! Positively Leicester Square.'

Channon stared out at the fields. Bowles had once spent six months with the Met and ever since had made fun of the rural life. 'We'll have to check that all the darts players went home as arranged,' he said. 'There are potential suspects by the dozen. It's really too much of a coincidence that there were so many people out there last night.' He took out his phone. 'I'll have a word with Jordan at the beach. He should be able to pull his scene-of-crime team off pretty soon – the tide will go against them finding anything else, and they've got the cliff top under cover in case of rain.' He didn't dial, though. 'No, we'll wait for the results of the post-mortem. Not only was a knife involved, those head injuries indicate a heavy weapon. The SOCOs can't have examined every pebble on the beach – not yet.'

They drove on in silence, slowing only once to allow a car with a Birmingham number plate to pass them. A man and woman were peering out with the air of people on new territory. 'Visitors to Roundhouse Cottages, do you reckon?' asked Bowles.

Channon nodded. 'Not the best start to their holiday,' he said drily. 'A murder within a hundred yards of the house and the landlord's family helping police with their enquiries.' Silently he added, to his own surprise, 'Poor Mrs Baxter!'

'Sammy isn't my girlfriend,' Luke protested, '–wasn't, I mean. I didn't know her all that well. I've just given her a lift a few times, that's all.'

The four Baxters were on their feet, confronting each other across the living room. 'How many's a few?' asked Rob.

'Three. Three times since she started going to her auntie's again. Last summer she had lifts in Jason Vine's car, but he got his A levels and now he's at Bristol.'

This was more an interrogation than the quiet chat they all needed, thought Sally. As for Samantha – she'd seen her once, playing a flute solo at the school concert: a slim blonde girl ... confident, she'd seemed, glowing with health and energy. 'Come on,' she said abruptly, 'let's go and have a coffee while we talk things through.'

They trailed into the kitchen, where Luke sat down with a thud. 'She's only as old as me,' he said for the second time. It was as if he thought the dead girl's age outweighed everything else.

Tessa took her mother's elbow and urged her to sit. 'I'll make the coffee, Mum,' she said solicitously.

Sally nodded, touched and at the same time irritated. Evidently it took a murder to bring out the best in her daughter... She herself was trying hard to grapple with the situation; her mind seemed to be moving slowly, creaking and grating like an engine in need of oil. She couldn't understand it; when something awful happened weren't you supposed to have a surge of adrenalin that clarified the mind and prepared the body for action? Instead of that she felt dazed and horribly lethargic.

From the look of him Rob felt the same. He was sitting quite still with his hands clasped on the table in front of him; only his eyes were moving, watching his daughter making the coffee. 'Did you know her, Tess?' he asked quietly.

Tessa handed the mugs around. 'I knew who she was, but I didn't really know her. Wasn't she in one of your computing groups?'

Rob stared at his coffee. 'Yes,' he said, 'she was a natural. She was taking it at A level.'

'Who?' It was Ben, from the doorway. 'The girl? Do they know who she is?'

Sally wanted to go and give him a squeeze,

but instead she just patted the chair next to her. 'Come and join in, love, we're just talking about it. Yes, they know. She's from your school but she lives on a farm nearer Pencannon. Her name's Samantha Trudgeon.'

Ben stared. 'She's doing A levels,' he said. 'She lives at Blue Leaze Farm – Malachi's dad works there sometimes. Her aunt and uncle own the Martennis Inn. Did – did she drown?'

'No,' said Sally reluctantly. 'No, the police think she was murdered, love. They might come back later this evening to talk to us all again.'

Before Ben could respond there was a peal on the old-fashioned doorbell. Rob went to answer it, and a moment later came back to the kitchen. 'Our first visitors,' he said grimly. 'The Binghams for Starfish Cottage. I've told them you'll show them where to go, Sal.'

Thanks a million, she thought. If she showed them the cottage she would have to tell them why there was a policeman on the gate, why they weren't allowed on the beach. She let out a shamefaced sigh. What was she griping about? She resented having to tell strangers that a young girl had been murdered, but only a few hours ago the young girl's parents had had to identify her body. She dredged up a welcoming smile and made for the door.

Silence had fallen at the kitchen table, and all at once Luke jumped up. 'It's not raining as hard,' he announced. 'Come on, Ben, let's go for a walk.'

'You'll have to tell the constable where you're going,' Rob reminded them sharply, 'and stay together.' Then he went back to staring through the window.

At his side Tessa threw her plait back over her shoulder. 'I suppose we'll get used to Luke being under suspicion,' she said briskly, 'but it feels a bit weird, doesn't it, Dad?'

Over the years Channon had found that he could pay close attention at a post-mortem as long as he didn't have to look at the face of the corpse. Actually the procedure was riveting: the careful removal of clothing, the pathologist's calm commentary as he looked for the outward signs of death, the constant whirring of cameras, the storing away of minute hairs and fibres and the scrapings from beneath the fingernails, the swabs inserted in every orifice of the body. Then the opening up and examining of the vital organs, the brisk recital of the contents of the stomach, where the degree of digestion could be helpful in establishing the time of death... It was technical stuff, a highly refined skill.

With Bowles scribbling away behind him Hunter, the chief pathologist, gave his preliminary report. He was relaxed but precise, warning, 'All subject to analysis and confirmation, but we're pretty safe on the following. Time of death midnight, give or take half an hour at the outside. She was in excellent physical shape – not a virgin, but no sign of recent intercourse – the immersion in sea water affects that, of course. Damage to the bra fastener and fingermarks on the breasts indicate some form of assault, but not frenzied. No teeth marks, no visible semen, but we'll test for it.

'Now this is interesting: these cuts to the inside of the right hand are obviously caused by an attempt to deflect a knife or to wrest it from the attacker. But there are also signs of attempted manual strangulation before the blows to the head finished her – damage to the thyroid ligaments, bruising of the neck, spotting around the mouth and so forth. So at first sight – and off the record – it's knifing, then attempted strangulation, and third time lucky – for the killer at any rate – blows to the head.

'Not only that ... there are scratches around the ankles and behind the waist above her jeans – could be brambles, gorse, certainly some kind of vegetation. Fracture of the right tibia, one of the bones of the left wrist and various bruises are consistent with a fall at about the time of death. Is that enough to start you off? Full report by, say, seven this evening.'

Intent on preserving a normal routine, Sally was preparing a substantial evening meal of pasta with smoked ham and mushrooms in a cream sauce, a large mixed salad and Luke's beloved ciabatta. For pudding there was passion fruit meringue, Ben's favourite, and to please Tessa she was even doing a starter, something she didn't usually bother with except on Sundays.

She'd been right about the adrenalin. It had surged forth at last and now she was full of nervous energy, fired by the compulsion to keep their home life just as usual. The big kitchen gleamed because she'd dashed around polishing everything in sight – windows, sink, the sunshine yellow Aga that was her pride and joy. She'd even tidied and rearranged the big pine dresser that stood against the only straight wall.

This room, she thought, pausing for a minute; this entire house had been a joy to decorate and furnish. It was her special talent, after all. Interior design had been her part-time job in Manchester: a window-dresser for furniture, room settings, kitchen equipment. Her flair for it had transformed their solid Victorian house and made it the envy of their friends. Here in Cornwall she'd used her talents on the roundhouse and its cottages and with all of them finished she'd been wondering what to tackle next, while at the same time anticipating a leisurely, sun-drenched summer in the garden and on that perfect little beach. Ben's beach ... he simply adored it. No, past tense – he *had* adored it, until today.

It had been a wearing afternoon, punctuated by phone calls from school friends and people of the village, all agog with horror about the murder. Tessa and Luke had dealt with their own calls, but rightly or wrongly – she wasn't sure which – she had intercepted those for Ben. Then Malachi's mother Zennie had arrived, apparently put out that her son had been involved in finding the body. 'He should'a kept out of it, Sally,' she said, tossing her mane of black hair. 'I said to him you should'a left it for somebody else to report, never mind you and Ben getting involved. I said to Georgie we don't want him involved with this lot.'

Sally found her attitude highly irritating. 'They could hardly pretend they hadn't seen the body,' she pointed out. 'As for being involved – Luke was one of the last to see her alive. That's what you call involved!'

Zenobia Gribble had always reminded her of a tigress, and now she narrowed her beautiful amber eyes and tensed her shoulders. 'Don't let him talk to the cops on his own,' she warned. 'You know what they're like. They'll pin it on him if they can't find anybody else. Made Georgie's life hell, they did, over that robbery at Danbilly post office, and then out of the blue a fella they'd got for something else confessed to it.'

Sally was desperate to get rid of her. 'Thanks, Zennie,' she said, aware that she was verging on rudeness. 'I can't ask you to stay because we've got a lot on this afternoon. I'll let you know what's happening.'

'What I wanted to say is that I'm not letting Malachi come down here for the time being,' warned Zennie.

That was rich, when half the time she hadn't a clue as to her son's whereabouts, and he'd been given many a meal at the roundhouse. 'That's up to you,' Sally said evenly. 'I'll see you, Zennie.'

She'd watched her visitor's curvaceous figure sway out through the gates, telling herself they had nothing in common apart from their sons. She could never fathom how Zennie's mind worked, yet sometimes she felt sorry for her, she didn't know why, unless it was because she seemed so out of place in a village like Curdower. She sighed; the interview had left her on edge, especially after what had happened half an hour earlier, when the tenants for Starfish and Sea Urchin Cottages had arrived within ten minutes of each other.

The Starfish couple had taken the news in their stride; in fact Mrs Bingham had seemed quite thrilled. 'I say,' she'd breathed, wide-eyed, 'a real murder! It's the nearest we've ever been to one, isn't it, Kenny? We'll just have to tour the area and so forth until we're allowed on the beach.' She had shrieked with delight on seeing the inside of their cottage, evidently unperturbed that they were in the middle of a police investigation.

Not so the couple who had booked Sea Urchin. Young, earnest, with a toddler and a young baby, they had been horrified at the news, refusing even to unload their car. 'You don't imagine we're going to *stay?*' demanded the mother, clutching the baby to her chest. 'We only booked here because it's almost on the beach.'

The father had been equally appalled. 'We haven't come all this way to get embroiled in a murder enquiry,' he said flatly. 'We want a refund – a full refund. You'll have to claim it on the insurance.'

Inside five minutes the toddler was fastened in his seat again and they were heading back up the road, leaving Rob clutching his cheque book, grim-faced. 'A great start to life as a landlord,' he said in disgust.

Later, the TV crews had descended, swarming right up to the police barrier for a view of the beach, and to Rob's fury trying to get close-ups of the roundhouse. 'Stay indoors, all of you,' he instructed the family. 'We can do without appearing on TV for

47

something like this.' They gathered together to watch the television news, which as always on a Saturday was brief and to the point. The murder got only a sentence on the national news, but more coverage on the regional network. There was a shot of the beach, and one of the coastal path with the thatched roof of the roundhouse in the same frame. There were also a few calm, measured words from DCI Channon, to the effect that more details would be issued shortly, but that anybody with information about this dreadful crime should ring a certain number. Sally watched him and for the second time felt a sneaking admiration. His words conveyed concern and compassion, but above all he himself exuded confidence and capability. She hoped it was backed by expertise.

Now, her mind circling endlessly, she was covering pear halves with tarragon mayonnaise for the starter. Why had Samantha been killed? How? Who had done it? At least she herself was at ease regarding Luke being implicated in some way.

He had strolled into the kitchen an hour or so earlier, asking 'What's for dinner, Mum?' as if the day was no different than any other day.

She told him, aware that this was the first time they'd been on their own since Channon's visit. 'Luke, I want to talk to you,' she said tensely. 'Sit down a minute.'

He perched on the edge of the table and said in a tone of mild surprise, 'You know, that policeman on the gate's a really nice bloke. His brother plays cricket for the county. Minor counties, of course, not like Lancashire.'

Sally gritted her teeth but stayed calm. Was there any point in alarming him? In passing on her own deep misgivings? No, there wasn't, but she had to find out now, while she had him on his own.

'Luke, do you realize that at the moment you're one of the suspects for killing Samantha? You can tell me what happened, you can tell me anything at all, but first – was what you told the inspector the truth?' She couldn't ask him if he'd been involved in the murder. You couldn't ask your son that.

A sunbeam, pale gold, was shining over his shoulders; she could hear the clock ticking and felt faintly aggrieved that it wasn't racing at breakneck speed. This, she thought, was her first-born child. She could read him. She would know if he'd been lying – if he was lying now.

He was staring at her, bemused. 'Come on, Mum,' he said pityingly. 'Do you take me for a nutball or something? They're investigating a murder, not somebody pinching a bar of chocolate. Of *course* I told him the truth!'

He was telling it now, she was sure of it. Her knees went weak with relief. Thank you,

God, she said silently, thank you. He wasn't involved in the murder, but could he have got her pregnant? Aloud she asked carefully, 'Was there anything between you and Samantha?'

Luke rolled his eyes. 'There was nothing between me and Sammy, Mum. I've given her a lift on my bike – three times. That's all.'

'Do you like her?' Sally realized they were skating back and forth between the past and present tense. Right now they were talking as if she were still alive.

'She's not bad – a bit bossy, I suppose. You know what girls are like when they're good at sport and have a place lined up at university. Some girls, that is,' he amended hastily, 'not all. If you must know, I really like Poppy, but she's keen on Dave Benson.'

Sally had met Poppy. She'd been to the roundhouse when Luke had a barbecue for his seventeenth. She was small and neat, with saucer-like eyes and shiny brown hair. 'Poppy's sweet,' she acknowledged. 'So did Samantha have a special boyfriend?'

Luke stared at his hands. 'Lots of the gang were keen on her,' he said. 'She could pick and choose among them if she wanted. Look, Mum, will you stop worrying? She didn't pick me, or at least not in that way. I was just convenient for a lift. End of story.'

'It's not the end of the story until they find

out who killed her, and why,' she retorted.

'I know,' he agreed, all at once contrite. 'It simply doesn't seem real that I was one of the last to see her alive – I keep forgetting that aspect of it. I think I'll go and give Bammo a ring.' Simon Bamforth, known as Bammo, was his close friend at school. Luke slid off the table and at the door turned to ask, 'What time are we eating, then?'

'Seven o'clock.' Sally stared at his departing back and felt sick with relief.

Chapter Four

Channon strode through a straggle of on-lookers and entered Curdower village hall, now taken over as the police incident room. Fresh from a meeting with his superior officers at headquarters he was impatient for action, flinging himself down at a trestle table to observe the scene.

His old friend John Meade was acting as office manager, and under his experienced direction things were moving at speed. Banks of phones had been installed, a couple of computers were already linked to the police network with more still to come, and on one wall was a large-scale map of the coast and farmland around Curdower. Next to the map Bowles was fastening a blown-up portrait of Samantha Trudgeon.

Channon writhed inwardly as he recalled her parents handing over the original photograph: the mother limp and unresponsive, the father red-eyed but dignified. How would he himself behave in a similar situation? Not that he had a teenage daughter, not that he had any children – not any more...

He stared intently at the girl's smooth young features, the grey-green eyes, the thick sun-streaked blonde hair which fell in front of one ear and was pushed behind the other. She was half smiling, giving him the odd sensation that she was approving their efforts.

Save it till later, Sammy, he told her photograph silently; at the moment we're getting nowhere, fast. Beneath his calm exterior he felt like a dog straining at the leash, eager for action. The first few hours of an investigation were vital: after that short space of time evidence was destroyed, clues disappeared, suspects jumped on trains and aeroplanes, witnesses forgot what they'd seen.

He now had a good detective constable as a personal assistant in addition to Bowles. Steve Soker was small, tireless and intelligent, an able second to the sergeant; he could be trusted to work alone and was excellent on computers. Just now he was in front of a terminal, listing information that had come in from interviews and phone calls.

He jumped up and came across to Channon. 'A few snippets before they're logged, sir. Samantha's teachers say she was bright and hardworking, but so far there's nothing unusual coming up – she was at school all day yesterday, which isn't always the case with second year A level students, though if they rely on school transport they haven't much choice. She was the outdoor type, apparently – good at games and pretty robust. She swam from Curdower beach last December for a dare, and she often went surfing up on the north coast.'

'Well, she wasn't wearing a wet suit yesterday!' Channon retorted. 'A levels, though ... arrange for a statement from whoever's in charge of final year students, will you?'

'Right.' Soker leafed through his notes. 'Several calls on the special line, sir. One quite promising, from a confident type called Blankett – that's as on a bed but with two t's – Maureen Blankett, runs a farm. She says Samantha walked across her land yesterday afternoon – seemed to think it might be significant, because a man passed in the opposite direction a few minutes later. A walker, she said, as the path isn't used much and it's only shown on large-scale maps.'

'Walkers usually keep to the coastal path,' said Channon dubiously. 'Bowles can go and see her right away. Anything else?'

'Yes, sir. There were sixty-six at the darts

final including fourteen women. Nearly all of them travelled by coach – one standard coach and a minibus. Only three private cars. We've got details of two, and a man's checking on the other.'

'I want to know who travelled with who,' instructed Channon. 'We'll need verification of travel arrangements and times, especially for anybody who went home on their own. Let me know as soon as we get the names of any casual visitors to the pub last evening – if not names, we need descriptions. And tell John Meade I want him as soon as he's free.'

Soker hurried off and left Channon staring intently at the image of Samantha Trudgeon. Once or twice in his career he had struck up a rapport with a murder victim, though he had never told anybody; it sounded cranky, as if he were dabbling in spiritualism. It had been nothing of the kind, of course; he'd merely come close to entering the victim's mind, which was what all detectives tried to do – but usually the mind they tried to enter was that of the perpetrator. Now, his team were setting in motion the tried and tested framework of an enquiry – not so far a full-scale major enquiry – it wouldn't come to that if he could nail somebody quickly ... if ... if... Amid the talk and bustle Channon simply sat there, deep in thought.

Every good detective he'd known had

possessed one quality which he believed should be prized above rubies. He himself had it – it was a gift, like a talent for music, or sport, or mathematics. The quality was intuition. Unmeasured, unexplained, it caused the mind to leap above the grim routine of investigation and corroboration to enter the realms of insight, instinct, imagination. Its arrival was sometimes sudden – the shaft of light in a dark tunnel – but more often it came from getting to know somebody's life, understanding their fears, their aspirations, who they loved, who they hated... Oh, yes, he prized his intuition above rubies – he nurtured it, fed it on arrests and convictions and the gratitude of heartbroken families.

Bowles appeared at his side, not bothering to conceal a self-satisfied smile. 'An e-mail from Hunter,' he said, handing over a long printout. 'His conclusions on the post-mortem.'

Channon looked at it. 'Did you happen to read the heading?' he asked gently.

Bowles stopped smiling. 'You mean "for your eyes only"? I didn't think you'd mind if I just glanced through it, sir.'

'I don't, as it happens, but some DCIs might.' He wafted the printout under the sergeant's nose. 'It backs your theory about the boy, presumably?'

Bowles was uneasy. 'Not conclusively,' he admitted. 'No sources of DNA, but in spite of the immersion in sea water they've found minute traces of engine oil and rubber on the bra. Also fibres caught in the buckle of her belt – red wool, possibly from a sweater. Could be oil and hand-grips from Master Luke's motorbike, could be his sweater – we can check on it.'

'It will have to go off to main forensic, anyway, but in the meantime we can work on it,' said Channon shortly. 'Now, we need to visit a Miss Blankett.' He'd changed his mind about sending Bowles on his own. 'She's a farmer. Soker has details. We'll go there first and call at the roundhouse on the way back. I'll read Hunter's report in the car.'

Bowles was put out that they were merely to call at the roundhouse, and it showed. Drumming his fingers on the table, Channon stared at him. 'All right,' he agreed, 'get a van to meet us there to pick up the bike, but they're *not* to approach the house until I say so. Right?'

'Right,' agreed Bowles, and concealed a triumphant grin.

Blankett's Farm lay among a network of narrow roads bisected by dirt tracks and ancient signposts. 'Good God,' said Bowles in disgust, reversing the car into a mass of yellow-green wild celery. 'It's like entering the Dark Ages! Who'd think we're only half an hour's drive from Truro?'

Channon had just finished reading about the intimate probing of Samantha's body, and he eyed their surroundings with a sense of release. Dark Ages or not, this was beautiful country. Cornish hedgerows in mid-May were rich in colour and the evening sun was brushing them with gold. Behind bluebells and wild garlic stretched pasture-land and fields green with young crops, while down to their left a fold between hills revealed the distant, copper-tinged sea.

The farm was immaculate. A curving drive climbed to a serene white house fronted by lawns and flowerbeds; the big yard was edged by well-kept outbuildings and beyond them towered huge modern barns. A biblical quote slid into Channon's mind: 'I will pull down my barns and build greater.' Somebody had done that here, right enough... Blankett's Farm breathed prosperity.

'Some place, for a woman,' muttered Bowles.

Channon had lectured on sexual discrimination. 'Sexist,' he warned automatically.

Bowles was unrepentant. 'It's not the result of her own efforts,' he said doggedly as they left the car, 'John Meade says it's been in the family for yonks. Daddy-oh Blankett left it to her.'

Channon strode ahead. Male-generated prosperity made it acceptable, did it? Bowles was a pain, at times. The owner herself answered the door and from force of habit Channon registered her description in his mental files. Medium height and build, strong features, skin good but weather-beaten, keen blue eyes, thick grey hair in need of a trim, a lightweight sweater over a neat, high-collared blouse...

He announced their names and rank, and she studied their IDs carefully. Satisfied, she let them in. 'I didn't expect a visit from so senior an officer,' she said, half smiling. 'Could I offer you a sherry? I usually have one myself at this time.'

Channon decided she was more a lady of the manor than a working farmer, though the brown sinewy hands showed signs of manual work. 'Thank you, no, Miss Blankett, and thank you for calling our special line. We won't keep you for long, we just want a few more details of your sighting of Samantha. Evidently you knew her?'

Maureen Blankett gave a restrained smile. 'I know most people within a ten-mile radius of my farm,' she told him. 'Certainly I know all the other farmers and their families and everyone in Curdower village. You may not have realized it travelling by car, but the Trudgeons are my neighbours.'

Channon hadn't realized it. Neither, he imagined, had Bowles. He waited.

'Blue Leaze borders the far corner of my land. Many years ago, before the Trudgeons were even heard of and certainly before his old-fashioned style of farming was back in fashion, the biggest meadow over there was dotted with trees and edged by woodland. You've seen the flowers at this time of year, the bluebells: leaze means meadow, or pasture – so, Blue Leaze.'

What an old bore, Bowles was thinking. Cut her short, Channon, and let's get to the Baxter kid. If he'd been in charge he'd have arrived at the roundhouse with a search warrant. The old girl, though, was more like a teacher than a farmer, and in one minute flat had made clear that she was landed gentry and the Trudgeons newcomers.

'Very interesting,' murmured Channon. 'So – you saw Samantha, Miss Blankett. What time was that?'

'I'd say just before four. She was in her school uniform. I was in high pasture – I'd just been checking the fences up there. Samantha was crossing my land on the public right of way – presumably on her way home.'

Channon noted the fractional tightening of her lips as she uttered the words, 'public right of way'. Farmers always protested otherwise but he was convinced that they didn't like footpaths crossing their land. 'Was it a common occurrence for her to use the path, Miss Blankett?'

'No, quite the reverse. I can't remember when I last saw her there. The school buses go all around the lanes, you know, dropping off pupils in various hamlets and at the end of tracks for isolated houses. I should imagine that Samantha is usually taken to the end of the single-track road that leads to Blue Leaze, leaving her to walk about half a mile, maybe three-quarters.'

'Did you notice anything unusual about her? Anything at all? We're trying to re-construct her last few hours.'

'No, she was strolling, as if she was enjoying it. A fit girl, I believe – on school teams for netball and hockey. She was carrying one of those coloured bags that they use instead of satchels.'

'Did you speak to each other?'

'No, I was too far away. I don't think she even saw me.'

'I believe a man walked along the path soon afterwards?'

Maureen Blankett leaned forward in her chair, regret in the direct gaze. 'Yes, and if I'd known what was going to happen I would have taken special note so that I could give you a full description. By the time he came along I was closer to the path, but still some distance from him. He was wearing a mid-blue casual shirt and khaki shorts. Boots, I think, with socks turned down over the tops.'

'Any backpack?' asked Channon keenly.

The farmer observed him closely and

decided that he was competent. 'Yes, a haversack. Medium-sized, I think, and dark-coloured. It may have contained only food and drink, of course – people do sometimes come to this area by car and then do a circular walk back to their vehicle.'

'And his appearance?' Come up with something good, he begged silently.

Maureen Blankett nodded in approval. He didn't waste words and she liked that. 'Fairish,' she said judiciously. 'Hair wavy or curly – certainly not straight or sleek, and quite short. I got the impression of a ruddy complexion. Build – fairly lean, I'd say, and average height.'

'And what age?'

'Well, I didn't get a clear view of his face, but he carried himself easily, like a young man – perhaps in his thirties. That's about all. I'm sorry I can't help you more.'

'Would they have passed each other?'

'Oh, almost certainly, but out of my line of vision. He came down the path maybe five minutes after Samantha had gone out of sight, but it's a long path, inspector, it skirts some of my best pasture.'

'What about your employees, Miss Blank-ett? Would any of them have seen him?'

'No – I've asked, but please feel free to speak to them yourself. I employ three men and a woman on my stock and my crops, and a man from the village on a casual basis.

Also a woman in the house, to leave me free for supervision, though I never ask any employee to do anything I couldn't do myself. I run a large farm, as you may have noticed.'

This frayed old Blankett was no modest violet, thought Bowles, but she had no cause to brag – it was all inherited. It would have done her good to inherit what his father had left *him* – a clapped-out old banger and a sheaf of bills.

By contrast Channon was finding her an unusual woman, one who might be interesting to talk to. In the past he had come across well-informed locals who had helped his investigations. But there was no time to linger. 'A most impressive property,' he agreed heartily. 'We may need a signed statement from you later, Miss Blankett. One last point – would you recognize this man again, do you think?'

Frank but regretful, the blue eyes in their network of lines looked into his. 'I'm not sure,' she admitted. 'Probably not. I didn't get a full-face view of him.'

A real life response, thought Channon. Photographic memory was the stuff of detectives' dreams. Two minutes later he was on the mobile to John Meade with the description of a fair man in his thirties, wearing walking gear.

They always used the dining room for the

main meal of the day, and Sally had laid the table with one of her grandma's damask cloths and the best china and cutlery. Well aware that she was going a bit over the top, she had cut fresh flowers from the garden and put them in a big crystal bowl as a centrepiece. She would keep things normal – better than normal – if the effort of it flattened her.

'A celebration?' asked Luke in puzzlement as they sat down. 'What's to celebrate?'

Tessa wrinkled her nose in distaste. 'Oh no,' she wailed, 'I've gone off starters. I thought I'd told you, Mum.'

'Not much for me, I'm not really hungry.' That was Ben, with an apologetic little smile.

The last to comment was Rob, who looked round the table and raised his eyebrows. 'What's for main course?' he asked drily. 'Fatted calf?'

'We've all had a trying day,' replied Sally, striving for calm, 'so I thought it might help if we had a nice, leisurely meal.' Her voice was rising and she couldn't control it. 'So for crying out loud,' she yelled, 'stop griping and eat!'

Ben blinked and stared guiltily at his plate. Seeing him, she let out a long, exasperated breath. He was going to have to toughen up a bit or life would rip him apart... 'Ben has an excuse,' she conceded more calmly. 'His stomach's upset.'

Even Luke seemed lost for words and they ate in a silence so deep the clink of cutlery seemed deafening. Some normal family life, thought Sally as she sliced warm bread and handed round the pasta. She had the sensation of the floor beneath their feet turning to dust and sliding away, leaving them on the edge of some bottomless pit. Was she tensed up or was she?

She observed Rob from under her lashes. Apart from their exchange in front of his computer they hadn't talked all day – not really talked, mind linked to mind. She would have to wait until they were in bed, the haven of their marriage, where everything was sorted out, everything shared – yes, everything. Their pleasure in lovemaking was undimmed, she was thankful for that. Maybe it wasn't so fierce, so passionate after twenty years, but it was deep and warm and satisfying. She needed it right now: the closeness, the giving, the comfort, the reassurance. The act of love was a release – it would take away their tension, calm them down.

They were still on their main course when the doorbell rang. 'I'll go,' offered Tessa, and a minute later came back followed by DCI Channon and Sergeant Bowles. She gave a helpless little shrug then stood indecisively between the detectives and her half-eaten meal.

Channon observed the scene impassively and addressed Sally. 'Apologies for interrupting your meal, Mrs Baxter, but if we could have a quick word?'

Rob was the only one who carried on eating and Sally shot him a look. He hated being interrupted during a meal and his attitude declared that he saw the visit as an intrusion. Surely, she thought in embarrassment, a murder was reason enough to intrude on anybody? She had been raised in a hospitable family, but even to her it sounded false and effusive when she said, 'There's plenty of food, inspector. Would you both like some pasta and salad?'

Channon refused politely and smothered a sigh. Who'd have his job? This woman, this mother, was clearly intent on preserving their family life, and yet it might never be the same again. 'If you and Mr Baxter could leave your meal for just a moment, madam, we'd like a word – with you as well, Luke.'

'Tessa – put ours in the Aga,' instructed Sally. 'You and Ben carry on with your meal.'

Tight-lipped, followed by a baffled and apprehensive Luke, Rob led the way to the sitting room, where even the white walls and jewel-bright rugs seemed gloomy after the gleaming lamplit table in the next room. Hurriedly Sally switched on the lights. 'All right,' said Rob impatiently, 'what's the problem?'

'We're trying to eliminate people from our enquiries,' replied Channon with practised diplomacy. 'In order to do that we must have items of clothing and so forth examined and if necessary sent off to one of the regional forensic centres, so please bear with me. We need to take away whatever your son was wearing last evening. All items of clothing.'

Sally was upset but not devastated. After all, her mind was at ease about Luke being involved. 'His things haven't been washed yet,' she said. 'Go and get them out of the laundry basket, Luke, and your sweater and best jeans – they're on the chair in your room.'

'Socks and shoes as well,' stipulated Channon.

The skin on either side of Rob's nose was white. 'You don't seriously think that my son had anything to do with it?' he asked tightly.

'We think a lot of things in the course of an enquiry,' replied Channon coolly, 'but what counts in the end is what we can prove in court. I have a police van waiting to take away your son's motorbike as well.'

'But you know already that Samantha was on the bike,' protested Sally.

Channon's dark gaze met hers. 'I must investigate,' he said simply. 'As yet we can give no details of how Samantha was killed, nor do we have a motive, but I can tell you that somebody was absolutely determined to take her life. As you know, Mrs Baxter, they succeeded in doing so only a very short distance from this house.' And, he thought, they used three different methods to achieve their aim, plus chucking her over the cliff. 'Luke's motorbike is simply one very small aspect of a complex investigation, and as it's here on your property I'd like your permission to remove it.'

Rob let out an angry, disgusted sigh and flapped a hand in agreement as Luke was returning with a bundle of clothes. 'They want to take your bike away for examination,' he told him wearily. 'We've given permission.'

Luke tightened his lips and remained silent, while Bowles laid the clothes and footwear on the settee. As they all watched he put each item in a separate plastic bag and sealed it, his eyes meeting Channon's as he bagged the red sweater. Last of all he sealed away Luke's treasured leather jacket.

'Put them in the van, sergeant,' said the older man, 'and Luke – perhaps you'd wheel your bike to the gate? I'll come with you to get it.' He turned to Sally and Rob. 'I'm sending two men over here in about an hour's time to take a detailed statement from each of you. No doubt you recall that I asked you to make sure that anything you say is accurate?'

Back at the table Rob and Luke finished their pasta, but it came as no surprise to Sally to find that nobody, not even her eldest son, was interested in the passion fruit meringue.

Chapter Five

Bowles had decided that at least two aspects of working with Channon were going to get on his nerves. The first was that the DCI was too soft – he should have pinned the Baxter kid down earlier in the day, before he announced who'd been killed. At that stage young Lukey-dukey might have tripped himself up by trying to stay in the clear. The other thing was that Channon didn't need food. He drank, of course – mineral water for God's sake – but food? What was that? He could have throttled the older man when he'd refused the offer of a meal at the round-house, and now he himself was ravenous.

They arrived back to find phones ringing, computers humming and men reporting back with completed questionnaires. Grey-haired and solid, John Meade was calmness personified. 'We've checked on every darts player, Bill,' he told Channon. 'Only three went home unaccompanied, two in cars and one on foot, and men are talking to them now.' He waved a hand at the open hatch of the kitchen. 'Eats,' he said simply. 'I've got the lady from the village shop doing sandwiches and tea.'

Channon appeared not to have heard, but Bowles was so hungry he could have kissed the young woman in charge, though she wasn't his type. No boobs, he told himself automatically as he asked for tea and sandwiches. Mouth full, he rejoined Channon, who was going through printouts with Soker. 'Who talked to the kids on the school bus?' the inspector was asking keenly. 'And those at the disco? Yates? I'll have a word with him. And is Mary Donald back from the Trudgeons?'

To Bowles he said, 'When you've finished eating, check with whoever interviewed the man who went home on foot. Unless he's pure as the driven I might talk to him myself.'

Bowles sat down at a table and relished his sandwiches, deciding there were no signs of being able to get off home. In his case home was a comfortable flat in Truro, and for at least the hundredth time he told himself how much better life was without a wife nagging about spoiled dinners and his long hours on the job. All right, so it wasn't exactly bliss having to see to his own laundry, nor having only breakfasts and the occasional takeaway at the flat, but it was freedom.

What a fool he'd have been if he'd let Sue have her way and they'd gone in for kids. Everybody knew they bled you dry after a divorce if kids were involved. Who wanted them anyway? Little devils, always yelling and giving cheek... He still couldn't quite believe that she'd been the one to finish the marriage. She'd found somebody else – the manager of a supermarket who worked set hours, so how boring could you get? No doubt the little wimp liked checking his shelves and his tills and having Sue next to him in bed ... she'd always been a cuddly armful.

For himself, he'd never thought there was anything wrong with their sex life, except perhaps that it wasn't adventurous enough. But empty? Thoughtless? Without consideration? That was what she'd said about it. He wondered now if she'd meant empty because he wouldn't agree to children, but at the time of the break-up he'd been in such a rage he could have gone and slept with every woman in Cornwall and fathered a multitude, just to get even...

He finished his tea and went to find out about the man who went home from the darts match on foot. 'George Gribble,' he reported back to Channon. 'Went to the

Martennis in his old banger, but it wouldn't start when he wanted to go home. Says he'd had a few anyway, so it made sense to walk home and go back for it this morning. He didn't see anything unusual on the way home. He's got a record, though – for receiving, a couple of years back. Also his wife's a sex-pot, so I shouldn't think he was trying for Samantha.'

'We'll have a word, all the same,' said Channon. 'Come on.'

Zenobia Gribble opened the door and narrowed her amazing eyes at the sight of the two detectives. 'Short of a suspect, are we?' she asked sharply. 'Well, you won't manage to pin anything on Georgie. You'd better come in – the neighbours have had one eyeful already. He's out the back working on the car.' She went to the kitchen and called, 'Georgie! They're here again!'

As she came back again a small, dark-haired boy came downstairs and stared at the detectives expectantly. 'Your men have already talked to Malachi,' said his mother, and turning to the child, 'Go an' play in your room. You can come an' watch telly in a minute.'

She hustled him back upstairs and the men waited in the living room. Too ornate for a cottage and a bit grubby, decided Channon, who had a squeamish streak about such

71

things. The place smelled of past fry-ups, as well, but maybe a man shouldn't expect too much on the domestic front when his wife looked like this one. Bowles had described her as a sex-pot, and in a low-cut gold top and skintight black leggings Mrs Gribble looked a sex-pot ready to boil over.

Long experience of ill-assorted married couples had failed to prepare Channon for the sight of George Gribble. The wife had given him a clear mental image of the husband: he would be the virile type, big and rather brash; talkative, with an easy, gypsyish charm, and if he didn't sport a moustache he would certainly have sideburns.

If they hadn't been on a murder case Channon might have allowed himself a smile at the sight of him. How wrong could he be? George Gribble was so nondescript he looked like a piece of old newspaper against the flocked gold wallpaper and red brocade of his living room. Short and thin, with wispy grey hair and tired blue eyes that flickered uneasily between his wife and the two detectives, he had the air of a dispirited old pony put out on poor grazing.

Channon was ultra-polite as he introduced himself. 'Just another word, Mr Gribble, we won't keep you for long. I believe you told my man you'd had a few drinks during the darts match? Can you recall how many?'

'Three pints,' said his wife with certainty.

'That's his limit, isn't it, Georgie?'

'It's my limit,' he confirmed, 'but just this once I might have had four, Zennie.'

Bowles looked at the wife but addressed the husband. 'The landlord of the Martennis tells us you had six or seven. Just as well the car wouldn't start, eh?'

The mockery was lost on Gribble. ''Twas the battery,' he said doggedly. 'Needs renewing, you see.'

'Yes,' said Channon, 'witnesses saw you with the bonnet up as people were leaving.'

'What if they did?' interrupted Mrs Gribble. 'He managed to get it home an' he's been tinkering with it ever since. He needs that car to get to his jobs. The farmers round here don't lay on door-to-door transport, you know.'

Channon thought that her manner was reminiscent of a mother defending a dim but troublesome child. He noted that Bowles had less to say than usual, perhaps stunned by the blatant sex appeal of the woman. He turned back to the husband and glimpsed the man's expression as he looked at his wife; it held – what? Resentment? Dislike? Bitterness? Well, well ... perhaps he wasn't the submissive little dimwit he appeared to be.

'Mr Gribble, I believe you saw nothing unusual outside the inn, or on your way home, and that you arrived back here just before twelve. Is that correct?'

'That's right,' agreed Gribble.

'As to your jobs, you work at Blankett's, I believe, and for Mr Trudgeon, of Blue Leaze?'

'An' Deacon, an' the rest,' interrupted Mrs Gribble. 'But all casual. Coupla days here, couple there. They're all loaded but they don't like laying out on casuals. Deacon'll work like a dog himself to avoid paying wages and Blankett's no better – gone berserk she has more than once when she thought Georgie was costing her money, an'–'

Channon ignored her. 'You knew Samantha, Mr Gribble?'

'Yes, course I did. A bright girl, an' pleasant with it.'

'And when did you last see her?'

Gribble pursed his lips in thought. 'Yesterday. I were doin' a bit extra for Mr Trudgeon, 'cos he was away for the day – I say it do seem hard they should'a been away when this happens, 'cos I can't remember the last time he left the place, even though he has a regular man on the pigs an' the herd an' a woman as helps with the crops. But what you was askin' – I was out in the yard when Samantha come a-wanderin'. About half four, it'd be.'

From what Channon had heard of Samantha she was hardly the type to go a-wandering anywhere. 'Did she spend much time out on the farm?' he asked with interest.

'Every day,' confirmed Gribble. 'Helped her dad keep it all on the computer, an' that. Proud of Blue Leaze she was – it being certified, I mean. Certified organic, that is.'

'Did she seem much as usual? In her manner, I mean.'

'Yes,' said Gribble, eyes wide and guileless. 'She saw to her fowls like she always did and then we talked a bit – uh – about her dad gettin' this award. That's where he'd gone – up to London to some environment do. His herd's been tested up, down and sideways and they're faultless, so he was given a commendation for that and for his vegetable crops.'

'But she didn't have the day off school to go with her parents?'

Gribble looked blank. 'No. Too busy gettin' ready for her exams, I expect. An' besides, she goes to the disco at school on Friday nights. If I'm at the farm late I sometimes give her a lift, then her dad takes her home.'

'But you didn't do that last night?'

'No. I was finishin' at five an' anyway, she didn't ask me. I expect she'd arranged a lift on the school minibus.'

'Thank you,' said Channon. 'Did you see Samantha leave the farm after you talked to her?'

'No,' answered the other carefully. 'She

hadn't been home all that long.'

Channon nodded. 'One more thing. I have men outside waiting to look at the engine of your car with a view to taking specimens of oil and so forth. If you object to the procedure I can get a warrant giving me permission to do so. Can I tell them to go ahead?'

Gribble was blinking uncertainly, his gaze once again on his wife, who threw back her hair angrily. 'What do you expect to find? Evidence he killed her? Come on, inspector – does he look like a murderer? He was back here when he said, an' he weren't drunk, neither.'

'Examining your husband's car is only one small part of a wide-ranging investigation,' replied Channon smoothly. 'We have to eliminate so many people it's a mere formality.' Silently he added, and we've as much cause to check on your Georgie as on anybody. Gribble might not look like a murderer, he thought, but he's a man who's keeping a watch on his tongue.

Zennie glared at her husband. 'We'll have to let them,' she said flatly, and to Channon, 'We want to watch what these fellas do, mind. I don't know what that old engine can tell you but we're havin' no planted evidence, are we, Georgie?'

'Definitely not,' said Georgie, and smoothed his upper lip with his forefinger.

Bowles decided they were wasting their

76

time. This little weed hadn't the energy to cross the road, let alone use three different methods to polish off Samantha. He looked at them both and wondered what they were like in bed. Talk about the lion lying down with the lamb – in their case it would be more like the lioness lying down with the clapped-out old donkey...

As he and Channon drove away a forensic engineer was lifting the bonnet of the Gribbles' old Escort, watched by a plain-clothes constable.

DC Yates gathered his wits and told himself that with luck he'd be off home by ten o'clock. It was always the same on a big enquiry – his mind went into reverse after twelve hours on the job. Now he leafed through his notes from talking to Samantha's fellow pupils, sorting out what might be of use to the man in charge.

Two solid hours of questioning kids – some tearful, some subdued, and some unable to conceal a certain excitement – had resulted in a meagre mish-mash of information. He'd had to work with a man he didn't even know when enquiring about the disco. 'Did you get anything significant?' Channon was asking now with interest.

'Nothing startling, sir. They all agree that their bus went past Samantha's usual dropping-off point – it was a new driver and he simply forgot. The roads are narrow over near Blue Leaze so she said it didn't matter about going back and to drop her off at a stile that was coming up.'

It didn't matter? thought Channon sombrely. If the man she'd met on that public footpath turned out to be the killer it mattered a great deal that the driver forgot to stop, but with luck he would never find out about it.

'Samantha seemed in her usual good spirits on the bus,' Yates went on. 'Said she'd see her special friends at the disco – she was being picked up by the school minibus to get to that, by the way. Oh, and Debbie Collier, one of her close friends, remembers Samantha saying she'd be going surfing. Debbie asked if there was enough wind for a good surf and Samantha just laughed and said she'd been kidding.

'They said she was expecting good grades at A level, but you'll hear about her school work from her director of studies, I expect. Nobody noticed anything unusual on the roads, no pedestrians, for instance, but the bus driver said that on his way back a grey van – unmarked – cut in front of him and shot off up one of the lanes. He didn't get the number.

'Nothing really interesting came up from the crowd at the disco. Samantha seemed OK and she went home with Luke Baxter.

Nobody thought there was anything going on between them, though one lad said that Luke had elbowed anybody else out of giving her a lift – maybe not significant, as the Martennis is so close to the Baxter place. Oh – apparently Samantha herself has given several lads the brush-off just lately, saying she's busy with her A levels.'

Yates fell silent, reflecting on what he and the other man had learned. Just lately he himself had been told he was a good interviewer, but if that was true he wasn't sure why, unless it was that he sometimes received answers other than verbal ones. A case of what was not said rather than what was: a fold of the lips, a narrowing of the eyes, the uneasy shifting of a bottom on a chair... When he pursued such unspoken answers he sometimes found out things that hadn't come to light before.

Channon was watching him, dark eyes alert. 'Impressions?' he asked. 'Anything strike you?'

'Nobody said anything against Samantha,' said Yates carefully, 'but I got a whiff of what might have been envy from some of the girls. She was very bright, she was pretty, she could pick and choose among the lads ... she was an only child whose parents doted. Then again, nobody said as much, but I suspect she was no angel. I think she might have been known to go for it – sex, I mean. That's all I can come up with.'

Channon nodded. He didn't see Samantha as an angel, either, just a lively young woman, well blessed with mental and physical attributes. The post-mortem had confirmed that she was sexually active, and they still needed knowledge of her current partner or partners. 'No hint of any of them having a close relationship with her? Or of anybody who had a grudge, or who actively disliked her?'

'No. I'd say she wasn't the kind of girl who gets herself disliked. Just envied a bit.'

'What about statements?' asked Channon.

'We've taken them, though not from every single youngster. Just about how she seemed, what time she left, transport for arrival and departure.'

'Well done. What's your name, by the way?'

'Yates, sir.' There was a touch of surprised resentment in the answer.

'I know that – your first name, I mean.'

'Dave, sir.'

'OK, Dave, and thanks. Get off home, now. I'll need you here first thing tomorrow.' When Yates had gone Channon beckoned DC Donald, who had spent hours with the Trudgeons and was now waiting to have a word. She was a fair wholesome-looking woman in her forties, highly competent and loaded with common sense.

At that moment she looked exhausted.

'Hello, Mary, you can give me any non-urgent info tomorrow,' he said. 'For now, just tell me how they're coping.'

'Devastated, but quite calm,' she said simply. 'They're consumed by guilt that they were in London, when as a rule they rarely leave the farm. Mrs Trudgeon's sister from the Martennis is spending the night with them and going home in the morning. She feels even more guilty, I think, because she didn't check on Samantha before going to bed herself. I'm afraid I told them you'd probably be round to have a word in person.'

Channon nodded. All victims had a need to speak to whoever was in charge, and Mr and Mrs Trudgeon would be feeling the need more strongly than most. 'I'll go first thing tomorrow,' he promised. 'Have our men finished in her room?'

'Yes, but I've warned the Trudgeons to leave it alone. They'll let you take the place apart as long as you get him. Not that they're terribly vengeful – just worried about it happening to somebody else. Mrs Trudgeon, though... I'm not sure if it's sunk in properly yet. They're really nice people – isn't it good we have proof that they were somewhere else when it happened?'

Channon nodded, knowing exactly what she meant. In a case like this the last thing he wanted was the father being guilty – or the mother, come to that.

Channon unlocked the door of his house and knew he'd done well to be back by midnight. There had been times in the past when he'd worked all night, come home for a shave and a shower and some breakfast, then gone right back on the job again. Now, though, he set his own hours of work, and tried not to expect the impossible, either from himself or from those under him.

It was silent in the hall, but he was used to that, and to the scent of wax polish and fresh flowers. Keeping the place up together was the responsibility of his part-time housekeeper, as was the cooking; she would have left something in the fridge, ready to heat up in the microwave. He had no objection to eating a hot meal after midnight; he rarely went to bed before two, anyway.

He liked his home. It was set apart from other habitation yet not isolated; a cream-washed old house surrounded by garden and within sight and sound of the sea, in a village about nine miles from Curdower. His mind still on Samantha, Channon poured himself a whisky and went up to run a bath. He could think in the bath better than anywhere else, and at that moment he needed to think about his priorities for first thing in the morning.

He lay there soaking and sipping at his whisky. Were they all fast asleep at the Curdower roundhouse, he wondered. Was Sally Baxter curled up close to her barely civil husband? Tomorrow he would read Baxter's statement and find out how well he had known Samantha – whether it was purely a teacher–student relationship. She'd been killed within yards of Baxter's home, after all. *His* home, as well as his son's. Bowles was wrong about the boy, he was sure of it.

Minutes later he went to the bedroom to put on his old towelling robe, and from force of habit switched on the lamp above the photograph of Claire and Danny. That old cliché, 'time is a great healer', was true; oh yes, it was true. He could look at their likenesses now and feel only a dull ache. The sense of being under torture, the rending apart with knives, the long bitter agony of loss were all healing with the passage of time. He'd had to leave the family home and set up here on his own – he couldn't have stayed on. Now, though, he was finding he could look back on the happy times and be thankful for them; he could visit the cemetery … what he couldn't yet do was to talk about his wife and son in casual conversation. People knew that and made allowances. One day he would do it, he promised himself, but not just yet … no, not just yet.

It was one o'clock in the morning and Sally was lying awake, one hand feeling the beat of her heart... How many beats between each crash of the waves? She started to count, but couldn't concentrate. How many waves had washed over Samantha? If there'd been a southwesterly gale behind the tide her body might have been lifted and carried to somebody else's beach instead of tucked neatly behind a rock on Curdower.

Poor Ben, he'd had to repeat the story of finding her when he made his second statement. Two different policemen came and they'd all had to add more detail to what they'd said already; how well they knew her, when they had last spoken to her. Rob had had to talk about her as a pupil, Luke as a friend, Tessa as an acquaintance ... and Ben, poor Ben, as a dead body washed by the morning sea. She'd found herself wondering what it must be like to go through all that if you were hiding something – if you were guilty.

It was rare for her to long for her mother, who had died of cancer when Ben was only a baby, but she wished she had somebody close – a sister or brother. She could have told them what was happening, shared her worries. They had few relations, her and Rob, but up to now it had only seemed to make them closer as a family. Mentally she reviewed her friends in Manchester, and decided against talking to any of them. Being embroiled in a murder seemed so over-the-top – so sensational.

At her side in the big bed Rob was restless. He too must be worried or he would be in the deep, peaceful sleep that always came to him when they'd made love. She recalled how she'd expected it to relax them both; they would turn to each other for mutual comfort, with desire almost a secondary aspect of the familiar expression of their love.

But it hadn't turned out like that. From the start Rob had been rough and urgent, gripping her thighs and hips until it hurt; kissing her breasts and her mouth so hard she'd had to push him away in order to breathe. 'Hey,' she'd protested, 'steady on, wild man.'

'I love you, I love you,' he'd gasped frenziedly as he reached his climax; then as he was shuddering with release, 'Sally, my Sally, don't ever doubt it – I love you...'

Afterwards there had been no lying close with his head on her breasts, no falling asleep in each other's arms, flesh to flesh. He had given her a sudden desperate squeeze and then turned on his side away from her; but not, it seemed, to sleep peacefully. He was tossing and turning; once he muttered something but she couldn't tell what it was.

Unable to settle, she slipped quietly from the bed and went to the window that faced the sea. Small and arched, there were four of them facing in different directions, but this was her favourite. People talked about the night sky being like black velvet, she thought, but right now the heavens looked grey – a dark steel-grey, the stars dimmed by the light of a dazzling moon. She could make out the coastal path as it climbed up towards the headland, the cliff-top thicket of gorse and brambles still bounded by police tapes, and – good grief – a man in uniform was there. What a job, standing guard through the night. Perhaps he had somebody with him, or a colleague down on the beach?

There were several little white bundles lying on the ground in front of the tape-bordered thicket ... what on earth? Then it dawned. They were flowers, the first of many, perhaps, from Samantha's school friends, from the villagers, maybe even from the customers of the Martennis Inn. There was nothing any of those people could do to express their grief and outrage, nothing apart from placing flowers as near as possible to where a girl they all knew had been murdered. That, and helping the police find her killer.

Sally thought of Channon's dark, steady gaze and was glad that he was in charge with Bowles as the underling, rather than the other way round.

Chapter Six

Malachi dug the toe of his trainer between the cobbles of the slipway and looked up at Ben. 'My mum doesn't know I'm here,' he said, dark eyes glinting. 'She says I'm to steer clear of your family.'

Ben observed his friend carefully. 'If she says that, why've you come?'

Malachi shrugged. 'It's better here than at home, an' anyway, she's still in bed. She's fed up because the police have been round asking questions.'

'What? You mean about–' Ben extended one finger and pointed to the rocks.

'Mmm.' Malachi wriggled his shoulders with a hint of bravado. 'My dad was walking home from the Martennis when the murder happened. He was too drunk to drive an' my mum keeps telling him off for having had more than his three pints.'

Ben tried to keep his face blank. He couldn't understand Malachi. For one thing he still seemed a bit – not pleased, exactly – but a bit *thrilled* about the murder. For another, he talked as if he didn't like his mum and dad. Of course he'd never seemed to like his mum all that much, she was too bossy, but now it sounded as if he wasn't worried that the police might suspect his dad of being the murderer.

Malachi watched his friend to see how he'd taken it. He liked Ben a lot, though he was a bit soft for a boy – too kind, too easily upset. It made him, Malachi, pretend he didn't care about things that he did care about, to show that although he was the youngest, he was the toughest.

Ben thought of his own mum and felt a warmth inside his chest. It was in the very same place as the wobbly feeling that came when he saw the morning sun shining on the beach. During the night he had realized that he might never have the wobbly feeling again, because the beach was spoiled now – spoiled for ever. He still felt a bit sick when he thought about that cold stiff hand with the blue fingertips.

His eyes began to sting and he had to blink very hard to prevent tears coming. Quickly he turned away. 'We can't walk along the high-water line today,' he said, 'not with the police still here. Come on, let's go to the den for a bit. Dad says I've to stay within calling distance.'

Together they headed for the dense thicket of shrubs behind the holiday cottages. In the tangled evergreen depths was the construction of old boards and sacking that was their own special place, their den. As they crawled towards it Malachi was wondering why the police were still poking about on the beach, and Ben was wishing that Malachi had stayed at home. It worried him, because he knew you shouldn't wish that about your best friend, even if he was only nine and three-quarters and you were nearly twelve.

Luke wandered into the kitchen and watched Tessa mixing orange segments with grapes in one of her bouts of healthy eating. 'I can't see why the police wanted my bike,' he said gloomily. 'They don't need proof that I gave Sammy a lift – they already know that.'

Tessa shot him a look. Usually he was so good-humoured he got on her nerves, but now he was in such low spirits she felt as if she quite liked him. 'You need a shave,' she said benignly, telling herself that a mention of his pathetic drift of whiskers was bound to cheer him up.

Sure enough he smiled and stroked the soft, reluctant stubble. 'D'you reckon? Maybe I'll leave it till tomorrow.' He watched her brewing a mug of herb tea and groaned in disbelief. 'Is this your *breakfast*, all this fruit and stuff? I'm going to have scrambled eggs with fried bread. Where's Mum, anyway?'

'Out,' said Tessa briefly.

He opened his mouth to protest, but changed his mind. 'It's only nine o'clock,' he pointed out. 'Where's she gone? Is she on her own?'

Tessa rolled her eyes and sat at the table. 'You think the killer's hanging around on the cliff path within spitting distance? Well, even if he is you needn't rush out to protect her – she's gone off in the car. She says she wants to think. In any case, we're supposed to get our own breakfast at weekends.'

'I know that.' He sat down facing her. 'Tess, have you any ideas on what the police could be after with my bike?'

She shrugged. 'It could be some obscure forensic test that we know nothing about, I suppose. Maybe even something to eliminate you. What does Dad think?'

Luke avoided her eyes. 'I haven't talked to him about it. He seems a bit edgy about us all being involved in a murder.'

'We're not *all* involved,' she retorted, at once forgetting her resolve to cheer him up. 'It's you who's suspect number one.'

Luke stared at her, his eyes suddenly hard. 'I gave Sammy Trudgeon a lift,' he said abruptly, 'because she asked me. I don't – I didn't particularly like her. End of story.'

'If you didn't particularly like her, why did you stay chatting to her outside the Martennis?'

'What?'

Tessa sat with her mug in one hand and her plait in the other, twirling and twisting it. 'That's what you told the inspector and his sidekick – that you and Sammy stayed chatting for a while.'

'That's right, we did,' Luke agreed slowly, chewing his lower lip. 'Just idle stuff. Out of politeness, really.'

'Really.' She mimicked his tone. 'That's all right, then.'

Luke got to his feet and took eggs from the pottery hen on the dresser. 'Thanks for the vote of confidence,' he said.

She was going a bit over the top, Sally acknowledged, leaving Luke and the rest of them and zooming along the lanes like a bat out of hell. She wouldn't be away for long, she couldn't be, not with this horror hanging over them, but she needed a spell of peace and quiet to get her mind sorted out.

As she neared the village she could hear the church bells, and felt a twinge of guilt because she wouldn't be in the congregation. She wasn't a devout Christian, she wasn't a regular worshipper, but she believed in God, or at least in the forces of good and evil, and so went to church or the tiny Methodist chapel about once a month. The force of evil was alive and kicking in Curdower, she told herself, but she couldn't face going to either place, not today. They'd be saying prayers for the Trudgeons and everybody would know that Luke was one of the last to see Samantha alive. They might even know that his motorbike had been taken away.

Now, on impulse, she skirted the village and headed for the highest point in the area, a patch of rough common land known locally as the Becky. Rob had found out that centuries ago a beacon had been erected there – a kind of makeshift lighthouse which had long since fallen into ruin. She slowed at a crossroads to give way to a car travelling east, and saw that inside it was DCI Channon, with a fair-haired woman at the wheel.

The tension inside Sally shifted and eased at the sight of the detective's dark profile and thick, grey-streaked hair. He had integrity, she was sure of it. She simply couldn't see him trying to pin a murder on Luke...

Minutes later she stopped the car on rough ground next to the ruins of the stone tower. It had been hazy down in the village, but up here the sky was clearing. She hoped that her mind would clear as well, and put an end to this – this what? Dread? No, dread was too strong a word – it was a ridiculous word. But ... there *had* sometimes been miscarriages of justice, cases of police incompetence or corruption. Dread wasn't a ridiculous word at all. It described her feelings exactly.

She got out of the car and stood leaning

against the bonnet. It was very quiet; not a sound to be heard apart from the sigh of the wind, the song of a lark high above her and the faint tolling of bells from Curdower church. She stared down at the patchwork fields and took the clean, salt-tinged air deep into her lungs. Luke had had nothing to do with Samantha's death, she was certain of it. But what had he been concealing when Channon called earlier in the day?

At the time she'd been so on edge at being questioned by the police that she'd seen nothing amiss in Luke's responses. It was in the silence of the night, after that fierce bout of sex – she refused to call it lovemaking – that she began to recall every word that had passed between her family and DCI Channon. Lying next to Rob and listening to the endless slap of the waves, a deep unease had unfolded itself in her mind.

Years of interpreting childish fibs and evasions had taught her to recognize the signs in her eldest, even at seventeen years of age. He had said: 'Her parents knew she might ask for a lift – they said it was OK,' and, 'We – we talked a bit and then I had a ride along the coast road.' Frank, innocent answers, delivered with conviction. Was she a mother out of a horror story to remember his hesitation when he said, 'we talked'? To recall the way he had avoided looking directly at anybody, and how he'd nibbled the inside of his bottom lip? All before he'd been told that the dead girl was Samantha?

Scenes from his childhood crowded her memory. 'She just got in the way when I was running upstairs' – that was what he'd said at eleven when he'd thumped Tessa for breaking his latest Airfix kit. 'I've finished my homework, so can I go and play footie?' – a twelve-year-old just chosen for the school team, whose homework wasn't finished at all. 'Oh, this kid at school left them with me because he didn't want his mum to find them,' – at fourteen, when she'd found the porn mags under his bed.

Incidents from his early days ... times when he'd stretched the truth a bit; nothing horrendous, nothing sinister, just a boy taking the easy way out of trouble. But the thing was, she'd always known when he was telling a lie or being evasive, because he always used to nibble the inside of his bottom lip.

Had he perhaps made a pass at Samantha, even though he was keen on Poppy, rather than simply 'talking for a bit' outside the Martennis? Was he scared to admit to it in case it incriminated him? Was she pregnant? He knew all about responsible sex – she and Rob had seen to that – but he was by nature impulsive and at his age impulse could overcome prudence. He couldn't have kept that from her, though, she'd have known. He might even have admitted it.

Was he, perhaps, shielding a friend who fancied Samantha? She didn't know the answer to those questions, how could she, but two things she did know. One was that he'd been telling the truth in answer to her questions yesterday, there in the kitchen, with the sunbeam shining over his shoulders. The other – and at this she grunted in deep resentment; the other was that for the first time in years, if not in their entire marriage, Rob was letting her down.

He was brushing aside her concerns for Luke – Rob, who was always as ready as she was to bundle the children off to the doctor if they were ill; Rob the devoted father who had insisted on talking to Ben's teacher when he'd had nightmares as a six-year-old, who long ago had taken a plump little Tessa on his knee for a cuddle and a chat the time she pushed another girl into the swimming pool at school. Rob, who was her rock, her safe haven when there was trouble.

But, she told herself with sudden honesty, the devoted father was disastrously lacking in patience with his eldest son, and had been for years. Not only that, he had given no support whatsoever to his youngest when the boy found a dead body on the beach... As for her, she was desperate for reassurance and he wouldn't even let her talk about the murder. This morning in bed he had called her a ghoul. 'For crying out loud, stop going on about it, woman,' he had snapped. 'You're nothing but a ghoul!'

All at once the wind blew more strongly across the hilltop and moaned through the ruined tower behind her. It sounds like a soul in torment, she told herself, shivering, and then straightened her shoulders and planted her feet apart. A soul in torment? Come *on!* Why was she agonizing, why was she laying herself open to premonitions of doom? They lived in a roundhouse where there were no corners for the devil, didn't they? Well then, if Rob either couldn't or wouldn't help her, she'd do it on her own. She'd make sure that the devil didn't come in, to the house or to the family. And that was that!

Channon took DC Mary Donald with him to see the Trudgeons, partly because she'd spent time with them the previous day, and partly because he thought that Bowles's abrasive manner would be out of place at Blue Leaze Farm. They had left the sergeant sifting through a pile of reports, apparently quite content, perhaps because arrests and intimidation were more in his line than giving out sympathy.

It was peaceful around the village green after the noise of the incident room; trees were whispering in a light breeze and a pale sun was struggling through a haze of cloud.

All was silent when suddenly the church bells rang out, slow and sombre and oddly muted. Well, it *was* Sunday, Channon reminded himself, but at his side Mary Donald gave a satisfied little smile. 'It's for Samantha, sir – they're doing a muffled peal – ringing right through till the special service at ten thirty.'

'Will her parents hear it?' That seemed important. 'Will they know it's for her?'

Mary nodded. 'They'll know, the vicar will have told them; and they'll hear – the sound carries for miles across the fields. Dave Yates was saying he's going to church, sir, on your instructions.'

Channon shrugged as he closed the car door. 'A long shot – just to see if anything strikes him. He knows most of the regulars, but they're expecting a big turn-up today.' As they drove away from the village he fell silent. Samantha's dead body on Curdower beach had been an affront, a brutal intrusion in this rural community, but now it seemed to him quite fitting that people she'd known all her life should be ringing the bells of their little church for her, and joining in prayers for her family. Like the bundles of flowers on the cliff top, it was something they could do in face of the unacceptable. Maybe the murderer would be sitting in one of the pews, feigning grief, pretending innocence. Channon wondered

97

if such a thing had been at the back of his mind when he asked Yates to go to the service, or had he been clutching at straws?

Up near Blue Leaze the breeze was stronger, blowing in from the sea. They left the car and Channon found himself practising reassuring phrases about finding the killer and how many men were working on the case. Together they headed for the low, stone-built farmhouse with the blue door. Rather different, he thought, from the gracious Blankett dwelling across the fields. Different, but with its own wholesome charm. Here there was a colourful cottage-garden in front of the house rather than orderly flowerbeds, rambling roses in new leaf around the porch instead of twin pillars and a neat white portico.

The same care was evident, though, as at Blankett's Farm; the yard was immaculate, the outbuildings well maintained, and beyond a low stone wall dozens of hens were pecking around in a field – part of the award-winning natural farming, no doubt. Sometime he would like to see over the place, but not now, oh, certainly not now.

'Jim Trudgeon's parents from Plymouth should be here,' Mary was saying. 'They'd been sent for before I left last night. There aren't any on the mother's side – just the sister at the Martennis Inn.'

'If they've arrived you can talk to the

grandma,' he ordered. 'Grandparents see a lot, and sometimes they're more objective than parents. Chat to her – get impressions.'

A small, grey-haired woman answered the door. The grandma in question, thought Channon, noting her puffy eyes and fixed expression. Obviously she'd shed tears, but had the full implications, the full horror of a murder in the family sunk in? He doubted it – he'd seen that look of blank incomprehension before.

Calm, capable, respectful, he introduced himself and Mary Donald, aware that he was exuding confidence and wondering how he could do it when so far he hadn't even developed a feeling for the case, let alone picked up a definite lead. The grandmother was shaking her head repeatedly. 'My daughter-in-law is under heavy sedation and still asleep,' she said wearily, 'but my son's in the yard somewhere with his dad. The work of the farm has to go on, you see.'

Channon nodded. 'Don't worry, I'll find them. Oh – we didn't seal up Samantha's bedroom, but I expect your son has told you about leaving everything just as it is for another day or two? No cleaning, no dusting, no tidying?'

Mrs Trudgeon senior wafted a hand, as if cleaning and dusting were beyond her comprehension. 'Whatever you say. We'll do whatever you want. Just go easy on my son, though. He's getting – he's getting angry.'

Channon sighed. This didn't sound like the quiet, restrained individual he'd seen the previous day, the man who had handed over the photograph of his only child. 'He feels helpless,' the grandmother explained. 'Guilty as well, because he wasn't here when it happened. He feels he should be taking action.'

'So would I in his place,' agreed Channon, 'but honestly, there's nothing he can do, apart from giving us information. We've taken over now, we're in charge. He'll have to trust us.' Silently he added: and at least he and his wife aren't suspects. Once, as a sergeant years before, he had been instrumental in convicting an apparently devoted mother of her young son's murder – a case that had caused him so much distress he almost left the force...

'DC Donald will explain what's happening while I go and talk to your son,' he said, and to Mary, 'I'll see you back at the car.'

He found the two men in one of the barns loading bales of straw on to a trailer; the father simply an older, greyer version of the son, who was now almost unrecognizable as the dignified man of the previous afternoon. His thick brown hair standing on end, he was tight-lipped and aggressive, shifting the heavy bales as if they were cardboard boxes. 'I can't hang around doing nothing,' was his greeting, 'nor act as if nothing's happened. I must know what's going on!'

'That's why I've come,' Channon told him gently. 'To assure you that we're doing everything in our power to find who's responsible for Samantha's death. There's a massive enquiry under way, Mr Trudgeon. We didn't bother you too much with questions yesterday, but I know DC Donald here asked you to list any friends of your daughter who aren't connected with school.'

'Friends? *Friends?*' the farmer repeated incredulously. 'For God's sake, do you think a friend killed her? It's a maniac on the loose, man – anybody with half a brain can see that!'

Trudgeon senior was looking as if he wanted to throw up, but he managed to put a restraining hand on his son's arm. Channon said quietly to the older man: 'It's all right, sir, we understand, but whether it seems sensible to your son or not we have to go through certain laid-down procedures. They're tried and tested and they get results.'

Jim Trudgeon flopped down on a bale of straw, and the other two did the same. As if slightly ashamed of his outburst, the farmer said flatly, 'Before the knock-out drugs took effect on her my wife and I wrote down the name and address of every person we could think of who knows Samantha, now or in the past, including a few young lads – you could call 'em boyfriends, I suppose. That's what you asked for, isn't it? I've got the list here.' He took some folded sheets of paper from his jacket pocket and looked at the detective with a touch of scorn. 'I simply can't see it could have been anybody she knew...'

Channon hesitated, but it would have to be said. 'She did go out again, Mr Trudgeon, quite late. She changed her clothes. We think she might have been meeting somebody.'

Jim Trudgeon stared as if it was the first he'd heard of it, but Channon knew he'd been told the essential facts within hours of his daughter's body being found. Clearly it hadn't registered why she'd been out on the cliff path at that hour. With a rush of compassion he changed the subject. 'We know that Samantha was good on computers, so it's possible there's a clue in the memory somewhere. May we take the PC base unit and modem for one of our men to work on? If there's farm business on it we'll look after it.'

Trudgeon was calming down now that something was happening. 'Samantha was clever,' he said. 'Quick, you know. She did all my letters and kept most of the farm's affairs on the computer. Once we knew she had an aptitude for it we got her a good one, though she says – she said, I mean – that it's already out of date. You can do what you like with it.'

'Thanks. I'll send somebody up for it later, and for anything else that might be useful. We'll be off now, and like I said, you can rest assured that we're doing our best.' The two men followed him out of the barn to find the hazy clouds clearing, while from the direction of the village, faint and slightly uneven against the gusting of the breeze, came the pealing of church bells.

Jim Trudgeon stood quite still and gripped his father's arm. 'They're ringing the bells for Samantha,' he said hoarsely. 'Can you hear, Dad?'

'I hear,' said his father brokenly. 'I hear, son.'

Quietly Channon went to the car, and when he looked back the father and son were clasped in each other's arms with the sound of the bells wrapped round them.

Zenobia Gribble examined herself warily in the wardrobe mirror. She never knew whether it would be her or a large-eyed child who stared back, a child in an outsize hand-me-down dress and too-small shoes. Today it was her full-grown, thank goodness, gypsy blood and all – her father's blood. It shouted out loud from the mass of dark hair and the golden skin, but she wasn't too sure about the eyes. Cat's eyes, her ma had called them, but her granny said they were the eyes of a tiger. What had they known about it, though?

What had they known about anything in that poky little house next to the pig farm the other side of Falmouth?

Now Zennie smoothed her hands over the curve of her hips, from force of habit giving a wiggle and a sway. She was wearing a tight skirt and top in emerald green, because she liked jewel colours; she liked animal prints and brocade and lurex – somebody had once told her they were exotic fabrics, and that they emphasized her appeal – her appeal to men, they'd meant. Ever since her figure first developed at fourteen men had been after her. They were fascinated by her, they wanted her, and by the time she reached sixteen, she'd known how to encourage them.

She'd encouraged the man who gave her Malachi, even when he hurt her so much she thought she would die. She encouraged him every day and every night for two weeks, because fool that she was, she'd thought he would marry her, that he would sail away with her in his big white yacht. What an innocent she'd been – an innocent little fool with an untouched woman's body ... untouched until the white yacht sailed into harbour.

She gazed at her reflection, remembering. She made herself remember because it helped her to keep her vow. He'd been twenty years older than her, and she'd imagined that all men must do to women what he'd done to her in the shuttered cabin on the big white yacht. She'd suffered what he did, even pretended she liked and understood it, because she wanted to sail away with him and say goodbye Ma, goodbye Granny, goodbye Uncle Ishmael, goodbye all you scruffy cousins with your grand, outlandish names. Goodbye the smell of pigs … and hello, wedding dress.

But nothing had been further from his mind. 'You asked for it,' he laughed, when his man was packing up and she cried. 'You asked for it and I obliged. If I've left you with something you don't want, then get rid of it,' and he'd slapped a wad of tenners in her hand.

Within the hour she'd watched him leave on the evening tide, her soft inner flesh still raw and her heart changing permanently from a sentimental dream machine to what felt like a solid chunk of granite in her chest. There, amid the grasses round Pendennis Castle, she had planned her future, vowing to attract men as a flame attracts moths. She would tempt them until they were gasping, and then she would refuse them, one after the other. Nobody – *nobody* would ever do it to her again – she'd see to that.

She sat on the rumpled bedclothes and asked herself why her life story seemed so old-fashioned. It was as though it had happened fifty or more years ago – the innocent young girl seduced by a scoundrel. She was out of place – out of her time. Grimly she looked at Georgie's neat bed across the room. Georgie, poor Georgie. Sometimes she almost forgot that solemn vow when it came to her husband. He believed he was Malachi's father, that the boy was a seven months baby. That was something else she'd messed up. When she found herself pregnant she should have used the money for the purpose it had been given, and stayed single. She could have been a model, she could have gone into films, but because she was a soft fool she'd hung on to the baby and married the kind, talkative little man who helped out at the pig farm.

It had been the surprise of her life to find that once he'd got over the shock of her accepting him, gentle little Georgie wanted what all the others wanted. She'd had to give it to him of course, to explain the baby. With a bit of subterfuge and help from her ma she'd even convinced him that he was the first; but kind though he'd been, considerate even, when it was over she hadn't been able to stop herself vomiting all over their new pink sheets. That had shaken him. It had shaken her as well, and then it happened the next time, and the next, so she told him he'd made her pregnant and steeled herself to refuse him. Kind he might be, but he was a man, and she'd made a vow about men.

Since then she'd always allowed him to kiss her – not on the lips, but on the neck or the hand or the inside of her elbow, and now he slept in a separate bed from choice, changing over the years from the good-natured, energetic man she'd married into the weak, faded individual who was still her husband.

Even worse than that, the little boy who'd been conceived during a series of sadistic rituals grew to look more and more like the man who had fathered him. He was dark, fortunately, so people thought he took after her, but she could see his father in his eyes and the turn of his head. She simply couldn't take to him. As for loving him … everybody was always on about love – on the telly, in films, in her magazines and romantic novels. She'd often tried to imagine what it was like, this love; she'd come to the conclusion that it must be a special sort of feeling, but she didn't feel anything special for Malachi. In fact it infuriated her when Sally Baxter and other women in the village so obviously doted on their children.

She went to gaze out of the window. Why did she have to live like this? What had she ever done to deserve it? Girls in their teens lived better lives than she did. They had mums and dads who made a fuss of them and taught them to read and write before they even started school. Samantha Trudgeon hadn't known she was born, passing exams, getting ready for university, wearing nice clothes and living on a posh farm. She'd never been kept off school to look after the young ones so her mother could have a day in bed. She'd never been shown up in front of all the class because she couldn't make head nor tail of her reading book...

Zennie stared at the church tower beyond the trees and felt stifled. Why should she have to stay in this stuffy little village? She didn't belong here. She belonged out on the open road in a painted caravan, with flowers in her hair and gold sandals on her feet. Maybe singing round a campfire at night.

But if she was out on the road in a caravan, who would stop the police from accusing Georgie of murdering that spoilt Samantha? Little Georgie, who wouldn't hurt a fly.

Chapter Seven

Eating a buttered scone and looking as if he could do with a bit of action, Bowles was waiting outside the incident room. 'We've got the walker,' was his greeting. 'He was in a bed and breakfast place the other side of Mevagissey.'

'Who tracked him down?' asked Channon with interest.

'A local constable. He'd been checking on B&Bs and came across our man as he was packing up to set off on the day's walk.'

'Has anybody talked to him?'

'No, the constable just checked he was the man who crossed farmland near Curdower and then rang in. He's holding him in case we want a statement.'

'Of course we want a statement,' sighed Channon. Routine must be followed, but a man who plodded along the coastal path and stayed at registered B&Bs didn't sound like one who could kill with such ferocity. He saw that Bowles was still chewing. 'Missed your breakfast?' he asked tetchily.

The younger man swallowed. 'The frayed old Blankett brought a big basket of eats for everybody,' he said. 'Scones and rolls and fruit cake – pretty moreish and probably all gone by now.'

A gesture in keeping with the Lady Bountiful image, decided Channon, but it was good of the old girl. He tried to picture her in a big apron at the kitchen table, and failed. He must remember to have another chat with her to get a bit of background on the locals. A woman in her position, an employer born and bred in the area, could get to know all sorts of things. 'Did you tell her we'd tracked down the man she saw?' he asked.

Bowles nodded. 'She said–' and here he mimicked an educated accent: '"Even though I hadn't seen his face, I expected you to trace him from my description, sergeant. However, I do realize that he isn't likely to be your number one suspect."'

'Well, he isn't,' agreed Channon, 'not unless he's been putting oil in a car or changing a fan belt. Have you had a chance to run a check on him?' Bowles wasn't one to miss the obvious, thank goodness.

'Yes. His name's Barry Miller, but there's nothing on him, so far.' He jerked his head backwards to the computers. 'They're still checking.'

'Go and see him,' instructed Channon. 'Suss him out. Get impressions. See if he saw Samantha do anything or go anywhere after she passed him, or if she spoke to anybody else. Get his statement and find out where he's heading on his walk in case we need him. Not much point in checking his gear. If he's guilty he'll have got rid of the evidence long since. And Bowles...'

'Yes, sir?'

'No unnecessary intimidation.'

Unabashed, Bowles grinned. 'Me? As if I would.' He grabbed a nearby constable and went off to his car.

Channon beckoned John Meade and handed over Jim Trudgeon's list. 'Start men on that lot, will you? They're Samantha's contacts from her dad. Basic enquiries only at this stage. And fix up with admin for a full briefing session at four o'clock this afternoon. Everybody to be there unless they have a watertight excuse, and even then I want a written progress note sent in.'

Meade nodded. 'I'll fix it. And do you want these? They're copies of the latest statements for you to look at – at least, those I think you'll want to read personally. I'll be working on the duty rotas if you want me.'

Channon went to his table in the corner and poured himself some water, then leafed through the statements and extracted that of Robert Baxter. He read it and found no real surprises – not that he'd expected any. Baxter hadn't left the house and garden all evening. He'd confirmed that Luke came in about eleven and he hadn't heard him go out again. Happened to look out towards the sea before going to bed at about eleven thirty – bright moonlight, no sign of anyone on the cliff path. As for school, in his own little group Samantha could be called the star pupil – a natural – her full-time computer teacher would confirm that. Baxter himself didn't know her outside school.

Then the statement of one James Tresillian, director of A level studies, who said that Samantha was a good worker, loads of application and very bright. Expecting good grades – As and Bs in Chemistry, Biology and Computer Studies, subjects needed for her chosen career in Food Sciences. Luke Baxter was also a very able pupil, expected to get good grades with an A in his best subject – Geography. Didn't belong to his father's group, as he wasn't taking computing at A level, but he would know all those who were.

Tresillian was full of praise for Baxter senior. His voluntary help was invaluable, especially with students doing business studies and accountancy. In fact, the school was hoping to offer him a regular part-time job when the budget allowed. The students liked him and he also helped them in environmental studies, a particular interest of his and one which appealed to the idealistic side of the young people. Because of his expertise on the subject they called him Mr Greenpeace, and no, he didn't think

Baxter had known Samantha outside school.

Not much to be suspicious of there, Channon acknowledged, though Mr Greenpeace's concern for the environment hadn't stopped him buying a gas-guzzling Discovery... He flipped through the bundle to find that Luke's own statement added little to what he'd said already, except that he'd changed, 'Sammy asked for a lift' to 'Sammy had asked me beforehand if I could give her a lift to the Martennis, so after the disco I said I'd take her, as I lived nearest the inn.' A slight but prudent adjustment in view of what Yates had unearthed about Luke elbowing another lad aside.

From behind his computer Steve Soker eyed Channon, but so far he had come up with nothing interesting enough to warrant interrupting the DCI's chain of thought.

Bowles found Barry Miller having a cup of coffee in the constable's neat little sitting room. He was lean and fair, with neat, unremarkable features, a mouthful of dazzlingly white teeth, and light green eyes. He seemed quite relaxed. I'll soon put an end to that, thought Bowles, introducing himself. 'We're sorry to inconvenience you, sir,' he said smoothly, 'but this is a murder investigation. A witness saw you on a public footpath in the area of the murder, some hours before it took place. Apparently the murder victim passed that way, also.'

Miller breathed out and smiled slightly, flashing the teeth. 'Yes, well? I pass several people in the course of a day's walk, sergeant. Where am I supposed to have seen him?'

Clever, thought Bowles, to pretend he imagined it to have been a man. Though if he hadn't watched television or heard a radio he couldn't know it was a girl. Not unless he was the killer.

'You were on a right of way across farmland near Curdower village,' said Bowles. 'You've agreed on that, I believe?'

'Yes, yes. Friday afternoon.'

'And did you have access to a vehicle of any description, Mr Miller?'

The green eyes widened. 'You think I borrowed a tractor?' he said mockingly. 'I'm on a walking holiday, sergeant. For exercise!'

This one was going to need taking down a peg. 'Please answer the question,' replied Bowles, biding his time.

'No, I did not have access to a vehicle.'

'Thank you. Now, did you pass anyone as you walked across Blankett's Farm? That's the one with the big white house, but you'll remember that, of course.'

Miller frowned. 'There was a long, curving path with fenced-off pasture on one side... I might have seen somebody. I think there was an old battleaxe prowling across the hillside. I remember her watching me from a distance and I wondered if she was going to object to me crossing her husband's land. They don't like public footpaths, you know, these blasted farmers.'

That at least was true, Bowles told himself. 'Can you recall anyone else, Mr Miller?'

'No, I don't think so, not on that stretch. Oh, just a minute! Was there a young woman? No – she was more of a schoolgirl – in school uniform, anyway. I remember her because the uniform seemed out of place in the fields. She was fairish, I think, and quite pretty.' Miller gathered himself together and sat upright in his chair. Behind him the uniformed constable managed to look both stolid and alert.

'Did you speak to each other?' asked Bowles.

'Just a nod and a good afternoon, you know the sort of thing. I remember thinking she must live on a farm, but she was heading away from the white house.' Miller let out a long, heavy sigh. 'She's the one you mean, isn't she? Somebody murdered her?'

If this was an act it was pretty good, Bowles told himself with grudging respect. There'd be nothing to connect this one with Samantha. He'd have showered and changed twenty-four hours ago, scrubbed his fingernails, cleaned his boots, gone through his belongings. 'Yes, somebody did,' he agreed briskly. 'Now, where did you spend Friday night?'

'A cottage not far from Curdower. Look – the woman gave me her card. She did good food. I had an evening meal there as well as breakfast.'

Bowles glanced at the card. 'We'll check with her,' he told Miller. 'Did you leave the house after your evening meal?'

'No, I turned in early and read in bed for a bit.'

That was easy enough to check with the landlady. 'We need to examine your back-pack,' he said briskly. 'We have reasonable grounds.' He didn't miss the relaxing of Miller's mouth at his words. They'd find nothing, and this cocky devil knew it, but the man's reply showed resentment.

'Reasonable?' he echoed. 'I saw her when she was alive, so I'm under suspicion of killing her, is that it?'

Bowles was unmoved. 'We don't reckon to miss anything when we're investigating a murder.' He turned to the local man. 'Constable, you have Mr Miller's belongings?'

The man produced a navy blue rucksack and Bowles examined the contents, deliberately taking his time. Nothing out of the ordinary, but then he hadn't expected there would be. He plonked it down on the settee next to Miller. 'Did the girl continue along the path when you'd passed each other?'

'Yes, I think so. I didn't turn round to watch her.'

'She spoke to nobody else, as far as you know?'

'There was nobody else around,' answered Miller. 'Is that all, sergeant?'

'Not quite,' said Bowles. 'We need you to make an official statement of what you've just told us. But first we'll make a note of your planned onward route and your home address in case we need to contact you again. You can give details to my colleague.' He let the DC take notes, telling himself that they'd get nothing on this one. As soon as they'd hammered out the statement somebody else could go and see the bed and breakfast woman. He, Bowles, would put his mind to something more rewarding.

'Look at them, gawping like morons!' Rob stared in disgust at the crowd on the cliff top. 'They'd be all over the beach if the tide wasn't up.'

He was with Tessa and Ben on the curved terrace outside the living room, watching as carloads of sightseers converged on the scene of Samantha's death. 'Some are bringing flowers, Dad,' pointed out Ben.

'And some have come for a second-hand thrill!' retorted Tessa. 'It was as if a signal went out as soon as the police moved their tapes.'

'They're not locals, anyway,' conceded her father. 'They'll be tourists. Well, I'm not having them peering at us over the hedge all day.'

Sally came up behind them. 'I don't see how you can stop them,' she said quietly. 'It's just morbid curiosity, the same as when people gather round a road accident.'

'Well, I'm not having them being morbidly curious about us,' snapped Rob, 'or if they are, we won't be here to see it. Who wants to go up to the north coast?'

'Hey!' Tessa was highly pleased. She liked the wildness and big breakers of Cornwall's other coast, and said so, frequently. 'Can we take a picnic tea, Mum?'

Sally was dog-tired from tension and lack of sleep, but Sunday lunch was eaten and cleared away. 'All right,' she agreed, 'if you all help get it ready and packed. Ben, will you go and ask Luke if he wants to come?'

Tessa marched off to the kitchen as if preparing picnic meals was part of her normal routine. Sally looked at her daughter's departing back and tried to stifle her irritation. Why couldn't she be pleased that Tessa was showing signs of becoming more helpful? Why? Because she herself was as tense as stretched wire, that was why. Tense because of Luke, though he had nothing to fear – she was sure of it. All the same, that unwelcome little picture edged into her mind again: her first-born answering Channon's questions, and nibbling the inside of his lower lip...

As for Rob, he was acting like a stranger – if a stranger could behave as he had done in bed last night. Now, he was leaning forward with his hands on the wooden balustrade edging the terrace – a solid, jointed construction in a Greek key design that he had fashioned himself. Like everything he made, it was both beautiful and practical.

Sally found herself staring at his hands. She had always liked them: they were big and capable, with flat square nails and a fuzz of fair hairs at the wrist. Vaguely surprised, she saw that they looked the same as they always did. Then she breathed out in self-mockery. Of course they were the same. Your husband's hands didn't change overnight just because you weren't on the same wavelength any more.

Summoned by Ben, Luke drifted out to join them. 'Mum,' he said morosely, 'it's really grim without my bike. How long d'you think it'll be before I get it back?'

'I don't know,' Sally admitted, and turned to Rob. 'What do you think?'

He shrugged. 'As long as it takes,' he told his son, 'so it's no use you beefing about it. Now, do you want to come out for the afternoon or not?'

Luke shot a look at his mother, resentment showing in the way he held his mouth. 'Not,' he said shortly. 'I'll stay in just in case they bring it back. I have some studying to do, anyway, and Bammo said he might come round.'

'Right,' said his father briskly, 'and mind you don't have anything to do with that lot outside. Sal – let's get moving.'

Just like that, Sally told herself grimly, and out loud said, 'The three of you can go without me. I'll stay here with Luke in case the police come again.'

Her eldest made no comment, and with a swing of the pony-tail went back upstairs. Rob stood there tapping the terrace with his foot. He was looking at her, his eyes very blue behind his glasses. 'I suppose that's best,' he agreed awkwardly. 'Look, Sal, I know I'm being a bit of a pig. I can't seem to get my head round all this – the family being involved and everything.' He opened his arms. 'I'm sorry, love, really I am.'

With relief she went into his familiar embrace, feeling the heat of his chest, breathing the clean body smell that she loved. 'You've been a lot of a pig, not a bit of one,' she told him. 'We've got to stay close, Rob, we've got to talk to each other until this thing's over.'

'You're right,' he said, 'as always. I do love you, Sally-bally. You know that, don't you?'

For a moment she stayed silent. How

should she answer? A bland, forgiving 'yes', when he'd let her down for thirty hours or more? But it was always so easy to see things only from one point of view. Suppose she'd let *him* down in ways that hadn't even occurred to her? She summoned a smile and leaned back to look into his face. 'Of course I know it,' she said, 'and I love you, you great hulk.'

With a hint of his old smile he kissed her on the mouth, just as Tessa said from the door, 'Mum – when you and Dad have finished are you coming to tell us what food we're taking? Ben wants filled rolls, but I want cheese and salad and crispbread...'

Giving Rob the look that had always been for him alone, Sally headed for the kitchen, smiling.

The briefing was in full swing, plain-clothes mingling with uniforms. Channon liked briefings, probably because he was good at them. Calm and concise, he was able to motivate the rank and file, believing that in order to be motivated they must feel involved, they must know what was going on and where the investigations were leading. In his rise to DCI he had seen how a painstaking slog by a constable could lead to a major breakthrough, and so he gave all ranks a chance to take part.

Already he had heard Bowles's report on

the walker, Miller, and that checks were being run on Samantha's contacts, so far without any leads. Also that the vicar and the Methodist minister knew the Trudgeons as well as they knew many a family in the scatter of villages in their care, but neither of them could make any useful contribution. Another aspect of the case, the forensic analysis on the oil and rubber, was taking time; the team in Truro were working on it, but the samples were so very small, and the immersion in sea water wasn't helping. Now he asked, 'Anything coming up on the darts players?'

Bowles, who had been silent for at least two minutes, spoke up again. 'They haven't finished working on them yet, but up to now nobody was on their own at the crucial time apart from our friend Gribble – oh, and two old guys who're a bit dubious. Went home together and they vouch for each other, but one was up for indecent exposure five years ago.'

'Get them cleared – or otherwise,' instructed Channon, 'and listen, everybody, we want nothing missed, nothing overlooked, nothing that's so obvious we don't bother to question it, and no – repeat no – jumping to conclusions. Now who are the men we put on chatting up the locals? Blamey, was it, and Loverack? Have you come up with anything?'

Loverack was small, loquacious and very

keen. 'Everybody's very cut up about it, sir, and the general opinion is that an outsider killed her – an opportunist thing. One old girl pointed out that half the teenagers are sex-mad druggies, but I think you could say she was a bit biased. Apart from her I haven't spoken to a single person who believes anybody local could have done it.' He was trying to be brisk and factual, but only managed to sound flippant when he concluded, 'Otherwise the universal topic is how fed up all the farmers are.'

There was a chorus of mingled agreement and scorn. Almost every man and woman there had connections of some sort in farming. Mostly they were in sympathy, but a couple of men were drawing an imaginary bow over a mournful violin. Bowles couldn't resist a gibe. 'Poor old farmers. What's up, can't they afford to run their Jags?'

There was a mutter of disagreement, and Loverack said doggedly, 'They're still suffering the effects of BSE, sarge, not to mention all the European rules and such. One fella has just put his house on the market to tempt the yuppies and sold his land to an absentee set-up in Holland. Another has stopped dairy farming and he's converting his stone barns to holiday homes.' He turned to Channon in apology. 'As for leads on the case, sir – none, so far.'

At his side Blamey was red-faced with

annoyance. 'They're not all rolling, like at Blankett's, sarge,' he pointed out, 'and even she must have felt the draught a bit. Old Deacon, now, up at High Bank, he's having to sell a piece of his land over near Blue Leaze, and the wife's cousin at Martennis Grise is having a bad time as well.'

Channon held up a silencing hand. Nobody would believe how often farming was talked about in the force, he thought. His own family background was in agriculture, so he would have liked to join in the discussion, but not at the expense of work. One thing had struck him in the exchange between the men. 'This man Deacon who's been forced into selling land. Who's buying it?'

'Trudgeon himself, I think,' said Blamey. 'The land butts on to his place, and he's doing well on his organic stuff, so I hear.'

Bowles was on his feet again, eyes narrowed. 'Are you talking of *Sam* Deacon? He's the old guy I was telling you about, sir, the indecent exposure.'

Loverack spoke up in protest. 'He'd had a few when that happened, sarge. They reduced the charge to drunk and disorderly and all he got was a fine. He's a decent enough old fella – a bit eccentric, maybe, but no killer.'

Channon's quiet voice cut through the sudden babble. 'We don't *know* that, Loverack. Somebody killed Samantha, and we don't know who, so we check on every single lead, however unlikely, and we keep on checking. Sergeant, when we've finished here take somebody – Yates here, or Soker – and investigate Deacon. Talk to the friend who was with him at the darts match and make sure he isn't doing a cover-up. If Deacon really is eccentric it's possible he's become unbalanced, or at the very least resentful that he has to sell his land to a much younger man – he could have wanted to make the Trudgeons suffer. Take it gently, though. We want co-operation from the locals, not bad feeling.'

Channon went back to his notes and looked at Dave Yates. 'Nothing struck you at the church this morning?'

Yates was guarded. The truth was that the whole set-up had left him close to tears, something he had no intention of revealing to anybody. The churchyard had been ablaze with azaleas and camellias, as if the very earth was paying tribute to Samantha, but inside the church it had been dark and cool and solemn, with a single vast arrangement of white flowers. He had found it unutterably sad.

'There was a full church, sir,' he said briskly. 'There were special prayers and some nice tributes to Samantha. A bit emotional, you could say, her young friends crying and that. No complete strangers that

I could see, but I checked with the vicar just to be sure. George Gribble was there, but not the wife or son. Samantha's aunt and uncle from the inn ... nearly everybody in Curdower, I'd say.'

'The Baxters?' asked Channon.

'No. I expect they were a bit wary of everybody knowing that the son was one of the last to see her alive. They don't attend regular, anyway. The Trudgeons weren't there, either, but nobody seemed to expect them. I weighed everything up, sir, but I didn't see anything that struck me as odd.'

And so it went on. No leads, no loose ends that couldn't be tied up. Just the usual routine of check, check, and check again. Channon looked round at the crowded faces, half expecting to see weariness, boredom, anxiety to get away, resentment at working all weekend. But no – the only hint of resentment was on Blamey's face as he looked at Bowles – maybe he was still seething about the sergeant's snide comments on farmers. The DCI shifted his shoulders impatiently. This might be farming country, but at that moment there were things far more pressing than BSE and bankruptcy.

'I've been in touch with the headmaster,' he said now. 'He's agreed that we can have access to the school at any reasonable hour, as long as we don't interfere in actual classes. Whoever I send in must report to him when they arrive.'

To close the briefing there were the usual questions from the ranks: some clever, some perceptive and some completely pointless. There were deadbeats on the force, the same as everywhere else, Channon told himself, but the majority were good hard workers, and in the end they'd get results.

Chapter Eight

It was seven thirty on Monday morning and Sally was worried for her sons. For Luke in case he was given a hard time at school because of being involved with the police, and for Ben – well – because he was Ben.

Ever since the murder she had felt the need to maintain a normal atmosphere in the family, but now it was dawning that she didn't even know what *was* normal in the circumstances. She had done boiled eggs and masses of toast and laid the kitchen table for everybody to eat together, which wasn't normal anyway. Now Rob was in his place leafing through one of his computer magazines, Tessa and Ben had come down, and Luke was in the next room answering a phone call from Bammo, who yesterday had offered him a lift to school on his pillion. A moment later he drifted in and announced in tones of doom, 'Bammo can't pick me up, Mum.'

'Well, you can cycle with Ben and Tess, I suppose,' said Sally, deciding that nothing would be gained by driving them all to school like an over-anxious mummy. 'Is there something wrong with Bammo's bike?' She asked because Luke would expect it, not because of genuine concern. In her view the disadvantages of motorcycling were so many and varied that a mechanical fault was hardly worth discussing.

Luke was intent on filling a cereal bowl to overflowing. 'I know he's been changing the baffles, but he didn't say it was that. He was a bit vague, actually. I expect he'll tell me more at break.'

I hope he does, thought Sally, suddenly wary. Was it more than coincidence that Luke's best friend was unable to give him a lift, today of all days? Bammo's parents were a staid couple nearing retirement. Had they perhaps objected to him keeping company with a police suspect?

Such an idea didn't seem to have occurred to anybody else. Rob was eating mechanically, intent on the latest computer news; Tessa was picking at dry wholemeal toast, having refused an egg and muttered darkly about cholesterol; Ben was chewing reluctantly and trying to look nonchalant; only

Luke was eating with any enjoyment. 'I'll give you a ring at lunch-time, Mum,' he said, 'to see if there's any news about my bike.'

Tessa fingered her plait and eyed him curiously. 'What are you going to tell everybody when they ask?'

Luke buttered more toast. 'Ask what?'

His sister rolled her eyes. 'About you being the last to see Samantha alive, of course, and having your bike impounded by forensic.'

At that Rob surfaced. 'Shut up, Tess,' he said irritably. 'He'll probably find himself the hero of the hour.'

'I don't see why,' she protested, 'and anyway, what am I supposed to tell my friends?'

'That because Luke gave Samantha a lift, the police are examining his bike as a routine measure,' said Sally tartly. 'You'll find that your brother isn't the only one being investigated, Tessa.'

Luke shrugged. 'You're a pain,' he told his sister, while Rob grunted in agreement and carried on reading.

Was Luke really as relaxed as he made out? Sally observed him as she unwrapped more butter. No, he wasn't, she decided. Minutes ago he had taken the tops off his eggs with great care rather than slashing at them as he usually did; now he was eating wholemeal toast with butter, when he invariably had honey as well – local honey, which he adored. And anyway, his jaw was too tight.

'You'll all have to expect a few questions at school,' she said carefully. 'Just answer them, but don't make a big thing of it.' She would have to have a word with Ben on his own before they set off. It would crucify him if he let himself relive the moment of finding Samantha every time he was asked about it.

Rob stood up and made a rare domestic gesture by taking his crockery across to the sink, then dropped a kiss on Sally's cheek and headed for the door. 'Busy morning ahead,' he said over his shoulder, and made for the stairs.

Sally tried to look unconcerned. He always dialled in to check the markets before eight. It was his usual routine, like making fresh coffee up in his workroom and appearing at midday for a lunch of odds and ends from the fridge. Was she being a fusspot to have expected a special word to the kids before he left them? Only Ben seemed to have noticed the omission. The blue eyes that were so like his father's were staring after him, reproach in their depths, and maybe uncertainty. She did a quick about-turn in her mind. 'Oh, I'd forgotten!' she lied. 'I have to go out early today. Any of you want a lift to school?'

There was no love lost between Bowles and

Soker. The DC thought the sergeant a coarse bully who was inclined to cut corners and Bowles saw Soker as a too-clever-by-half computer freak who should have stayed in uniform.

Bowles was barely civil to the younger man as they drove into the yard at Pengally Farm, which to him looked a complete mess. He eyed the unswept yard and a manure heap steaming gently behind a wall. 'I suppose this is what they call a working farm, is it? A pity they don't get round to doing the work!'

Nearby an elderly man was tinkering with a tractor, and Soker wondered uneasily if he'd heard the gibe. Unperturbed, Bowles flashed his card and introduced himself and the younger man. 'Mr Deacon?'

'No. I'm Will Baldwin. If you've come about that bad do on Friday night, Sam an' me can vouch for each other. We were at the darts match together.'

Bowles eyed him with interest. So this bald old badger was the alibi, the friend who'd 'stake his life' on Deacon? Bearing in mind Channon's orders about taking it gently, he decided that a bit of gentle grilling might reveal something, and managed a smile. 'Ah, yes, Mr Baldwin. We have a copy of your statement here, and we're just checking a few details in order to build up a background to the crime. We don't seem to have it on record that you're employed by Mr Deacon, but I see you're working here?'

Baldwin nodded calmly. 'I give him a hand now and again, on a friendly basis. He's short of help, you see, with Georgie Gribble only here a coupla times a week. If he's got a lot on I come over for a bit, 'cos time hangs heavy now I'm retired. Me an' me wife used to run our own place at Low Level, but we got as we couldn't stand the hassle. She died a twelve-month back.'

Bowles never offered sympathy about things that were past and done with. He consulted his notes. 'You live alone now, Mr Baldwin?'

'That's right.'

'And last Friday evening you travelled to and from the Martennis with Mr Deacon?'

'That's right. I brought him back here.'

'It must have been a terrible shock to you both when you heard about Samantha being killed?'

'That's right,' agreed Baldwin for the third time. Soker detected a gleam of mockery in the faded eyes and felt like telling Bowles that his 'let's humour the old chap' treatment wasn't working.

The sergeant's next question, however, showed that he had seen the hint of mockery and was far from amused. 'Mr Baldwin, I take it that you know about Mr Deacon being charged with indecent exposure some time ago?'

Baldwin's lips tightened. 'Yes, I know. An' you'll know, sergeant, that the charge was reduced to drunk an' disorderly.'

Bowles nodded. 'Did you agree with the charge being reduced?' Soker squirmed and searched his memory as to whether this line of questioning was in order or simply a typical Bowles ploy of stretching the rules.

Baldwin hooked his thumbs under his ancient braces. 'I don't see it's relevant, but I don't mind telling you that I did agree with it. Sam had had a few, that was all. He's never been one to carry drink, but he likes his bit of fun. He simply went a bit too far that night.'

'I see,' said Bowles, as if he saw much more than had been revealed. 'Perhaps you'd direct us to Mr Deacon?'

Baldwin pointed along an overgrown hedge bordering a field. 'He'll be down there, somewhere. It's the old sheep-dipping pens. He's looking them over to see if he can sell anything for scrap.'

They trod a tangled path, trampling bluebells underfoot and brushing aside the branching wild celery. ''Morning,' called a voice. 'A bit early for snooping, isn't it?' A wiry old man with a beard and a wide-brimmed hat was leaning against the gate of the sheep pen, waiting for them. 'Hard up for suspects?' he asked mildly.

Bowles went through the introductions and told himself that this was a cocky old devil if ever he'd seen one. He looked like an out-of-work actor with his long wavy hair and face fungus, not to mention the hat.

'We have a few more questions, Mr Deacon,' he said silkily. 'We can either talk to you here or you can come back with us to the incident room at Curdower.' That should take the wind out of his sails, he told himself.

Sam Deacon smiled, revealing remarkably good teeth. 'I reckon that doesn't take much deciding,' he said, and pointed to a half-rotten bench. 'Take a seat.'

'We've spoken to Will Baldwin,' Bowles told him, 'and he's confirmed what you both said in your statements about the darts match. Now, though, we'd like information regarding your relationship with the Trudgeon family.'

Soker sat there impassively and wondered if the sergeant had ever heard of the word subtlety. Bowles, however, noted the slackening of the jaw beneath the short grey beard and congratulated himself. The out-of-work actor here hadn't expected that one. 'I haven't got what you'd call a relationship,' Deacon protested. 'They run the next farm. Part of their land butts on to mine. That's all there is to it.'

'You've recently sold land to Trudgeon, though?'

'Yes, I had to let it go,' agreed Deacon. 'He gave me my asking price so I'm not complaining.'

'Did you expect to get what you asked?'

'Yes. It's a good stretch o' land, and anyway, Trudgeon could afford it. He admitted as much to my face. It's clear to me that those who have it will spend good money on that organic stuff of his.'

Bowles shook his head in sympathy. 'As if an old-fashioned farmer like yourself has been producing rubbish, eh?'

Deacon shot him a sideways glance. 'Organic farming's coming – in fact it's already come – and it's here to stay. The old ways were fine – we grew good crops an' raised good beasts, but in the end we got a bit entangled in chemicals and such and we were let down by the folk who worship money – them an' all the funny buggers in the EEC.'

Bowles would have liked to sing a verse of 'Tell me the old, old story', if he'd been sure of the words, but he restrained himself, and said, 'It must have been very hard for you in the last year or two, but can I take it you were happy with the sale of your land?'

'I wasn't happy that I needed to sell it,' Deacon told him, 'but I was happy enough to get what I asked, with no quibbling. What's more, de-tec-tive ser-geant, if I hadn't been happy I certainly wouldn't have shown my disappointment by murdering

Trudgeon's little girl. It's money I'm short of – not the blood of a youngster.'

For a moment Bowles was at a loss for words. The old man gazed across his land and went on, 'When she was little I used to see her on her dad's tractor when he was in his top field. Sometimes she'd wave and blow me a kiss.'

A load of slop, Bowles told himself sourly. He was conscious that he hadn't handled either of them very well, and he suspected that Soker was concealing a sneer. Nevertheless, Deacon's words had the ring of truth. Flasher or not, they were wasting their time on him.

He and Soker were almost back in the village before he recalled that two days earlier he'd thought exactly the same about a certain Mr Miller.

The incident room was as lively at seven in the evening as at any other time, and Channon was taking a call from Eddie Platt at the forensic laboratory. 'Eddie!' he said above the background noise. 'Is there news on the motorbike samples?'

'No match,' came Platt's deep tones. 'The bike's in the clear, Bill. We'll let you have it officially, of course.'

Channon found himself sagging with relief. He'd attended more lectures than he could count on not getting emotionally involved and staying detached from both suspects and victims, but in his climb to DCI he had found that lectures couldn't govern feelings. He hadn't, he really hadn't wanted to confront Mrs Baxter with news that her son was the murder suspect. 'What about the other lot?' he asked. 'From the Escort?'

'Now we're talking,' said Platt with satisfaction. 'Positive on the oil – at least, ninety-eight per cent positive. The age of the engine has helped with that. We're still on with the rubber. The difference was clear on the bike samples, but not those from the car. You know the drill – results have to go to regional for confirmation and a full documentation, but I reckon you'll be safe to go ahead and take the oil as definite.'

For seconds the detective didn't reply. George *Gribble?* he thought in disbelief. Faded little Gribble? He hadn't been so surprised on a case in the last twelve months. There'd been something a bit odd in Gribble's manner, it was true, but he'd put it down to unease at being questioned, and the presence of his wife. Clearly it had been more than unease – it had been guilt!

At the other end of the line Platt was saying in perplexity, 'Hello? Hello, Bill?'

'It's OK, I'm here,' he said. 'I was just a bit stunned, that's all.'

Platt laughed. 'I thought DCIs were never surprised!'

'That's the others, not me,' retorted Channon wryly. 'Thanks to everybody over there. Oh, you've got the address – will you arrange for the bike to be returned as soon as poss, and the clothes?'

'A van has to go to St Austell this evening. Shall I ask them to drop it off?'

'Brilliant! I'll see you, then, Eddie.' He looked round for Bowles and found him hovering nearby. 'No match for the oil and rubber on young Baxter's bike,' he told him, and wondered if the sergeant was registering his avoidance of I-told-you-so overtones.

Bowles stared, his pale eyes meeting Channon's dark ones. 'Do we take it Lukey-dukey's in the clear, then?' he asked edgily.

'Yes, for now,' said Channon. 'We were expecting the fibres from his sweater to match those on Samantha's belt, weren't we, and we already know there's no trace of beach residue on his footgear or jeans. I'll call at the roundhouse myself to tell them. They deserve that – the family must have been in turmoil.' The sergeant remained silent, so he pointed out gently, 'You haven't asked what forensic said about Gribble.'

Bowles's jaw dropped. 'Aw, no! Not that little nerd? The crafty little swine!'

'The oil's a match, not the rubber – not yet, anyway, but we'll go and see him and have him in. Get a couple of men to go in a second car to collect samples of clothing.

Not that we'll find anything of interest unless he's thicker than I take him to be. Three minutes and we're off. We'll go by way of the roundhouse.'

Bowles opened his mouth, but seeing Channon's expression, closed it again. Off in three minutes but delayed by twenty because of a detour to the Baxters'? He was right. The man was soft.

All was quiet in the roundhouse and Sally was loading the dishwasher. The day hadn't been so bad after all, she thought. Ben had weathered it better than she'd expected, emerging from school looking relieved rather than fraught. 'Everybody was OK about it, Mum,' he said, 'except some of them thought it must have been exciting when – you know, on the beach ... and assembly was horrible. The head gave a little talk about Samantha and some of the girls were crying. He said the police are doing a wonderful job.'

Now Ben was upstairs doing his home-work, and so was Tessa, who had joined them after school in high good humour. It seemed she'd been the centre of attention in her form, with everybody eager to hear all the details. There had been tears, of course, and sympathy, but Sally gathered that some of them had been a bit envious of all the excite-ment at the roundhouse. Who, she wondered, could fathom the minds of teenagers?

Only Luke had been morose, slouching to the car and slinging his gear in the boot. She had manoeuvred her way out between school buses and a scattering of cars, asking him casually, 'Everything all right?'

'A couple of kids seemed to think I'd topped Samantha,' he announced flatly, 'and as for Bammo, he came on his bike after all. He said it was just a bit unreliable.'

It had dawned. Sally looked at him in the rear view mirror and hoped that Bammo's parents would feel they'd been a bit over-protective when it was all sorted out. She hoped more than that, of course, but tried to push it all to the back of her mind.

She was reflecting on all this and tidying the kitchen when the doorbell rang. Outside was DCI Channon, on his own, but at the gate were two police cars with Bowles in one and two uniformed men in the other. Her heart gave a single, heavy lurch. 'Oh – hello,' she said weakly. 'Come in.'

Without more ado he stepped inside. 'A brief call, Mrs Baxter,' he said quietly. 'Don't worry, there's nothing wrong – quite the reverse. Our forensic people have finished with Luke's bike and found nothing suspicious on it, or on his clothes. He should have everything back later this evening.'

There was a thud on the landing and Luke appeared, looking down on them both from the top of the stairs. 'Hello, Luke,' said Channon. 'I've just called to say your bike's in the clear, and so are your clothes. We'd like you to keep yourself available, though, in case we have more questions, but so far we're satisfied. I've just been telling your mother that the bike will be here sometime this evening.'

Luke smiled, and Sally realized how much she'd missed that wide, radiant grin in the last two days. 'Hey! Thanks a lot, inspector!' With a twirl and a leap he turned on the stairs and made for Ben's room, leaving his mother facing the detective.

Sally knew she was clutching at something and found it was the dishcloth. She was so relieved she could have tossed it in the air and kissed Channon's stubble-dark cheek. 'You must be so busy, yet you've taken the trouble to come and tell us yourself,' she said, smiling. 'I do appreciate it.'

'I'm glad to do it,' he replied. 'You'll have been worried.'

'I was,' she agreed, 'but not because I thought Luke had done anything wrong.'

'No, of course not. Just because you're his mum.'

It was there again, the fleeting rapport between them. He understood what she'd been through – he must be a father himself. 'Do you have children?' she asked with interest.

His face changed, as if shutters were being closed over an open window. 'I had a son,' he said stiffly. 'He and my wife were killed in a car accident.'

'Oh!' Already emotional, Sally felt her eyes fill with tears. She swallowed and said hoarsely, 'I'm sorry – really sorry.'

He nodded his head, backing away through the doorway. 'That's all right.'

'Just a minute,' she said, sniffing and wiping her eyes with the dishcloth. 'Can I take it that my family are free of suspicion, now, about Samantha?'

Channon studied her face for a moment: the wet brown eyes, the rosy tan, the wide, full-lipped mouth. Not pretty … attractive, more like. He sighed. If she'd been the most beautiful woman on earth it wouldn't have helped if her son had killed Samantha. 'Nobody's completely in the clear until we charge whoever's done it and get a conviction,' he said, shaking his head. 'Goodnight, Mrs Baxter.'

'Goodnight, Mr Channon.' She watched him walk back to the car, where the sandy-haired Bowles was revving the engine. That's one in the eye for you, sergeant, she thought wearily, and closed the door. Questions trudged across her mind like troops squelching across a battlefield. Why wasn't she rushing upstairs to tell Rob? Why had she cried when Channon spoke of his wife and son? She knew the answer to that one – because she'd sensed his anguish and knew how he must feel. And why on earth had she wiped her eyes on the dishcloth?

With a sigh made up of relief and exhaustion she sat down at the kitchen table. The sun was streaming in, spilling gold over the jug of flowers on the table, and she fancied that her beloved yellow Aga was looking supremely content. Things were all right again. Life was liveable after all, life was lovely, life was golden. Except that a girl was dead.

She could hear the three young ones upstairs, with Luke talking nineteen to the dozen. It seemed he hadn't gone to his father's workroom... She got up to go and tell Rob the good news herself.

Chapter Nine

The cottage windows needed cleaning, but the little garden showed signs of industry and imagination. Perhaps it was Gribble's handiwork, thought Channon. The man himself opened the door, with his wife at his side and his son wide-eyed behind him.

'Go to your room, Malachi,' ordered his mother, and the child went upstairs. Zennie was far from pleased at another visit, especially from four of them. 'What is it this time?' she asked impatiently.

'If we might come inside?' suggested Channon.

George Gribble led the way indoors and Channon tried to put a name to his expression. Troubled? Anxious? No ... wary, that was it. Hardly surprising, in the circumstances.

'We'd like you to come to the police station in Truro to help with our enquiries, Mr Gribble,' he said impassively. 'Also, we need to take away for forensic examination everything you were wearing on Friday evening. And I want my men here to go through your belongings – we have ample grounds and if you refuse I can obtain a search warrant without delay.'

Zennie was incensed. 'You *what?*' Tears of anger glinted in her amazing eyes, but she blinked them away with a twitch of the head. 'What do you think you'll find? I've told you already he was back here when he said he was!'

At times like this Channon wondered why he was in the force. 'Your clothes, Mr Gribble,' he persisted.

'I've washed 'em,' Zennie announced with satisfaction. 'Shirt, trousers, pants, vest and socks. They're in the kitchen with the ironing.'

Bowles couldn't resist a sharp glance at Channon. If he'd been in charge they'd have taken this place apart as soon as they knew Gribble had gone home on his own from the darts match.

'And your shoes?' asked Channon.

'You can have 'em if you want,' said Gribble, in the benign tone of a man offering a cutting from his garden. 'They're in the bedroom. Grey canvas with tan laces.'

The two men went off upstairs and Zennie looked at her husband in bafflement. He'd never, ever, got the message that you didn't co-operate with the police, you put obstacles in their way. Everybody grew up knowing that – except Georgie.

'Right,' said Channon. 'We'll leave my men here, and you're at liberty to watch them if you wish, Mrs Gribble. Shall we go?'

'Are you *arresting* him?' asked Zennie incredulously.

'Not at this stage. We'd like him to come in voluntarily.'

'No chance!' she snapped. 'He's going nowhere if you don't say why you're questioning him. We want a reason, don't we, Georgie?'

Channon could have sworn that the hint of a smile touched Gribble's mouth. There was something odd here. He'd never taken anybody in for questioning – not for murder, anyway – who acted as cool as this one. The little man nodded and said: 'It's all right, inspector. You can give your reasons in front of my wife.'

Bowles was dying to speak, but Channon silenced him with a look, telling himself that this couple were seriously weird. If Gribble had managed to work out their grounds for taking him in, why did he want his wife to hear what they were? As for her, she couldn't have the slightest idea what was coming.

'Very well,' he said heavily. 'Mr Gribble, the sample of oil which we took from your car on Saturday evening is a match with traces found on the bra of the murder victim. A trace of rubber was also found on the bra, but that is still being compared with samples from the fan-belt of your Escort. Also, we are examining fingermarks on the breasts of the victim.' He turned to Zennie. 'All this gives us ample grounds for an arrest, Mrs Gribble, so we're being considerate, to say the least.'

He had the mad idea that she was deflating, like a blow-up doll with a leak. She was breathing out non-stop, as if she wanted her lungs to collapse. The low-cut red top displayed her impressive cleavage, and he found himself wondering if her breasts would be the first to shrink. At last she took in air with a hiss of unbelief. She wafted a hand. 'Georgie,' she said faintly, inviting him to deny it.

Gribble merely turned his hands palm upwards and lifted his shoulders, 'Looks as if I'll have to come an' answer your questions, Mr Channon,' he said equably.

Arms spread wide, teeth bared, Zennie leapt in front of him and faced the policemen. 'Are you saying he handled her tits? *Georgie?* Can't you see he wouldn't do it?'

With one hand Georgie smoothed back his wispy grey hair, and with the other eased his wife to one side. 'How do you know I wouldn't?' he said.

She gaped at him and in turn Bowles gaped at her. He hadn't seen anything as sexy in years as this open-mouthed woman with her mane of wild hair and her skintight clothes – he could have bundled her into bed on the spot. Yet her husband here had been touching up a schoolgirl.

Evidently stunned into silence, Zennie made no reply. She didn't even move, but leaned against the door of her red and gold room as if she hadn't the strength to stand upright. She uttered no word of farewell as the three of them left, and seemed oblivious to the policemen upstairs.

Intrigued and yet puzzled, Malachi had been listening from behind his bedroom door. Why should his dad have touched the tits of a girl who went to Pencannon School? A girl who was nearly grown-up? A girl who'd been murdered? His dad was an old man. He couldn't – he couldn't have killed her. Could he?

Channon would do it by the book when it came to interviews, Bowles warned himself wearily. Everybody knew that stretching a point here and there could bring a quick result and let you get on with the next thing; but from the start they had to face Gribble across the table, with the recorder switched on and Channon calmly announcing the time and date. To his amazement the DCI's first question was, 'Now, George, it's better if we're on first name terms, isn't it?'

For crying out loud, thought Bowles, why not wrap him in cotton wool and have done with it! He had to swallow a snigger, though, when the little nerd replied, 'Yes, if you say so, Mr Channon. What's *your* first name, then?'

'I've got three, George. They're Detective, Chief and Inspector, so let's get on. Now – did you see Samantha Trudgeon after the darts match?'

'Yes, I did.'

'Where did you see her?'

'Going out the yard of the Martennis toward the cliff path.'

'And what time was that, George?'

'A bit after eleven. Quarter past, maybe.'

'You spoke to her?'

'Yes. She were a bit surprised when I appeared. I'd been in the car park an' she couldn't a' seen me.'

'So what did you say?'

'I asked her where she were goin' at that time.'

'You were surprised to see her setting off somewhere?'

'Yes. Her mum and dad wouldn't a' liked it.'

'And what did she say when you asked her that?'

'She said she couldn't tell me.'

'And what did you reply?'

'I said I'd have to tell her dad.'

Channon could have smiled. This sounded more like an exchange between a stern uncle and a naughty ten-year-old than a seedy old lecher and an attractive young woman. 'What did she say to that?' he asked curiously.

'She got a bit snotty.'

'I can imagine, George. Maybe she didn't like you knowing she was going off on her own?'

'She weren't exactly goin' off on her own. I'm pretty sure she were goin' off to meet somebody.'

'So what did you do?'

Gribble smiled. 'She were a pretty girl,' he said. 'Fresh, like. Fair-skinned.'

'We know,' put in Bowles impatiently.

'What happened next, Gribble?'

Gribble looked at the sergeant. 'It's first name terms,' he pointed out primly, 'an' I'm answerin' Mr Channon.'

Bowles subsided in fury. This was on the record, for God's sake.

'Go on, George,' said Channon gently.

'Well, I stood firm. Said her dad wouldn't like it an' neither would her auntie. They were still clearing up inside the pub, see. The lights were still on, an' that. I said I'd go an' tell her auntie. I'd had a few, see.'

'So?'

'So she said, sort of wheedlin', "What can I give you, Georgie, to keep quiet?"'

'And what did you say to that?'

Gribble's faded blue eyes stared across the interview room. 'I shouldn't a' done it, but it were a chance in a million.'

'Of course it was,' agreed Channon, 'you don't pass a chance like that up. So what did you suggest?'

'I said, "Give me a feel of your tits an' I'll forget I've seen you."'

'Right. And she agreed?'

'Quick as a flash. Oh, she shrugged a bit and pulled her face, but she yanked her sweater over her head quick enough.' Gribble stared at the table, remembering. 'She were wearin' a white lace bra. It gleamed, sort of, in the moonlight. Well, I grabbed her. I – I'm not proud o' this, mind.

I should a' let her unfasten it herself, but I whirled her round an' – an' wrenched at the fastenin'.'

For the first time his gaze included Bowles. 'You'll have noticed I weren't surprised you'd got on to me? Well, I do watch the telly, you know. They're always on about forensic these days – how you can identify a single hair, an' so forth. Well, I'd been under the bonnet of me car, an' me hands were dirty, so as soon as you took samples from the Escort I guessed what you were after...

'Well, she leaned forward an' let me take hold of her. Just for a minute. I must have squeezed her too hard, though, because she squeaked and said, "OK, that's your lot, Georgie. You keep your promise, now." She didn't know, an' neither did I, that I'd have to break me promise by talkin' to the police. She wriggled herself back into her bra an' pulled her sweater back on, then she patted me on the cheek. Looking back, I'm glad about that ... it meant no hard feelin's, see? Then she went off along the cliff path towards Curdower.'

'And what next?' asked Bowles, who felt he'd kept silent for long enough.

Gribble wagged his finger and tutted. 'I'm tellin' your boss,' he reproved. 'What next? I went home, that's what.'

'You went home,' repeated Channon

gently. 'And Samantha went off to meet somebody on the cliff path above Curdower beach. Who do you think it could have been, George?'

'The lad from the roundhouse, I reckon.'

Bowles leaned forward intently, but kept quiet. 'You mean Luke Baxter?' asked Channon.

'Yes. He'd given her a lift home from the disco.'

'How did you know that, George?'

'They were together when I went outside at about half past ten. His bike were there an' he were holdin' his helmet.'

'Why did you go outside, George?'

Gribble shifted on his seat. 'I had a few quid put away under the dash for emergencies. I decided to use some of it for my last pint.' He shot a look at Bowles. 'Yes, for my fifth – or it might even have been my sixth.'

'And you saw Samantha and Luke Baxter talking?'

'Not talkin' – arguin'. They were by the tall hedge that goes behind the pub, an' they didn't see me. I stayed for a bit to make sure she were all right, but I needn't a' worried. She were givin' as good as she got.'

Bowles was listening with reluctant respect. Maybe there was something to be said for the soft approach. If he'd been doing the questioning he wouldn't have got all this

152

out of Gribble; he would have frightened him into his shell long ago. Channon, however, was forging gently ahead. 'Did you hear what they were arguing about, George?'

'Not really. There were a lot of noise from the darts match – shoutin' an' whistlin' an' that. The lad were doin' most of the talkin' – but very low, like folk do when they're menacing somebody.'

'So he was menacing her? Threatening her, do you mean?'

Gribble hesitated, all too aware of the implications of what he was saying. He sighed. 'Yes, I'd say he were threatenin' her, and she didn't like it. She didn't like it at all.'

'Were they still talking when you went back inside?'

'No, I stayed there until he went off on the bike and Samantha marched round the back – to help with the clearin' up or to go to her bed, I suppose. Then I went back to the darts.'

'Thank you, George.' Channon announced the time and the end of the interview, and switched off. He left a constable in the room and beckoned Bowles outside. 'Well, what do you reckon?' he asked, dark eyes thoughtful.

Surprised at his own conclusions, Bowles said: 'I reckon the little creep's on the level, and not just because he's implicating the kid, either. It all fits, doesn't it? We know she'd changed her clothes, and she wouldn't have done that to meet George. She wouldn't have arranged to meet him at all. He's admitted having a feel, but that's not an offence, unless it's without agreement. There's more to him than meets the eye, and his relationship with his wife must be pretty odd, but I think he's telling the truth.'

'So do I,' agreed Channon soberly. 'So do I. We'll let him go home for now, pending anything incriminating being found there. And we'll have Luke Baxter in for questioning.'

'He's involved somehow,' agreed Bowles, 'but don't forget all his gear's in the clear, so if he finished her off on the beach he must have done it starkers.'

'That's true,' agreed Channon. 'I'll give it some thought, and I think we'll call it a day for now, sergeant. We can ring the round-house first thing and tell them we want to talk to Luke. There's no point in letting him go off to school and then dragging him out of the classroom. I'll see you in Curdower in the morning.'

Bowles was only too willing to go off duty. His flat was less than half a mile away, and he'd be in time for a decent meal at a little place he liked. The woman who ran it was his type, but unfortunately she doted on her husband.

Channon thought about Luke Baxter.

Depression was settling on him like a damp, heavy cloak, and he could think of nothing that would lift it from his shoulders.

'Oh, I thought I must have missed you, sir!' A breathless woman constable stopped Channon on his way upstairs. 'There's a call for you from a Mrs Sunning. She says she's tried to get you on the special number at Curdower and she keeps getting fobbed off.'

'Is it about the case, then?'

The WPC wriggled her shoulders. 'I couldn't pin her down, sir. She keeps on about her drains and how it's costing her good money, but she says it's information for your ears alone.'

'Put her through to my office, will you?' Channon went upstairs, thinking that he might not be another Sherlock Holmes, but he didn't work for Dyno-rod, either. He picked up the phone and announced himself in full.

An aggrieved female voice seemed unimpressed by his rank. 'And not before time!' the voice said. 'My name's Annie Sunning and I run a bed and breakfast house on the road from Mevagissey to St Austell.'

'I see. I believe you want to speak to me in person, Mrs Sunning?'

'Well, I know you're in charge because I saw you on the telly, but I wanted you because when my husband's cousin Leonard had burglars you were very good with him. You were a sergeant, then.'

Fame at last, Channon told himself wryly. 'Oh, I see. So what is it?'

'Constable Lammis called on me yesterday asking about a gentleman walker – a Mr Miller. He took him away to his house for a talk, and then later on I had to give a statement to two of your young men.'

'Ah! Is something bothering you about that, Mrs Sunning?'

'It's my drains, inspector. In a profession like mine you can't afford to have blocked drains. Last night I had a lovely married couple in my twin en-suite, and this morning when they flushed the toilet it wouldn't clear. They weren't pleased, I can tell you. They said it was embarrassing, which I had to agree – it is. The wife said she wasn't used to that sort of thing and I had to tell her neither was I. For the sake of goodwill I had to knock five pounds off their bill. I mean, it doesn't seem right, does it?'

'Maybe not,' said Channon, 'but what has this to do with our enquiry?'

'I'll tell you if you'll let me!' came the irate reply. 'There aren't many plumbers out our way, and if you can get one they charge the earth, so I put up my No Vacancies sign – which was losing me good money before I even started – and waited for Derek to come home – that's my husband.'

'And he cleared the drain?'

'Yes, after a struggle with the S bend and thinking all the house would be blocked, and this is why I'm ringing. What was blocking the drain was a pair of lace panties and a matching bra. They were streaked with bleach, and that, but you could see they'd been dark red – wine-coloured, sort of.'

Channon gripped the receiver hard. This was a new angle. 'And who was in the room the previous night?'

'Mr Miller, 'cos I let my twin en-suite as a single if nobody's booked it. Better that than leave it empty, you see. Now the two young men who took my statement told me you'd wanted to talk to Mr Miller in connection with the young girl who was murdered over at Curdower. Well, he was a nice enough young man, I'll say that, but it seemed strange to me that he'd been on his own in my twin en-suite the night before the drains were blocked with women's underwear. Mind – I'm not saying that poor little girl on Curdower wasn't wearing any, but – well – I wondered, you see. I thought you should know.'

'You thought right,' said Channon. 'Well done, Mrs Sunning, and thank you. You've still got the underwear?'

'Yes, in a bucket of disinfectant.'

'Good. Leave it as it is in the bucket and

I'll send somebody over for it right away. My men will take a brief statement from you.'

'But will I be recompensed for my losses?'

'Give full details to my men and we'll look into it. That's all I can say at the moment, and thanks again.'

He leaned back in his chair, recalling that it had been Bowles who interviewed Barry Miller and reported back that he was unlikely to be involved, and that there was nothing of interest in his gear. Not up to the sergeant's usual standard – he could wait until next morning to learn of the latest developments. The question was, had the man flushed the bra and pants away when he heard Constable Lammis arrive?

Could it be that Samantha had been wearing the wine-red set when she met Miller on her way home from school? She hadn't been averse to removing her bra for George Gribble – would she have removed both bra and pants for the much more appetizing Miller? And would he then have carted the bra and pants in his backpack along the coastal path? Did he, perhaps, see them as some sort of trophy?

Channon picked up the phone again and asked for the incident room at Curdower. He wanted to see that bra and pants and oh, he wanted to see Barry Miller.

Zennie was at the window when the police car dropped Georgie outside the cottage. She was so relieved to see him she had to force herself not to run out to the gate.

It was nearly nine and Malachi was in bed. She never let him stay up late, but tonight she'd had him upstairs by eight o'clock. He'd kept asking questions and if she hadn't felt like a wet rag with worry she'd have slapped him one to shut him up. How could she think, how could she get her mind in order when he kept asking things? Awful things?

What should she have said when he asked whether men who were married were allowed to mess about with schoolgirls? What *could* she have said when he wanted her to tell him for certain that his dad wasn't a murderer? She'd been so shattered by Georgie's calm admission that for the life of her she couldn't answer the child. She simply told him to get himself some milk and go to bed.

She watched her husband walk up the path beneath a sky streaked with purple and gold; his grey hair looked pink, even the flowers at his feet were tinted with rose. The lane outside was so peaceful, she thought, but inside her head it was bedlam; questions were leaping about in there, screaming and yowling. She started taking deep breaths to calm herself. In ... out ... in ... out...

When Georgie came in the first thing he

noticed was her eyes, which looked enormous in a face that was sickly white beneath its coating of make-up. He told himself it was a wonder he wasn't tying himself in knots worrying about what she was going to say, but the truth was that he simply didn't care, and because he didn't care, he felt that he was in charge. 'Well, Zennie,' he said, tossing his jacket on the settee, 'here I am, an' they haven't accused me o' murder – at least, not yet!'

She didn't know what to say to him, she who always had a hundred words to his half-dozen. He seemed to be expecting a reply, so almost in a whisper, she said: 'I'm glad you're back.' It was true, she thought, it was true.

He raised his eyebrows and sat down. 'So am I,' he admitted. 'There were a lot o' questions, but I reckon they believed me when I said I didn't kill her.'

'I should hope they did,' she retorted, with her first flash of spirit.

'Mind, I had to tell 'em somethin' I'd thought to keep to meself.'

'What?'

Georgie shrugged with a hint of guilt. 'He's nice enough, young Luke Baxter, but somethin' I said might'a got him in trouble.'

Hard lines, thought Zennie. Luke had parents who'd look after him, which was more than she'd ever had. Right now she was more interested in her and Georgie. Tensely she stood waiting for him to continue.

'Don't keep standin' there as if it's a funeral!' he said irritably. 'An' where's Malachi? In bed?'

She flopped down in the opposite chair. 'I sent him up early. He was going on an' on, asking this, that an' the other.'

'Had he heard what was said?'

'Yes. He wanted to know if married men are allowed to mess about with schoolgirls.'

Georgie pursed his lips as if tasting something bitter. 'An' what did you tell him?'

'Nothing,' she said in the new, quiet little voice. 'I just sent him to bed.'

He tapped his fingers on the red brocade of the chair. 'Aren't you goin' to ask why I did that with Samantha?'

She said carefully, 'One reason could be that she's a fast little madam.'

'Yes,' he agreed. 'An' another could be that what I'm refused at home I look for elsewhere.'

She'd expected that. It had been clanging in her brain since he left the house. She felt she must look weak, slumped in the chair, so she straightened her back and stiffened her shoulders. She couldn't strengthen her voice, though; it came out as a croak. 'She was one of a long line, then?'

'Oh, yes,' he said bitterly, 'they're queuin' up, aren't they? Women trample each other in the rush to get at me. Talk sense, Zennie.'

Something was turning over in her chest, like a weight being pushed aside to make room for another that was even heavier. 'You didn't – you didn't ever pay for it, then?'

He leaned forward and rested his elbows on his knees. 'As a matter of fact, I did, when I were desperate. Three times in all, three times in ten years. They were cheap tarts, but at least they didn't vomit when I'd finished.'

'I couldn't help that, Georgie. I didn't plan it – it just happened. Once I was pregnant I realized I couldn't do it again.'

'Once you were pregnant,' he repeated thoughtfully. Suddenly he jumped to his feet and made for the stairs, while she gazed at him in bewilderment. She heard him go into Malachi's room and a minute later he came back. 'Fast asleep,' he said. 'He's heard enough to upset him for one night.'

'What do you mean? What else might he hear?'

He shook his head pityingly. 'Zennie ... Zennie. Let's stop pretendin'. I've gone along with it all our married life, just to give you a bit of self-respect an' – well – because I used to love you. You were expectin' when you used to talk to me over the fence at the pig farm. Did you think nobody knew you spent days an' nights with that fella on the yacht? Did you really think *I* didn't know?'

Still bolt upright in her chair, she stared at him. This was the most horrible night of a horrible life. Worse than when she saw them sailing away in the white yacht; worse than when she told her ma she was going to go ahead and have the baby ... and the most horrible thing of all was what Georgie had just said.

She swallowed, and it felt as if a brick was lodged in her throat. 'You said you went along with it because you used to love me.' Used to, used to, *used* to, went the mad chorus in her head.

'Yes,' he said. 'I loved you for years, Zennie. You're so gorgeous to look at, you're so clever, so quick ... you used to make the blood sing in me veins. But over the years it dawned on me that love needs nourishin' to keep it alive – an' my love didn't get nourished, did it? You could say it died o' starvation. I don't blame you, I blame the swine who hurt you so bad you had to hurt me to get even with him, me an' all the men you teased into wantin' you just so you could refuse 'em.

'I used to think I'd make you like me a bit by givin' you all the things you wanted – a fine house an' pretty clothes an' gold bracelets, but I'm not that sort o' fella– I haven't got the – what do they call it – the earnin' power.'

She was short of breath, now. 'I didn't know you wanted to give me pretty things,' she gasped. 'You never told me that. You never told me you loved me, either.'

'No, I didn't, did I? An' you know why not? Because I thought you'd laugh at me, an' I couldn't face that. The funny thing is, it doesn't matter to me now whether you laugh or you don't. An' what's even funnier is that now it doesn't matter, there's somethin' come up that might well pay for pretty clothes an' gold bracelets an' maybe an amber necklace. You told me once that you'd seen some amber that matched your eyes...'

All at once he got to his feet again. 'So I'm goin' out,' he said.

She didn't ask where he was going. All she could think was that he'd said he didn't love her any more. That word love again, she was always hearing it – it haunted her. For the very first time in their marriage, she wondered if what she felt for Georgie was love. Did love mean you cared what happened to somebody?

She ran after him to the door, grabbing his arm to delay him. 'I thought you said the car's on the blink?'

'It is. I'll ride me bike. It's too far to walk at this time'a night.'

'Georgie, when you come back, shall we talk?'

He shook his head. 'It's a bit late for talkin'.'

'Yes, I know, but if I talk, will you listen?'

'I'll listen,' he agreed soberly, 'an' as soon as I get this little bit extra, I'll go out an' buy you somethin' nice. You should have nice things, Zennie. You should have had a nice husband – a big strappin' fella, handsome – not somebody like me. So though there's nothin' left for you an' me ... when I come back, I'll listen.'

Outside the light was fading and the street lamp shone at the end of the lane. Everything was grey and blue and gold. Then, in the gesture which was all he'd been allowed for nearly ten years, he kissed her; once on her wrist and once on the inside of her elbow. Then he got out his bicycle, switched on the lamps, and rode off down the lane.

Channon was in the forensic lab, waiting for the arrival of the underwear from Mrs Sunning. He had contemplated asking the Trudgeons if they would identify the garments as Samantha's, but decided against it. Time enough to subject them to more stress if and when he got a confession out of Miller.

The door crashed open and the genial Eddie Platt breezed in, wearing the blazer of a local male voice choir. He greeted the quiet technician in the corner and said to

Channon, 'My night on call again – the second time in a month I've had to leave 'em short of a baritone.' He shrugged out of the blazer and took off his tie. 'What's coming in, then, Bill?'

On hearing the tale of the underwear he groaned in disbelief. 'Aw! First it's traces of oil and rubber soaked in sea water. Now it's God knows what on more underwear, but this lot's been flushed down a loo and impregnated with toilet cleaner; it's blocked a drain, been bombarded with other people's faeces and urine, and then to cap it all, bunged in a bucket of disinfectant! You don't ask much, do you?'

'You've dealt with worse,' said Channon unfeelingly. 'You know I can't bypass forensic at this stage if I'm to present a case. What I want to know is whether it's worth me waiting here to have a look at it or shall I get off to Curdower to deal with the suspect? That's if he hasn't done a runner. I simply can't see him sticking to the pre-arranged route he gave to Bowles.'

Eddie Platt's head jerked round. 'Bowles has dealt with him? My God, your suspect must be a smooth operator to have got past that one – he'd have his own mother in for questioning if he could.'

'He's not a bad detective,' Channon pointed out, 'just low on personal appeal. So is it worth my waiting?'

'You know damn well it isn't,' retorted Platt. 'Get off and search for your drain-blocker. I'll ring you direct on your mobile with a prelim report, but don't bank on me finding much.'

'Thanks, Eddie. I'll need a description and the make, if you can decipher it, and the original colour.'

The analyst was taking out a plastic apron as he left.

Luke had been watching the road from an upstairs window and was at the gate when the van arrived with his bike. Sally expected him to leap on to it and zoom off at once, but instead he examined the machine carefully, as if expecting damage. Then he stroked the metalwork before wheeling it gently to its home in the shed.

Seeing his mother watching he raised a sheepish grin. 'Just thought I'd give it a bit of a polish,' he said, 'and then I might go for a ride.'

Sally smiled, telling herself she'd smiled so much since Channon's visit it was a wonder her jaws didn't ache. Rob seemed happier as well, eyeing them benevolently from across the garden. Maybe he'd been just as much on edge as her, but in his case it had shown in being distant and irritable. All at once she'd had enough of gauging everybody's reactions. She needed to get away from the family, away from the house. On impulse she went to talk to Rob. 'I need a change of scene for a few minutes,' she told him, 'so I'm going along the cliff path for a bit.'

With the setting sun behind him he gazed down at her, his face dark against the sky but, illuminated from behind, his hair shining in a golden halo around his head, like an old-fashioned painting of a saint. She expected a hug or a kiss in acknowledgement of things being all right again, but in a far from saintly tone he snapped, 'God above, woman! Luke getting his blasted bike back doesn't mean they've got the killer. What are you trying to do, put yourself next on the list?'

'What?' He was right, she thought in confusion, and she was wrong to contemplate walking *there* in the gathering gloom. 'I didn't think,' she said limply, and burst into tears, a loud wail that held a hint of hysteria. This is a release, her mind insisted behind the noise, a release from worry and tension.

And then the Rob she'd loved since she was nineteen years old was there for her, strong arms, warm chest, a big hankie to dry her tears. 'Come on, sweetheart,' he whispered, kissing her wet eyes and the palms of her hands. 'All this has been too much for you. If you want to get away from the house I'll come with you. It's all right, Sally-bally... Don't cry – everything's all right.' His arms around her, they walked down past the holiday cottages towards the beach. And everything *was* all right. Everything was wonderful.

Jane Bingham was watching them from the window of Starfish Cottage. 'Here, Kenny,' she called, 'just look at them like a couple of lovebirds. You wouldn't think the police are in and out of the house all day long, would you?'

Channon found the incident room fairly quiet, with just one computer humming and John Meade as calmly competent as he'd been at eight that morning. He came and greeted Channon at the door. 'Miller should be here soon, Bill. I've sent two cars; one to the address he gave Bowles and another in case he's done a runner. No joy with Gribble, I take it?'

Channon gave him a brief update, and concluded, 'We'll have to talk to Luke Baxter, of course, but Mrs Sunning's blocked drain has made me put everybody else on hold. Has anything come in?'

'Routine reports mostly, with nothing on any of the youngsters who knew Samantha. But Bill, you're as good as there with Miller, aren't you?'

'I should be,' agreed Channon dubiously, 'but keep an eye on Deacon, just in case. How soon can you get off home? We might have a busy day tomorrow.'

John Meade gave him a look. 'You're joking. I'm not going home till you've talked to Miller!'

Zennie was weary of everything going round and round in her head so she had a bath and changed her clothes while she waited for Georgie to come home. It was funny but all at once her jewel-bright separates seemed wrong. The plunging necklines, the skin-tight skirts – she had the feeling that they weren't the sort of clothes a wife should wear; at least, not a wife who – who cared just a bit about her husband.

In the end she put on a swirly black dress with gold daisies embroidered round the hem and a bodice that was high at the front and low at the back, a reversal of her usual style. She'd bought it at a rummage sale because it had the look of a gypsy about it.

When Georgie saw what she was wearing, would he think she'd changed? She wasn't sure she *had* changed, all she knew was that something inside her felt different. She hoped he wouldn't be long. He'd said it was too far to walk so he hadn't gone to the roundhouse, which was only five minutes down the road, or to the incident room, which was even nearer.

Had he cycled to one of the farms? To Sam Deacon's, or Blankett's, or to the

Trudgeons? Had he got a special job to do there? 'Somethin's come up,' he'd said, 'a little bit extra.' Was he – could he be hoping to make a bit out of telling Jim Trudgeon what he knew about Luke Baxter? No – he'd be more likely to get money from Sally and Rob for keeping quiet about Luke – if he got any at all.

Money and Georgie didn't go together. He'd never, ever, earned more than the basic rate for farm labouring, a bit from selling eggs when he used to keep a few fowl in the shed, and a bit more the time he raised bedding plants from seed. Lack of money was why she'd worked as a waitress in half the cafés in Truro, jobs that sometimes ended in the sack for 'looking too sexy' or 'appearing too provocative'. Lack of money was why she now worked part-time in the back room of a supermarket when she'd have liked to be at home watching telly...

So was he at this very minute trying to change all that? To her own amazement Zennie found she couldn't raise much interest in the money. She just wanted to talk, and she wanted Georgie to listen.

Chapter Ten

'He was your suspect and you gave him the all clear,' pointed out Channon calmly. 'If you want to be in on the interview, get over here.'

Relenting about not telling Bowles, he had rung him at home. The sergeant, relaxing after a good meal and planning a solitary early night, was highly mortified to hear about Miller. 'Good God,' he exploded. 'He was cool as they come, sir, but he didn't strike a false note. I could have–'

'Save it,' interrupted Channon briskly. 'I've just had word we've got him. He was off out somewhere, but we got to him just in time.'

'I'm on my way,' promised Bowles, adding as he put the phone down, 'and I'll make the cocky devil sweat if I get the chance!'

Malachi was sitting under the hedge at the side of the road. It was a favourite place of his – a broken-down stone wall backed by tall bushes and surrounded by flowers. Bluebells, yellow cat's-ear and wild garlic, all glimmering in the half-light – to him it was a magic grotto and he was the wizard who lived there.

His Batman pyjamas weren't as good as a wizard's cloak, but he was wearing them because he'd sneaked out of bed while his mum was having a bath. Earlier on he'd pretended to be asleep when his dad checked on him, then he'd sat at the top of the stairs, listening. He hadn't been able to understand everything they said, but he thought he knew, now, why his mum couldn't be bothered with him. It was because his real dad had been a man with lots of money and a yacht, who had hurt her and then left her, so she'd had to find somebody else.

It would be a good idea, he thought, to call one man his real dad and the other his Gribble dad. He wondered where he'd have been living if his real dad had married his mum – not that he'd ever want to live with him ... not even if he was a millionaire.

He was glad about one thing; his Gribble dad hadn't murdered Samantha ... but it had sounded as if Ben's brother Luke had something to do with it. He didn't like that part of it any more than he liked the rest of what they'd said. His Gribble dad had sounded different – loud and a bit bossy, while his mum had sounded quiet and sort of – dead. Their voices kept sounding in his head, like when he and Ben had shouted in the cave on Martennis beach and the echo had rung back from the wet walls, over and

173

over again.

Another thing he wanted to think about was that though he didn't really like his mum, when he heard her talking in that new, sad little voice he'd felt as if he wanted to go and climb on her knee and put his arms round her neck, like he used to do when he was little with his Gribble dad. It was getting cold under the hedge, but he had too much to sort out in his mind to go back to bed just yet. He was so busy thinkng that he didn't even hear the approach of the motorbike. The first he knew was when the headlamp shone and the big bike screeched to a halt in front of him.

'Malachi! What are you doing out here?' It was Luke, Ben's brother – the one who might be a murderer, wearing a black and silver crash helmet. Forgetting that he'd always admired Luke, Malachi shrank back among the vegetation and wished he'd stayed in bed.

Luke opened the visor of his helmet. 'Why are you out here?' he repeated.

''Cos my mum and dad have been havin' a row,' answered Malachi, tears not far away. 'My mum doesn't know I'm here, an' my dad – well, he's gone to tell somebody somethin' he knows – somethin' he'll get money for. Somethin' he saw on the night of the murder!' Oh, he shouldn't have said that, he thought in panic, but the words just came out of his mouth on their own. Fearfully he looked at the figure in the black jacket.

But Luke didn't seem angry, just curious. 'He's gone to the police?' he asked. 'To the incident room?'

It was nice being asked important questions, even if the one who was asking might have murdered somebody. 'No, it was too far to walk,' Malachi muttered, 'so he's gone on his bike.'

'Malachi!' It was his mum this time, rushing towards them like a whirlwind. 'How often have I told you to stay in your bed?' Seeing the motorbike and its rider, she grabbed her son and held him by the shoulder, close to her side. 'What are you doing talking to Malachi?' she demanded.

Luke sighed. He'd never been able to understand this woman. She was so unlike his own mother she might as well have come from a different planet. 'I saw him sitting under the hedge, all on his own, and I stopped to see if he was all right,' he explained.

'He'll be all right when I get him home,' snapped Zennie. 'His dad's up on the farms, somewhere, but he'll be back soon, an' then–' Still clutching the child, she fell silent and backed away. Better not say too much, she warned herself, in case she'd been right about Georgie trying to get money for telling what he knew about this one. Downright dangerous he looked in his black, in spite of being Sally's son. She hurried Malachi back to their lane and then along to the cottage.

Luke sat astride his machine, watching them. Then he shrugged and switched on. The engine roared, the lights speared ahead and he rode off into the gathering dusk.

The interview would take place at the incident room, in the old-fashioned kitchen for privacy. A line of brown-painted cupboards behind him, Channon looked at the chipped white sinks and two huge enamel teapots on a shelf. Not exactly official surroundings, he told himself, and wondered how long it would be before he was back home and putting his meal in the microwave.

He couldn't help having doubts about Miller being their man. If he'd been guilty surely he would have done a disappearing act after being interviewed by Bowles, rather than continuing along the coastal path? As for the name and home address he'd given, that was being checked by the Bristol force at that very moment.

Bowles arrived first at Curdower, having had a shorter journey than the men bringing in Miller. Pale eyelashes flickering, the sergeant looked sour and uncomfortable when confronted by Channon. 'I'm sorry, sir,' he muttered reluctantly. 'I could have handled it better. He was a bit cocky, you see, but he rang true. I never thought for a minute he was our man...'

Channon waved a hand. 'I'm not saying he is, sergeant, but we've enough to merit a going-over, wouldn't you say?'

There was no answer to that, so they sat and waited, the one with a full stomach, the other with increasing hunger. A single computer was humming and through the open door the village green lay silent beneath stars that were suddenly bright as the moon slid behind cloud. A call came through from Bristol, confirming that a Barry Miller, aged thirty-seven, married with one child, did indeed live at the Filton address he'd given.

Minutes later the car arrived, and flanked by uniformed men, Miller came in looking fit and tanned in grey shorts and a yellow shirt. He shot a glance of pure dislike at Bowles, but listened impassively as the senior man introduced himself. Edgy, judged Channon, but hardly quaking in his shoes... He led the way to the kitchen and Bowles followed with Miller.

Once they were seated, he switched on and went through the preliminaries, starting the questions in his most gentle and disarming manner. 'You're on a walking holiday, I believe, Mr Miller?'

'Yes, for a week. I finish next Wednesday. Look – I told your sergeant everything I could about seeing the girl, and–'

Channon simply lifted a forefinger and Miller fell silent. Bowles ground his teeth. The iron finger in the velvet glove, eh? Maybe the whole hand came later.

Channon continued: 'You stayed with a Mrs Trelewyn just outside Curdower on Friday night, I'm told?'

'Yes.'

'And the following night, on the St Austell road from Mevagissey, you stayed at a house called Sundance, a bed and breakfast establishment owned by Mr and Mrs Sunning?'

Miller shot a glance at Bowles. 'Why ask when you know?'

'This is for the record, Mr Miller,' warned Channon pleasantly, 'so we want it right, don't we? I believe PC Lammis called on Mrs Sunning yesterday just as you were packing up ready to set off on your day's walk?'

'That's right. He asked if I'd been in the Curdower area on Friday afternoon and when I said I had he took me to his home to wait for the sergeant here.'

'Did you hear Constable Lammis arrive at Mrs Sunning's?'

'No. The first I knew she brought him up to my room.'

'I see. So you didn't attempt to get rid of anything from your backpack?'

'Such as what?' Miller's pale green eyes stared into Channon's in perplexity. 'If you've found a gun I can assure you it's not mine.'

'We haven't found a gun, Mr Miller, but we have in our possession a bra and pants which had been flushed down the toilet adjoining your room.'

Miller sighed wearily. 'Don't tell me, inspector – the girl wasn't wearing any undies!'

Channon's dark eyes glinted with anger, but he suppressed it. 'No, I won't tell you that,' he agreed blandly. 'I'll merely remind you of something. This is a murder investigation. I'm asking the questions and I want answers. What were you doing with a lacy, wine-red bra and pants in your possession?'

'Prove they were mine,' rejoined Miller. 'Prove they were hers, for that matter.'

'We have men working on it,' Channon told him. 'I ask you again, why did you have the bra and pants?'

The green eyes were hard as pebbles in cold water. 'Why don't you find out who was in the room the night before me?'

No wonder Bowles had been taken in, thought Channon. This was a confident customer, devious and intelligent. He consulted a copy of Mrs Sunning's statement. 'The occupants of the room for the three nights before you arrived were Mrs Sunning's two sisters on a family visit. I really don't see two middle-aged ladies blocking their sister's drain, Mr Miller.'

Miller gazed down at his hands and didn't speak. Got him, thought Bowles, and at that moment Channon's mobile rang. With a word of excuse the DCI left the room, saying to Bowles, 'He's all yours!' He told a constable to go and sit in and as the door opened again caught the sergeant's first words. 'Right, that was the nice one – I'm the nasty!'

As he'd expected, it was Eddie Platt on the phone. 'Bill?' came the cheerful voice. 'Tell your landlady she has all the bacteria known to man down her drain! Not to worry – so has everybody else. No clear traces of the wearer left on the knickers, though I'd have expected something in spite of the soaking. Either she had immaculate genitals or she'd put the pants on just before taking them off again. Originally dark red, both items fairly new, and with consecutive sales codes. Moderately expensive but not exclusive, because they're from the old firm – Marks and Spencer. Do you want them keeping as they are, or laundering? I can say for sure that you'll get no forensic evidence from them.'

So nothing to pin on Miller. Channon gazed across the room. 'Get them laundered, Eddie, if you will, in case I have to show them to the parents. Oh, I'll make a note of the codes, and the sizes too, if you can decipher them.'

A minute later he was back in the kitchen, where Bowles was looking bad-tempered and Miller tight-lipped but calm. Channon sat down again. 'That was news on the underwear, Mr Miller. You must find it convenient to pick up a matching set at Marks. No saleslady, just pay at the desk.'

Miller stared back woodenly. 'They were from Marks? So what?'

Channon's voice was icy. 'So I think they were yours, Mr Miller. Bought by you, worn by you, for your own pleasure.'

The green eyes were suddenly alive, glinting with panic. Bowles was dumbfounded. He hadn't sussed Miller as a cross-dresser. What did he do, swap clothes with the wife? Wait a minute – Channon was a wily sod; was this a ploy to put Miller off his guard?

But the walker had slumped in his chair. 'Go to the top of the class, inspector,' he said quietly. 'Yes, they're mine. I've done it for years when I get the chance.'

Channon leaned forward, all gentle sympathy now. 'That's why you had them with you on the walk? Because you were alone? Why didn't you tell me this as soon as you were brought in?'

'Why do you think?' asked the other bitterly. 'You might start wanting to check with my wife, and she doesn't know. I'm not proud of it, but I can't get rid of it. It's just something I have to accept. I – I need it.'

'So you *did* hear Constable Lammis arrive?'

'Yes, yes, yes! I thought my backpack might be examined so I flushed them away. I felt bad about the drains and so forth. I'll recompense the landlady.'

Channon stood up. 'Thanks, Mr Miller. That's cleared a few things up for us.'

'Can I go?'

Channon shook his head reprovingly. 'I've reminded you once and I'll remind you again, this is a murder investigation. We need more than *your* word, Mr Miller.' He jerked his head to Bowles and said to the constable: 'Give him what he's entitled to but keep him here till I tell you he can go.'

To Bowles he said, 'We're going to the Trudgeons'. Inspector Meade has warned them. You drive.'

Bowles was irritated to find things moving faster than he'd anticipated. 'You think Miller's on the level? You gave him the perfect get-out.'

'That was intentional. I think he's telling the truth, but I'm about to try and make sure – if I can. Sizes,' he said heavily. 'Sizes, Bowles.'

'You mean Miller's?'

'Miller's, Samantha's, and the underwear, which is size sixteen, Bowles. You saw the body, give a guess at her size.'

Bowles recalled lean young limbs, breasts so firm they splayed out only slightly as she lay on the slab. Taut hips and buttocks ... a slim, active young body. 'Ten? Twelve?' he ventured. 'It's hard to tell, sir.'

'I agree. That's why we're going to the Trudgeons'.'

Bowles didn't like dealing with the bereaved. 'Can't we telephone?'

'We could, but if I was Samantha's mother I'd expect a visit to ask about my daughter's choice of underwear, let alone her size. Come on, it's getting late.'

They made for the car. Bowles didn't ask if the older man had eaten. What was the point? He never seemed hungry.

This time Ellen Trudgeon was awake, a pale, slim woman with good skin and thick fair hair in a well-cut bob. Carefully made-up, she was wearing a white cotton shirt and banana-yellow trousers, as if about to visit Truro for an afternoon round the shops. Next to her Jim Trudgeon looked unkempt in grubby jeans and a checked shirt, the stubble thick on his jaw. His parents, sitting in front of hot drinks at the big kitchen table, were clearly exhausted.

'Chief inspector, isn't it?' asked Ellen with interest. 'I'm sorry I was asleep the last time you called. We've had a rather tiring time, as you know.'

Channon kept his reactions under strict control. Just tiring? When your teenage daughter had been murdered? He shot a glance at her husband and almost groaned. Jim Trudgeon was ravaged – his face lined and scored until he looked the same age as his father. The farmer widened his eyes and gave the smallest shrug of his shoulders, but the message was clear: 'She's being very odd – make allowances.'

He nodded slightly to show he understood, while at his side Bowles kept a low profile. 'I'm sorry to call on you so late,' said Channon, 'but if I could have a word – perhaps just with you and your wife, Mr Trudgeon?'

The parents stood up, almost with relief, and took their milky drinks away with them. 'Could I offer you tea or coffee, or a sandwich?' asked Ellen with concern. 'You must have to work such unreasonable hours.'

Channon felt like saying that murder was unreasonable as well, but instead he assured her that they were used to long hours, and no, they didn't need food or drink. 'We've come to ask for information which may be rather distressing for you. It's about your daughter's underclothes.'

'You said she wasn't touched!' protested Trudgeon. 'Not in that way.'

'That's correct. There was no sexual interference with your daughter.' That was stretching it a bit, remembering Gribble, but why tell this anguished father that his daughter had let an odd-job man squeeze her breasts? 'Like much of our work,' he said soothingly, 'this is merely a case of elimination. Mrs Trudgeon, perhaps you can tell me if your daughter had a set of lacy, wine-red underwear? A matching bra and pants from Marks and Spencer.'

'Not that I know of,' answered Ellen carefully. 'Though she sometimes treats herself to something new out of her allowance. If that's the case and it hasn't been in the wash I might not have seen it.'

Present tense, Channon told himself. This was rejection of the facts – refusal of them. Her husband let out a noisy breath, as if to disassociate himself from his wife's attitude as much as her actual reply. Channon ploughed on. 'Her size, then, Mrs Trudgeon. Could you give me that?'

'She's only seventeen and still growing,' said her mother dotingly. 'She's still a size ten.'

'Thank you,' said Channon. 'That's cleared up a little matter that was troubling us. We won't detain you any longer.'

Jim Trudgeon came to the gate with them, and Channon touched his arm. 'Your wife hasn't accepted it yet?' he asked gently.

'No! She keeps talking as if she's at an afternoon tea party, all polite and we must look after the visitors. She's had a couple of sessions with a counsellor but it's made no difference. I'm sure she thinks Samantha will walk in at any minute. I can't stand it!'

'She'll have to face it sooner or later,' Channon told him with compassion. 'If you're still worried about her in, say, forty-eight hours, ring our welfare department and they can put you on to a qualified psychotherapist. And Mr Trudgeon – I should prepare myself for a difficult time when she has to accept it, if I were you.'

'A difficult time?' repeated Trudgeon derisively. 'What do you think I'm having at the moment?'

They were in the car going back to the village. 'Are we letting Miller go?' asked Bowles.

Channon was grim. 'There's no option. We have no proof that the underwear's Samantha's. It isn't even her size. We can't hold a man for blocking a toilet with his own bra and pants – that's if they *are* his own. Even if we had them here we could hardly insist on him trying them on for us.'

Bowles grinned. 'What a picture, eh?' He was happier now it looked as if he'd been right about Miller. 'There's always Lukey-dukey to question,' he said cheerfully, and drew up with a flourish outside the village hall. It was quiet inside, with John Meade still hard at work.

'We're letting Miller go, so send him back by car,' Channon told Meade. 'Bowles here will bid him a fond farewell.' He looked across the room at the three men behind the tables. 'The nightwatchmen OK? You get off then, John, and I'll do the same. I'll be in with Bowles at seven thirty in the morning.'

A minute later Channon was driving home, his headlights making tunnels of the roads with their tall hedgerows. Home, he thought; the silent, empty house that had at last become a home of sorts. A meal, a drink, a bath, and then some exercise – of the mind. A mental review of progress on the case and a long, hard think about how to handle Luke Baxter in the morning.

Chapter Eleven

Jim Trudgeon was getting up. It was five o'clock, half an hour earlier than his usual time, but if he'd spent another minute next to Ellie's sleeping form he would have pushed her out of bed.

She'd been asleep *all night*, muttering and twitching a bit it was true, but asleep nevertheless, while he'd been wandering the house and pacing the yard, his mind in turmoil. He'd watched his livestock at rest, caught the lift of a barn owl's wings and seen rain clouds obscure the face of the moon. Any sight, he'd thought, was better than that of his wife fast asleep.

Now he threw on some working clothes, knowing that she couldn't help being in this state of refusal, or rejection, or whatever the doctor called it. But what about him? He was in hell. He needed his wife and she wasn't there. In her place was this ultra-polite stranger who kept making tea in the best china pot and twittering about nothing. His own parents were devastated but at least they were in the real world – if he hadn't had them to turn to he'd have gone mad.

Mad ... was Ellie mad? Had it turned her brain? He opened the front door and breathed air that smelled of rain. The countryman in him noted it, but the father in him was thinking of a bright-eyed little girl; the husband of a wife who had been silent and withdrawn when they were given the news. He'd received no comfort from her then and she'd asked for none from him. She simply sat there, motionless, refusing food and only drinking when she was bullied, until in the end the doctor gave her a strong sedative in the hope that when she awoke she'd be able to face what had happened.

Before she went to bed she'd helped to make out the list of their daughter's friends for the police, though even now he didn't know if she understood the reason for it. Then she'd gone listlessly to her drugged, enviable sleep.

Day was breaking as he walked through his front garden. It was starting to rain but he paid no attention because he was looking back to when Ellie awoke. She'd dressed herself in smart casual clothes, made up her face and ignored any reference to Samantha except to pretend that she was still alive. His mother said: 'Give her time, Jim. It'll sink in with time.' But would it? He didn't know, he didn't know anything except that he was in agony.

It wasn't yet fully light, but his feet followed a familiar path, one that slanted across a meadow to the top field named not for its position but for its yield in crops, which was the highest of all his arable land. Last year's potatoes had been the best ever, so he was hoping for similar success with this year's forage crop. As he walked, the first touch of serenity began to lay itself across his tired mind. The feel of the grass beneath his feet, hard and dry and eager for rain; the cool kiss of that rain in his hair, on his skin... It was registering now – this was just the thing to keep his crops coming on. Soon it was a downpour, but he continued to head for the top field, and when he reached it, stared thoughtfully into the silvery half-light. His life might be in chaos, but out here it was always the same; nature was his friend, he worked with it, believed in it. Calm was returning to him and with it came compassion for the wife he loved. Compassion for Ellie, but a deep, abiding anger for Samantha.

In command of his emotions again, he was turning to go back to the house when through the slant of the rain he caught sight of somebody standing at the other end of his field, amid his young fodder beet. There was no public right of way there, so who on earth could it be at this hour? Irritated, Trudgeon headed for the man, who stood with head bent and arms outstretched, as if welcoming a child.

Then for the first time in days Trudgeon let out a laugh. It wasn't a man – it was a scarecrow! But it wasn't one of his. He used them, they represented all that he believed in, but he hadn't set it up. So who had? Puzzled, he made for the turnip-headed figure. Was it some sort of joke? No – it would take a strange sense of humour to play a joke on his family at a time like this. Could it be a message, then? Not everybody was in favour of organic farming, for instance. He'd had many an argument about it in the pub.

Half expecting to find a note pinned to the jacket, he tramped over the young beet and stood straddle-legged in front of the scarecrow. He lifted the heavy head by its straw hair and floppy old hat, but the face that looked up at him wasn't made from a turnip. It was a real face, a man's face, deeply mottled and quite lifeless; the eyes were staring as if in amazement, the mouth stretched wide, the tongue lolling.

Bile rose in Trudgeon's gullet and he let out a high-pitched howl. He coughed and spluttered, gaping in horror and trying not to vomit. It was George – little Georgie Gribble. Drops of rain were landing on his bulging eyeballs, lengths of rope fastened his neck and his ankles to an upright spar of wood, each wrist was tied to the cross-brace. The hat was too big and Georgie's face looked like a small purple gargoyle under the dirty straw.

Pain ripped through the farmer. 'Georgie,' he whispered, 'who's done this to you?' Self-preservation made him look over his shoulder at the empty field and its dark hedges. Should he be frightened? Should he be angry? Yes, and yes again, but it was simply too much for an exhausted man to deal with. He sat down on the wet earth and wept.

Channon was shaving when the call came through from the incident room. 'It's DC Hallows from Curdower, sir.'

'Yes, Hallows, what is it?'

'We've had an emergency call, sir, from Mr Trudgeon.'

The wife, thought Channon, she'd gone

over the edge. 'Carry on,' he said. 'I'm listening.'

'He says he's found a body, sir, out on his field. He's a bit upset. He says it's murder.'

Channon's mind had been in focus since he awoke. 'Did he recognize the body?' he asked crisply.

'Sir – he says it's George Gribble.'

God *above!* For seconds Channon was silent, then he said: 'Hallows, write this down. First – ring Inspector Meade and tell him I say he's to get in immediately. Second – send a uniformed constable up to Blue Leaze at once. Tell him to say I'm on my way and until reinforcements arrive he's to follow procedure for a suspicious death – cordon tapes and so forth, and he's not to leave the body, not even for an instant. Third – ring Sergeant Bowles and get him in. Fourth – let's see – make sure Trudgeon tells nobody about this apart from the immediate family. That applies to you as well – nobody to be told unless they're in the force. Is that clear?'

'Yes, sir, but what about Gribble's wife?'

Channon sighed. Who'd have the job? The little tigress had been humiliated, and she wasn't the type to take it calmly. Could she have killed her husband? 'She'll have to wait,' he said heavily. 'She's automatically a suspect so I want to tell her myself. Try and get hold of Mary Donald to go with me. I'll ring Truro HQ myself and they can notify the police surgeon and the chief pathologist. I'll be on my way in less than ten minutes and I'll go straight to Blue Leaze.'

Relief echoed down the line. 'Right, sir, thanks, sir.'

In seven minutes flat Channon set off in heavy rain, telling himself that this killing was probably by the same hand that had killed Samantha. He'd like to know, though, why Gribble's body was on Trudgeon's land. Trudgeon himself had been in quite a state, of course, what with grief and anger and worry about his wife. If he'd heard rumours about Gribble being taken in for questioning he might possibly have attacked him as an act of vengeance; killed him, even, though if that was the case he would hardly have rung in to report it. His mind producing theories and as quickly rejecting them, Channon sped along the empty roads, spray shooting high on either side of the car.

A constable in waterproofs was waiting for him in front of the stone farmhouse. 'The body's in the next field, sir, if you'd follow me. The SOCO's just arrived, with more on the way, and the police surgeon's rung through to say he's already set off.'

'Quick work,' said Channon approvingly, and followed the man through the downpour. Rain like this would make it almost impossible to find vital clues around the body, and nobody had yet arrived with the customary waterproof cover. He'd asked no questions about cause of death, he reminded himself, so what was he going to find?

Later, whenever he recalled Gribble as a scarecrow, Channon wondered why he hadn't found the sight horrific. But to him at that moment it wasn't horrific, it was sad – awfully, terribly sad, because Gribble looked pathetic. Drooping on his wooden cross like some weak parody of a crucifixion, the little man had even less dignity in death than he'd had in life.

'Poor devil, eh, sir?' muttered the constable on guard, while the scene-of-crime officer clicked away with his camera permanently on flash. Channon put on the obligatory anti-contamination gear to approach the body, his eyes narrowed in concentration. Strangulation, this time, apparently, but it had at least been quick, judging by Gribble's look of surprise.

There was the sound of car doors slamming, and a moment later men converged on the field, the surgeon and Bowles among them. For once there was no brisk comment from the sergeant; no 'I've seen worse when I was with the Met.' He simply stared in disbelief. 'Poor little blighter,' he said, shivering. 'It looks like the devil's been at work here.'

Channon shot him a look. The devil had been mentioned before on this case – now where had it been, and when? Ah – at the Baxters' ... he'd quoted the old saying about no corners in a roundhouse.

Meanwhile the organized chaos continued; the full force of the law swarming over the scene of a crime. 'You hardly need me to certify death on this one,' observed the police surgeon briskly. 'He's very, very dead. Time – several hours ago – before midnight, I'd say. Probably strangulation, though with a very fine cord – maybe the old garrotte. The post-mortem will clarify that, and everything else you want to know.'

Photographs and more photographs were taken; samples of earth and vegetation removed. Eventually, the body was taken away as well, complete with straw hair and the hat, but by then Channon had left the scene and was dealing with Trudgeon.

The farmer was close to collapse, his parents hovering nearby brewing tea for everybody, but of his wife there was no sign. 'She's still asleep,' mumbled Trudgeon in amazed embarrassment. 'Inspector – I've told your men all I can. I'll make a statement of it if you insist, and then I have to go to bed. My dad's going to organize the work for me – just for today. I feel – I feel ill.'

'No wonder,' said Channon with sympathy. 'Just a brief statement of how you found the body, and the exact time, if you can recall. The officer here will print it out and then if you'll sign it... And perhaps your parents could just say whether or not George Gribble called here late last evening? I'll put good men on to it so we won't need to keep you for long.'

Trudgeon stared at him woodenly. Channon decided he was close to breaking point, too exhausted to pretend or to conceal. He might be an unlikely murderer, but he'd been here on his farm all night. He could have killed George well before midnight, then gone for an early tramp in the rain to 'find' him. They'd better search that ground out there, and search it well – and the hedges, and the outbuildings. Just as well extra SOCOs were on their way.

Zennie Gribble was face down in bed, reluctant to grapple with a new day. She'd waited up for Georgie until the early hours, wrestling with mental images of him with another woman, because that was where he must be – he'd got his money and he'd used it to pay for a woman. Not that he'd find one in Curdower, or Martennis, maybe not even in Pencannon – he must have paid Ted Lightfoot to take him to Truro in his taxi.

So much for promising to come home and listen to her, so much for buying her something nice... For once she hadn't wanted something nice, she'd simply wanted to talk to her husband. Everything was jumbled up in her head; that knocking noise was in her head, wasn't it? No – it was the front door! Georgie was back without his key! She threw on her gold satin robe and ran down the stairs, ready to pretend she didn't know where he'd been.

But it wasn't Georgie at the door, it was DCI Channon with a policewoman. 'Oh!' said Zennie. 'He's not here. He – he had to go out.'

'When was that, Mrs Gribble?' asked Channon.

'What? Last night, soon after he got back from Truro.'

'Did he tell you where he was going?'

'No, an' I didn't ask. I was – well – I was a bit upset. He went on his push-bike.'

'How about you, Mrs Gribble? Did you go out after he left?'

'Me? No. That is – yes – for a minute. I'd looked in on Malachi an' his bed was empty, so I went an' found him out on the road, sitting in the hedge, like he does. He goes out there in his pyjamas though he knows I'll tell him off. I had him back indoors in a coupla minutes. What *is* this, anyway? Georgie said you'd believed what he told you about Samantha.'

Channon observed her closely. If this was an act it was pretty good, but now for the final test. 'Mrs Gribble,' he began, 'I'm afraid we have bad news about your husband.'

'Oh God, he's had an accident!' Remorse swept through Zennie. She'd been picturing him with a woman, but he'd been lying injured out on the roads. 'He would ride that old bike!' she said wildly. 'He's in hospital, isn't he?'

'If we could just come inside for a minute.' It was the second time he'd said that on this doorstep, thought Channon.

Zennie led the way indoors. 'Tell me,' she said hoarsely. 'Has he broken a limb?'

Channon took a deep breath. 'Worse than that, I'm afraid. George is dead, Mrs Gribble. He's been murdered.' He told himself that the best actress in the world couldn't make themselves lose colour as she did at that moment. Mary Donald moved quickly to her side, but already Zennie was doubting what she'd heard. She put up a hand and cupped her ear, like a very deaf old woman. 'Would you say that again?' she asked carefully.

'George is dead, I'm afraid,' repeated Channon. 'He's been murdered.'

Zennie's skin took on a waxy sheen. She leaned against Mary and for a long moment was silent, staring emptily in front of her. Then she pushed the policewoman away. 'How?' she snapped. 'Where? I won't ask why, because I know why. It was because he was going to tell what he knew, for money.

Going to tell Trudgeon who'd killed his daughter.'

With a single look Channon warned Mary against the slightest wrong move. 'But George didn't know who'd killed Samantha, did he?'

Zennie leapt forward and grabbed him by the front of his jacket. 'He knew *something*,' she snarled. 'An' Luke Baxter knew that he knew it! Malachi told him!'

Luke again! Channon's heart plummeted, but he kept a straight face. 'Malachi saw Luke Baxter? Did you see him too?'

'Yes I did,' she answered with venom, 'face to face. Malachi told him that his dad knew somethin' about the murder – he admitted that to me later, because it worried him – an' then I arrived while they were talking an' – an' I let slip that Georgie was up at one of the farms.'

'But you've just said that he didn't tell you where he was going.'

'He didn't. He said it was too far to walk, so I knew it wasn't the Baxters', nor anywhere in the village.'

'I see. Thank you, Mrs Gribble.' No tears, he noted. 'Is there somebody we can contact to come and stay with you for a while? A relative or a close friend?'

The beautiful eyes stared into his and he thought they looked as dead as her husband's. 'I don't have nothing to do with my family,' she told him quietly, 'an' I have no friends. They don't like me in the village.'

'Then WPC Donald will stay with you,' he said gently. 'Later on, we'll have to ask you a few questions about when you last saw George, what time it was, and so forth. I'm afraid we'll have to question your son, as well.'

At that there was a sniffle and a muffled wail from the stairs. Malachi appeared at the door, wiping his eyes with the back of his hand. 'I shouldn't'a told him,' he mumbled brokenly, 'but I didn't know he were goin' to kill me dad. I didn't know, Mum!'

Zennie looked at the child as if she'd never seen him before, then she held out a hand to him. Slowly, hesitantly, Malachi went to her. He laid his head against her stomach and put his arms around her waist.

Zennie didn't embrace him. She didn't move, and still she didn't weep. 'We don't need anybody with us,' she said doggedly. 'We don't need anybody at all. Malachi an' me – we'll be all right on our own.'

Chapter Twelve

It was 7.15 a.m. and extra staff were arriving at the incident room. Headquarters had made a rapid decree that as the Gribble killing was almost certainly linked to the Trudgeon case, the joint investigation should be upgraded to a full-scale major enquiry. This meant that Channon would have the benefit of increased funding and more manpower.

Always at his best under pressure, he had already reassured his superior, who was demanding progress reports before there was any progress, and had just conferred with John Meade on how to deploy their forces. More computers were being installed and now he was trying to snatch a moment for thought between noisy verbal bulletins from the telephone staff.

'Gribble spoke to a mate outside the pub at a quarter to nine, sir!'

'We've put a trace on a Discovery seen near Blue Leaze at about ten o'clock.'

'Two men are on their way to Pengally Farm to see Sam Deacon.'

'George was spotted cycling away from the village well before nine.'

'Sergeant Malley's taken a DC to check on Barry Miller, sir.'

Order, method, routine: the strength of an enquiry, thought Channon, but where in all this turmoil was his precious intuition? Fast asleep, apparently. As for the little scarecrow-corpse in its rain-washed field ... if Trudgeon wasn't the murderer – and he doubted very much that he was – Gribble was either followed to Blue Leaze and killed when he arrived, or he'd been attacked elsewhere and, dead or alive, taken to Blue Leaze to be tied to his ghastly crucifix.

So far there had been scant information on the body – just the police surgeon's report and the duty pathologist's confirmation of strangling with fine cord and the tying up of wrists and ankles. Not even, so far, a definite time of death; that would come from the official post-mortem, scheduled for 10.30 a.m. As for evidence at the scene of death, the SOCOs were examining every inch of Trudgeon's land and the nearby lanes and hedges, so far without success.

He asked himself whether there was any point, now, in keeping quiet about it being Gribble who was dead, or for that matter about the manner of his death. He beckoned John Meade. 'You know I put a ban on telling anybody about Gribble, and the way he died? Has word got out, do you reckon?'

Meade shrugged. 'You know the rural grapevine. Farmers are early risers, and I've no doubt somebody saw lights and all the activity up at Trudgeon's place. Add to that the fact that it was a while before we got the screens and covers up, and it's more than likely that somebody either saw George as a scarecrow or simply sussed that he was killed out on the field. Folk certainly know somebody's dead because we've already had offers of help. Oh – I've just had word there's a pre-fab building arriving soon for extra office space. I thought it could go on the green outside.'

Channon looked around the crowded room. 'Not before time by the looks of it, John.'

Meade nodded. 'More space and more nourishment. I've got two women making tea and toast. Do you want some?'

Channon hated to eat on the job, but he'd left home without any breakfast. He accepted a mug of tea and some buttered toast and saw that Bowles had done the same and was chewing with an air of edgy impatience. 'What about Lukey-dukey, sir?' he asked. 'Are we having him in?'

Channon was ashamed of his reluctance to do any such thing. 'Yes,' he said, 'of course we are – for voluntary questioning. We don't have any evidence, don't forget, merely witness say-so. I can't leave here just yet, so ring the Baxters, will you, and tell them to keep Luke at home. Don't put them on their guard by giving the impression it's crucial, and say we'll be there by about eight thirty.'

Eyes narrowed, Bowles picked up the nearest phone. Before long Luke Baxter's gleaming motorbike would be pensioned off and his equally gleaming pony-tail would be given a trim by the barber of a remand centre or he, Bowles, was a Dutchman.

Channon was examining his own feelings of distaste for what was to come. He hadn't been reluctant to have Gribble in, had he? Why, then, was he dragging his feet with Luke Baxter? Because he was a likeable young lad, or because he, Channon, was on the same wavelength as Luke's mother? God only knew that over the years he'd given and received enough advice on not getting personally involved with either victims or suspects, but there was something about the Baxter family that caught at him, and it wasn't all good. Somewhere, too deeply buried under routine and reason and common sense, was something else – something he couldn't bring to the surface. He shrugged. It would come to him with time – it always did.

He was making himself go through the Trudgeons' statements when Steve Soker's neat, wiry form appeared at his side. 'Steve,' he said, 'I thought you'd gone into hibernation. What have you been doing?'

The DC wriggled his shoulders. 'I've been here, sir, on the usual paperwork, but snatching time on the computer whenever I could. You said to see what I could do with Samantha's stuff.'

'So I did,' agreed Channon. 'Well, have you come up with anything?'

'School work, of course, and a whole load of farm data, but–'

'But what?' Soker was a good lad but time was pressing.

'Well, I can tell she was bright, sir. She has codes and passwords that I haven't managed to crack. Shall I spend more time on it?'

Channon waved a hand. 'Yes, yes, but I might need you on something else.' Then he paused for thought. They were getting nowhere fast on Samantha, and as for Gribble, they hadn't even started. 'Keep at it,' he ordered. 'Should I get you some help?'

With the confidence of youth Soker shook his head. 'No, sir, I've got the ability and I like doing it.'

Channon smiled. 'Off you go,' he said.

Men were setting out to talk to farmers in the area around Blue Leaze when a visitor strode into the incident room and surveyed the ranked computers and telephones. 'Good morning, chief inspector,' said Maureen Blankett crisply. 'I can see why I couldn't get through – all your telephones are in use. Surely you need more lines installed?'

Channon swallowed a sigh. He could do without a lecture on management from the lady of the manor, however concerned she was. 'Good morning,' he replied. 'I can assure you that we're upgrading our capacity, but it all takes time. Now, if you wouldn't mind, this room is for police personnel only.'

The farmer nodded approvingly. 'Quite right, but I won't keep you for more than a moment. I gather something unpleasant has happened on Trudgeon's land? I saw lights, heard cars, put two and two together and hoped it didn't add up to more trouble for Jim and Ellie. Then half an hour ago one of my men said he thinks there's been violence done over there. If that's the case I feel I should tell you that we expect whoever is perpetrating these acts to be caught without delay. This is English farming country, inspector, not murder mile in Naples.'

'You don't say,' murmured Channon.

'I must make it clear that it's unacceptable in Curdower.'

'I quite agree, Miss Blankett. Now – is there anything else?'

The direct blue eyes widened. 'Of course there is! Why do you think I'm here? I tried to telephone you to say that my junior stockman found a bicycle in the hedge not far from my main gate. I've seen it and it's the type that George Gribble sometimes rides. I can't see him leaving it there and walking home. And another thing–'

'Hah!' Channon was highly pleased. 'Don't touch it,' he warned, 'just leave it where it is for the forensic team to examine.'

'Forensic? To examine George's bike? Don't say something's happened to him? Not to little George?'

'I'm afraid he's dead, Miss Blankett, and we're treating it as suspicious.' And how, he added silently. 'I can't tell you more, but our men will be out to see you before long. Everyone in the area will be interviewed, and statements taken from those in the immediate vicinity of Blue Leaze.'

Maureen Blankett's crisp, lucid way with words had deserted her. 'But – that is – I mean – the other thing is – one of my barns, the one we use for small pieces of equipment, well – it was open when my man arrived, the door swinging loose and letting in the rain. He says a wheelbarrow's gone missing, and maybe other things as well ... we don't know, we're not sure...' A lock of crisp grey hair had fallen over one eye, and all at once she looked an old woman.

Channon beckoned a WPC. 'Stay with Miss Blankett until she's fit to go home,' he said, and to the farmer, 'I'll have men up at your place within half an hour, so will you telephone instructions that nothing must be touched, nothing moved, no floors swept.'

The sinewy shoulders were already straightening. 'Very well, inspector. We'll do all we can to help. What about Mrs Gribble? Do you know if she's being looked after?'

'When I spoke to her she wanted to be alone with her son, but perhaps another woman could help?' He nodded his thanks, his mind already forging ahead. A wheelbarrow, eh? To cart a dead body? Things were moving, at last.

One day of 'all sit down together for breakfast', thought Sally, and they were back to everybody drifting in when they felt like it. She'd done scrambled eggs for Rob, who by now would be at Truro station to catch an early train to London Paddington. Tessa was eating a bowl of chopped fruit and Luke attacking a mountain of toast and honey. 'You're going on your bike, I take it?' she asked him.

He nodded, eyes gleaming. 'I'm calling for Bammo in case his baffles are playing up again.' Evidently his friend's brief neglect was forgiven and forgotten...

Ben came in then, wafting his English homework. 'You know that last page of my essay, Mum? I've altered it, and it's a lot better.'

Sally smiled. *He* was a lot better, as well. That worried little crease above his nose had disappeared. They were all back to normal, she thought: Luke on top of the world now he'd got his bike back; Tessa up to the minute with her homework, as usual, though still obsessed by healthy eating; Ben less tense about what had happened on the beach, and once again engrossed in his beloved English Lit. As for Rob, he was back to normal, as well. His kiss when he left had been one of their long-standing little secrets from the children. Outwardly a gentle farewell, but actually a quick, open-mouthed meeting of lips that said it all. Today its message had been, 'I love you and last night was great!' She sat down with coffee and a croissant and kept on smiling.

When the phone rang Tessa said, 'Finish your breakfast, Mum, I'll go.' She came back blinking uncertainly. 'It was that sergeant. He says to keep Luke at home because the inspector wants to talk to him again. I asked him what about but he wouldn't say. They'll be here at about half past eight.'

Luke rolled his eyes. 'They're not after my bike again, are they?'

Nobody answered. Silence descended and for long seconds the only sound was rain against the window. Three pairs of eyes stared at Sally, who felt a familiar sensation building up inside her chest. Dread was back – cold, sinew-wrenching dread. But why? This wasn't unexpected. Channon had told Luke: 'Keep yourself available in case we have more questions, but so far we're satisfied.' This meant that they did have more questions, but did it also mean that they were no longer satisfied? Did it mean–

'What about Ben and me?' asked Tessa. 'You can't drive us to school if the police are coming.'

Sally forced herself to reply. 'And you can't cycle in this downpour. I'll run you both to the village and you can get the local bus to Pencannon. That'll give me time to be back here by half past eight. Just make sure you're ready, both of you.'

Ben's eyes were swivelling uncertainly from one to the other, the little crease back above his nose. Luke, always one for action, jumped up from the table and announced, 'I'll ring Bammo to tell him I won't be calling.'

Tessa tossed her plait over her shoulder and came round the table. 'I don't think it'll be anything much, Mum,' she said awkwardly, and all at once circled Sally's shoulders in her arms and gave her a hug.

Touched and surprised, Sally looked up. 'Thanks, love,' she said. Relief battled with remorse as she acknowledged that her daughter really was changing. Had she been too tied up with the boys to see it? Had Tess been thinking that her brothers came first? It was true that because Rob always clamped down on Luke, she, Sally, had tried to make it up to her son in dozens of little ways, and as for Ben, well – he was Ben – gentle and hesitant and needing her. In protecting her sons, had she neglected her daughter? Was it the reason Tessa was so coolly self-sufficient, so self-absorbed? Was it what lay behind years of her being uptight and uncommunicative – clinging to her father rather than her mother?

This was mad, trying to analyse Tessa in one minute flat when in the past she'd spent hours agonizing about where she'd gone wrong with her. On impulse, she caught hold of her daughter's hand and planted a kiss on the palm, pressing her fingers down on top of it as she used to do when Tessa was little. She wouldn't have done it a few days ago – she couldn't have – they hadn't been on those sort of terms. Now, she fancied that an unspoken message passed between them: Things are going to get better. We're going to start understanding each other...

Soon, Sally promised herself, she and Tessa would talk – really talk, but right now Ben was intent on saying something. 'Tessa's right, it can't be anything much. Luke's bike was in the clear, don't forget. Inspector Channon said so. I – I liked him, Mum.'

'So did I,' agreed his sister, 'but we can't

211

say the same for the sergeant, can we? Come on, let's go and get ready.'

They were upstairs when Luke came back. 'Mum,' he said hoarsely, 'do you know what Bammo's just told me?'

'No. What?'

'Somebody's just rung his mum to say that George Gribble's dead. People are saying he was murdered.'

Sally gaped at him. 'How?' she asked. 'When? Where?'

'And why,' finished Luke grimly, 'but nobody knows the answer to that one. Bammo said it was during the night, over at Blue Leaze Farm. Malachi was telling me last evening about his dad expecting to get money because he knew something about Samantha. Then his mum arrived and said his dad was up on the farms.' Luke leaned forward with his hands flat on the table. 'Mum – if old Gribble's been murdered it's connected with Sammy – it's got to be!'

Sally's mind became crystal clear. Zennie – odd, beautiful Zennie was now a widow, Malachi was without a father, but she couldn't even think about that. What concerned her was that the two of them had told her son where George had gone, and why. And he – Luke – had been out on his infernal bike late in the evening.

She waved a silencing hand. 'Let me think,' she said tensely. Lots of people would have been out and about: going to the pub or over to the Martennis, visitors out for a late stroll, the group of adolescents under the chestnut tree near the church, and of course, the constant to-ing and fro-ing at the incident room. Rob himself had gone out before they went to bed – he'd left his smallest laptop in the computer room at the school and he'd needed it to take to London.

'For now I think we'll just tell Tessa and Ben that Malachi's dad's had an accident, Luke. That'll prepare them for what they'll hear at school. Sit down for a minute, will you?'

Reluctantly he flopped down in the chair opposite. 'Don't get in a state, Mum,' he warned. 'I can't see Channon taking me for a double murderer.'

'Neither can I,' she admitted. 'All I'm saying, Luke, is be prepared. Zennie might have told him that she and Malachi talked to you last night.'

The clear hazel eyes stared into hers. 'So?'

She shook her head. 'So I don't know. I think I'd better get in touch with your dad.'

'He'll be on his way,' he protested, 'and he'll be back this evening, anyway. Leave it, eh, Mum?'

Sally was watching him carefully. Not a single, solitary nibble of his lip, she told herself in relief. 'All right,' she agreed. 'I've just got time for a quick shower before we set off.' She jumped up, but Luke grabbed her arm.

'You can trust me, Mum,' he said soberly. 'I've done nothing wrong – nothing. Do you believe me?'

'Of course I do. You're my son, Luke. I trust you, and I love you.'

He gave a small, embarrassed grin. 'That's all right, then,' he said.

Channon was as polite as ever but deadly serious, following them into the big, circular room with Bowles at his elbow. This, thought Sally, would be no friendly chat.

'Is your husband here, Mrs Baxter?' was his first question.

'No, he's on his way to London by train. He usually goes on Tuesdays.'

'I see. Well, I'm afraid we have to question Luke, so exactly how old is he?'

'Seventeen,' she said warily, 'seventeen last October.'

'I see,' said Channon again, and his dark eyes were unreadable. 'In that case we're allowed by law to question Luke without a parent or independent responsible adult being present. However, you can come with him if you wish.'

'Come with him?' she repeated blankly. 'Where to?'

Bowles let out an audible sigh. Channon

was a DCI, for God's sake, not some thicko plod, yet he couldn't bring himself to spell it out to her. Why didn't he just take the kid in and give him a grilling? Straightfaced, he intervened. 'We're asking Luke to come with us to Truro police station of his own free will for questioning.'

Sally swung round on Channon in protest, but it was Luke who asked, 'On what evidence?'

'We don't need evidence, Luke,' answered Channon quietly. 'Just reasonable grounds for suspicion.'

'But my bike was in the clear! You said so yourself.'

'That's right, it is. We need to talk to you about quite different aspects of our investigations.'

Plural, thought Sally, more than one investigation. The name Gribble trembled on her lips but she kept it back. She could hear her own breathing, noisy and very rapid. 'What *are* these different aspects?' she asked.

'We don't have to reveal them, madam,' said Channon smoothly. 'Shall we go?'

'No, we shan't!' she snapped breathlessly. 'We're not going anywhere until I know more. Are you arresting my son?'

This was the mother defending her young. Channon shot a warning look at Bowles. 'As the sergeant said, Mrs Baxter, we'd prefer Luke to come with us voluntarily.'

'And if he refuses?'

'Then I'm afraid we'd have to insist.'

'You mean arrest him?'

'Yes.'

Luke stared in open disbelief, his jaw sagging. Then all at once he gained command of himself and amazingly, gave a small shrug. Channon saw it and his heart sank. 'Luke,' he said heavily, 'we're hoping that you can help us with our enquiries concerning the murders of Samantha Trudgeon and George Gribble.'

This couldn't be happening! Sally bit her lip so hard she tasted blood. She was confused and out of her depth, but one resolve filled her mind. It would be over her dead body if Channon pinned a false charge on Luke. They couldn't refuse to go to Truro, but would it be taken as a sign of guilt if they asked for a solicitor?

As if sensing her turmoil, Channon looked her in the eye. 'I'll keep you informed of your rights at all times,' he said gently. 'And for the record, I try very hard to avoid accusing somebody who's innocent.'

Sally's breathing slowed. She'd trusted this man from the moment they first met. She trusted him now. With a small nod of the head she attempted to tell him so, and said, 'Luke and I will go in my car, Mr Channon, so that we won't have to trouble you for transport back.' Then she turned to her son and said, 'I think we'd better go, Luke.'

He shrugged again and picked up a denim jacket, then they all walked out into the rain.

Chapter Thirteen

Malachi thought it strange that his mum had started to be different before his dad was murdered, rather than after. Ever since she knew that his dad had messed about with Samantha she'd been talking in that funny little voice and wearing a dark dress that didn't show her boobs. Now she was sitting in one of the red armchairs, staring in front of her but not actually looking at anything, so he got himself some bread and marmalade for his breakfast.

He wondered if they'd be able to have a funeral for his dad, or whether the police would keep his body for ever and ever. And what about going to school? If he asked her whether he should go it might look as if he didn't care about his dad, but he did care – a lump kept coming in his throat and stopping him from swallowing his food. Food – that was it! He'd make his mum some breakfast! He could brew tea and he could make toast. He used to make toast with his dad, sometimes, and they'd have it

217

with Marmite or peanut butter.

He'd been thinking about his two dads and how he'd been going to call one his real dad and the other his Gribble dad, but somehow it didn't seem such a good idea any more. He didn't care about the rich man on the yacht, he just wanted one dad, the one he'd always had – but he was never going to see him again. He wouldn't come home any more ... they wouldn't watch telly together any more...

With a sniffle and a deep sigh he got out the china cup and saucer that his dad had won on the fair at Falmouth. Perhaps she'd shout at him for doing it, but even if she did it would be better than listening to that whispery voice. He found her sitting very straight, her eyes all smudged, but from make-up, he told himself, not from crying. He moved the gold coffee table in front of her and then brought in the old wooden tray with her breakfast.

As if coming out of a trance, Zennie shook her head and focused on her son as he hovered behind the tea and toast. She opened her mouth to say she didn't want it, then saw that he'd used the rosebud china, and that it was thick with dust; there was even dust floating on top of the tea. Normally such things didn't bother her, but now it pained her to see the pink rosebuds looking dirty, because for once it had been a happy time when the three of them went to the fair. Georgie had won the cup and saucer and had bowed low as he presented it to her. Then he'd kissed her – on the wrist, of course.

'Do you remember the night your dad won this, Malachi?' she asked.

'Yes,' he said, and two fat tears slid down his cheeks.

Zennie stared at his wet face. Another man's son was crying for Georgie, yet she herself couldn't raise a tear. There was an empty space where her heart should be, a great, gaping black hole. Just when she'd found out that she cared about Georgie, just when she'd decided that she could never again let him turn to another woman, he'd been taken away from her. Taken away, and she didn't even know how he'd died. Was it a punishment on her for having made him live without love?

Pain and loss and exhaustion were in her eyes as they looked into those of her son. Malachi stared back, desperate for a cuddle but knowing she wouldn't give him one. He was consumed by feelings he didn't understand, and though he tried hard to keep quiet, he let out a whimper, and then a wide-mouthed howl. 'I don't care about that other dad!' he wailed. 'I only want one dad and now he's dead!'

Zennie was startled. 'You were listening!'

she accused. 'You weren't asleep at all when your dad checked on you!' Georgie wouldn't like this, she thought – he hated it when Malachi heard something he shouldn't. 'But Georgie won't know, will he?' asked a cold little voice in her head. No, maybe he wouldn't, but she must try to make it all right. 'We were just arguing a bit, me an' your dad,' she said. 'It didn't mean nothing.'

'Oh, yes it did,' contradicted Malachi. 'I knew what me dad meant about that man with the yacht. I don't want that dad,' he repeated, 'I want me real dad!' He pushed his way past the breakfast tray and stood with his thighs touching her knees.

Zennie was aware that something was turning over in the big black hole where her heart should be. She'd never felt close to this child, yet in his own way he was broken-hearted at losing Georgie. She examined his features. Was she imagining that he didn't look as much like the man who fathered him as she'd thought? She patted his hand. She'd never expected to get any comfort from him but somehow, listening to him cry, she didn't feel quite so alone.

Sally sat at one side of the room while Luke faced the two detectives across a small table. Channon had asked her not to interrupt, so she was steeling herself to keep silent – not easy when her whole being was geared up to do battle on behalf of her son.

She hadn't tried to contact Rob; things had moved too fast and in any case she would have alarmed him for nothing if Luke was sent home inside ten minutes. Now, though, with Channon announcing names and dates and times for the tape, she was consumed by fear. Luke was clever, the whole family knew that, but she doubted whether he'd grasped the seriousness of his position.

Channon started in the calm, reasonable tone that had so appealed to her at their first meeting. 'Now, Luke, we want to take you through what you've already told us when we chatted at your house and in your signed statement. Is that quite clear?'

Luke nodded. 'Yes.'

'You've told us that Samantha had asked you about a lift before the disco, and that you agreed to take her as a pillion passenger because the Martennis is close to your home. Is that correct?'

'Yes,' said Luke again.

'But a witness at the disco told us that you were so keen to give her a lift that when somebody else offered, you more or less insisted on her going with you. Why was that, Luke?'

Sally leaned forward. This was new. Please God, she begged silently, let him be careful how he answers. Channon was a good man

– she was sure of it – but he had to do his job.

Luke merely shrugged, and said, 'There was always somebody willing to give her a lift, but I'd already agreed to do it – it was convenient and besides, I like to have somebody riding pillion.'

'Somebody? You mean anybody, or Samantha in particular?'

'Anybody.'

Bowles broke in. 'Were you attracted to her?'

Luke sighed. 'No, I wasn't. She was pretty and good fun and everything, but I wasn't keen on her, if that's what you mean.'

'Was she perhaps keen on you?' asked Channon.

Luke gave an odd, tight little smile that seemed to Channon far too old and cynical for his years. 'No,' he said evenly, 'I don't think so.'

'So what time did you arrive at the Martennis?'

'I've told you – about ten thirty.'

'And you chatted for a bit?'

'Yes.'

'What about, Luke?'

'Oh, you know, music and stuff ... how the disco had gone ... our favourite bands, that sort of thing.' Luke's clear eyes were guileless, his manner co-operative; he nibbled the inside of his lower lip as if he was on edge but trying hard to be helpful. Sally watched the childhood mannerism and her heart thudded.

'So,' continued Channon, 'it was an amicable chat?'

'Yes.'

'But Luke, I have a signed statement from a witness who watched you and Samantha talking. This witness insists that you were arguing with her, that you might even have been threatening her.'

'But there was nobody there!' Luke protested. 'That is – I mean – we were just talking.'

Well, well, thought Bowles, young golden boy *was* lying, after all; just look at the wary eyes and tight mouth, the way his arms were tucked against his ribs. Let Channon sort this one out, he'd got plenty out of Gribble by his softly-softly approach.

'I didn't say we agreed about everything, inspector,' said Luke persuasively. 'We were just talking about things that interested us. In any case, where *was* this witness? I don't recall an audience.'

'He didn't intrude,' agreed Channon, 'but he got the impression of a strong disagreement. If you did have an argument, Luke, now's the time to tell me about it.'

For long seconds Luke seemed to consider that, and glanced sideways at his mother. 'Maybe a difference of opinion,' he conceded, 'on – on what singers we liked. It wasn't an argument.'

'I see. And you left Samantha at what time, Luke?'

'About twenty to eleven.'

'Did you see her go inside?'

'No, I told you before, she went round the back. Then I went for a quick spin.'

'And got home when?'

'Just before eleven. I was in bed by about ten past.'

'Now, Luke, this is very important, so please think before you answer. Did you leave the house after ten past eleven?'

'No, I didn't.' That had needed no thought.

'Very well. You got your bike back last evening. Did you go out on it?'

'Yes. I was so glad to have it back.'

'Where did you go, Luke?'

'Into the village, then out on the lanes.'

'Did you speak to anyone?'

Luke glanced at Sally, as if to say, 'You were right,' then related his encounter with Malachi and his mother.

'So what impression did you get as to George Gribble's whereabouts?'

'That he'd gone to one of the farms. Malachi's mum said as much, and Malachi told me that his dad knew something about Samantha, and that he was going to get money for it.'

'So where, exactly, did you go next?'

'Up round the Becky, then along to Pengally Farm, then left at the crossroads and along the lanes for a bit until the long downhill run to the sea – past Blue Leaze.'

'Did you see anyone, or any vehicle?'

'Not Gribble's old Escort, if that's what you mean. A green Rover passed me near Blankett's and I saw the back of a tractor going into one of Trudgeon's fields. Then I went for a bit of a run on the Mevagissey road.'

'Did you stop anywhere, Luke?'

'Yes, at the Fat Lamb – it's a pub on that road.'

'What time was that?'

'Oh, just before ten. I had a Coke, then a kid I knew came in and we talked a bit and had a game of pinball.'

'Give the name of this friend to the sergeant. We check everything, Luke – everything, and now we'll take a break for a minute, I think.' For the first time he turned to look at Sally. 'Could I have a word, Mrs Baxter? Outside.'

She couldn't wait. Once out of the room she told him, 'I want a solicitor for my son before he answers any more questions. Are we allowed that?'

For reply Channon took her by the arm and led her into a small empty office. 'Please sit down,' he said gently. 'Yes, you're allowed a solicitor. We might not need to detain him much longer, though.'

'I want one in any case,' she said. 'I want to phone my husband about it, if I can get hold of him. He might still be on the train.'

'Yes, I should talk to him about it,' he agreed, and then closed the door. 'Mrs Baxter, strictly speaking I have to be circumspect in what I say to you as the parent of somebody being questioned, but I must ask if anything struck you as odd about Luke's answers?'

Sally opened her mouth to say no, and as quickly closed it. This man knew, and knew *she* knew, that Luke was being evasive about his talk with Samantha. It went against all she believed in to withhold something from the police when it came to a murder enquiry, so she looked warily round the prosaic little office for signs of a tape machine.

'We're off the record,' Channon assured her. 'Trust me – I only want the truth.'

This, thought Sally, was the worst moment of her entire life. Would talking frankly to this detective make things better for Luke, or worse? She twisted her hands together, and it came to her that people actually did do that in moments of anguish. And then, because she felt alone and horribly confused, she let herself be governed by the trust that Channon aroused in her, the trust he'd just asked for. 'He's hiding

226

something,' she muttered, gazing down at her hands, 'and I don't know what. But against that, he's told me he's done nothing wrong, and I believe him.' Channon stayed silent, so she explained, 'I know him, you see. I know my son.'

'I can tell from experience that he's hiding something,' said Channon, 'and you can tell because you're his mum. Would you speak to Luke for us? Tell him not to conceal anything. If he gives us the truth it might hurt somebody else – one of his friends, maybe, but I can't see it hurting him. Will you have a word with him, Mrs Baxter?'

She let herself be taken back into the interview room, where Channon beckoned Bowles and the constable and left her alone with Luke. She gave him a hug, and her arms still round him, said, 'Luke, Mr Channon thinks you're holding something back about your talk with Samantha. He's asked me to talk to you about it.'

Luke shrugged away from her. 'He thinks that because it suits him! What do *you* think, Mum?'

'I don't think – I *know*,' she said. 'I know you didn't kill Samantha or George Gribble, but I also know that you're concealing something, for reasons I can't even guess at. Don't do it, Luke. I beg of you, don't do it. It will only harm you in the end.'

The hazel eyes looked into hers, wide and

bright and angry. 'You're losing your judgement,' he said tightly. 'Channon's trying to stitch me up, and you're backing him! I can't believe it! I've said all I'm going to say about talking to Samantha. He's only harping on that because he can't come up with anything else.'

This was her first-born son, she thought dully. Her lovely, lovely boy, trying to fob her off – lying to her. 'I've known you since before you were born, Luke,' she said quietly, 'I know you better than you think. I'm going to go and ring your dad.' She left him still sitting at the table, his hands clasped in front of him.

Outside the room there was all the bustle of a busy station, with Channon and Bowles waiting in the midst of it. 'Luke denies hiding anything,' she told them. 'If you have fresh questions I want a legal representative, and now I'm going to try and get hold of my husband.'

'I'll show you the public phone,' said Bowles politely.

'Rob? It's me. Can you speak?'

'Yes,' came the familiar voice with a touch of impatience. 'I'm just about to take a taxi to the City, love. What's up?'

Relief at having him listening made her gabble. 'Rob, we're at Truro police station. They've got Luke here for questioning.

They asked him to come in of his own free will, but if he hadn't agreed they'd have arrested him!'

The silence at the other end of the line was like cold breath on overheated skin. 'Rob?' she said uncertainly. 'Are you there?' The dialling tone told her that he wasn't. Fumbling, she redialled, but the line to his mobile was dead. She stared at the receiver and shook it, as if that would bring him back on the line. She left it for long seconds and then tried again.

'Hello,' came his voice, and she said wildly, 'Oh, thank God, I thought you'd gone! What happened? Did you hear what I said before? We're at the police station in Truro. Channon's got Luke here for questioning. Rob, can you come back? I need you here.'

'Calm down. They said Luke was in the clear, didn't they? What are their grounds for having him in?'

'Questions, they said – helping them with their enquiries. Rob – they're asking him about George Gribble as well as Samantha.'

'What's he got to do with it?'

'He's dead. Murdered. Last night. Rob, I'm worried sick. Can you come home?'

There was another unnerving silence. 'Rob!' she cried. 'Are you there?'

'Yes,' he said tightly, 'I'm thinking. I've got a packed schedule today, and several clients to see. I suppose I could get the next train back and ring them on the way.' His reluctance to do any such thing came over the line as clearly as if he'd put it into words.

She was stunned. 'Your son is being questioned about a murder – about two murders,' she told him, 'but don't let it prevent you from seeing your clients!'

Silence again, then he said, 'I'll take the next train home and go straight to the police station. Will *that* do?'

God *above*, she thought in fury, he's going all uptight again, just when I need him. 'Yes!' she snapped. 'And for crying out loud don't switch your mobile off on the way!' The sense of let-down was a pain in her chest, but she tried to speak more calmly. 'Listen, I've told Channon I want a solicitor, and he says that's OK. Who shall I say I want?'

'Why ask me?' came the reply. 'We've never used a solicitor down here, and we can hardly send to Manchester for one. Can't they put you on to somebody at the station?'

'I'll ask them,' she said quietly, and hung up on him. That, she told herself bitterly, is the man who made love to you last night, the man who said you were the most wonderful woman in the world. But last night everything had been all right, hadn't it? Today everything was all wrong, and there lay the difference.

Chapter Fourteen

It was still raining when they set off from Truro, with Sally keenly aware that this was an opportunity to talk to her son in private, and Luke staring silently through the windscreen.

Before they left the station there had been another long session of question and answer from Channon and his sergeant – the same questions, the same answers – and then the senior man had simply thanked them for their help and said they could go home. It had been anticlimax time with a vengeance, and they'd said little to each other as they went to the car.

Now Luke asked, 'Is dad coming back, then?'

'Yes, I told you. He said he'd get the next train.'

He shifted restlessly in his seat. 'Well, can't you ring him again and tell him not to bother?'

Sally gritted her teeth and stared at spray from the lorry in front. 'No, I can't,' she said shortly. 'He might be on his way by now, but even if he isn't I want him here. You're a murder suspect, Luke, whether they have grounds for it or they don't. Channon said he might contact us again later in the day and if he does I want your dad here and a solicitor on call.'

Luke sighed. 'I suppose there'll be nothing to stop me going in to school when we get back?'

For answer she pulled off the road and stopped in the entrance to a field. 'What's up?' he asked warily.

She switched off the engine and the drumming of rain on the roof seemed deafening. 'What's up?' she echoed. 'Channon has two witnesses – three if you include Malachi – who've given him cause to think you're implicated, that's what's up. It's clear to him – just as it's clear to me – that you're concealing something, no matter how much you deny it. I want your dad in on what's happening, and I'm damned if you're going to sail off to school as if you haven't a care in the world!'

He glared at her. 'I'm fed up with all this! I gave Sammy a lift. We talked. I never saw her again. I went out on my bike last night, just like I said. I did nothing, I saw nothing. End of story! And if I can't go to school I'll do some revision at home.' Antagonism coiled between them like barbed wire.

She made one last effort. 'Luke, we've always communicated, you and me. Don't shut me out, not now. I told you the other day that you can tell me anything – anything at all – as long as it's the truth.' She wiped her eyes with the back of her hand. The last thing he needed was a weepy mother.

The bright hazel eyes looked deep into hers. She saw his lips parting, ready to frame words, then closing tightly together. At that moment she couldn't tell whether he was a boy or a man. He swallowed as if his throat was parched and took hold of her hand. 'I'm not a fool, Mum,' he said, 'and I'm not trying to hurt you. Anything I say, or don't say, is for a very good reason. I promise you I won't put myself at risk. Now, can we leave it?'

There was no doubt now – it was a man speaking. Calm entered her heart and spread to her mind. 'All right,' she agreed, 'we'll leave it. You and I won't speak of it again, but I'll have to talk it over with your dad.'

'That's up to you,' he said.

Still at the station in Truro, Bowles answered a phone call and waved the receiver at Channon. 'It's Curdower – the incident room. Our friend Miller's playing naughty boys.'

Channon was on edge after his abortive session with Luke Baxter. 'What's that supposed to mean?' he asked irritably.

'He's being naughty,' repeated Bowles.

'He can't, or won't, say where he was late last night. Inspector Meade wants to know if they should bring him in again.'

Channon took the phone. 'John? What's all this? It must have been well after nine by the time we dropped him off last night and he couldn't have got back to Blue Leaze without transport. Has he a car?'

'No, but I've just had a call from the lads. The landlady of his B&B says that as soon as we'd dropped him off he went out again and she doesn't know what time he came back. She gives her guests a key if they want one and she'd given him his before we picked him up.'

'And what does he say?'

'He'd already left when the lads got there – apparently ready to call off his holiday a day early. They tracked him down on the bus back to St Austell and the train for Bristol.'

'So what did he say about last night?'

'So far he's stalling, Bill – as cagey as hell. But the lads have asked around and the man who runs the local garage says that at tea-time he hired a car out to Miller. They don't know when he returned it – he left it in the yard and put the keys through the door as arranged.'

'All right,' agreed Channon, 'grab the car in case we need it for forensic and get him in again – but only if the men are sure of their facts. If they're wrong he'll be shouting victimization – he's crafty enough. I can't see it leading us anywhere, though. Surely he wouldn't have tried anything just after we'd had him in? How could he have known where Gribble would be last evening? What reason could he have for killing him ... unless of course Gribble had seen something? Did they *know* each other, for God's sake? Gribble didn't sound to me as if he shared Miller's little foibles about female clothes. Get him in anyway, and we'll be back with you as soon as we can – we have to attend the post-mortem in a minute. Put him somewhere on his own till I get there and let him stew – it might soften him up a bit.'

He hung up and turned to Bowles. 'You heard that. Let's go.' He kept on talking as they walked through the rain to the pathology department. 'Miller won't say where he was last evening, but if he was at Blue Leaze he must have had a previous connection with Gribble. What, for crying out loud?'

'We don't know – yet,' said Bowles grimly. 'What we do know is he's a cocky sod. If he's put one over on me I'll have his guts.'

'If he's a double killer we'll both have his guts,' promised Channon drily, 'whether he's put one over on you or the Archangel Gabriel. Forget him for a minute. What did you think of young Baxter?'

Bowles didn't want to answer. He'd thought a lot about Luke, and knew quite well that his own attitude to the teenager had been biased. He'd been biased against suspects before and it hadn't helped his career; he'd had to warn himself against it more than once. Now he was regretting his attitude. Envy had twisted his judgement: envy of Luke's lifestyle, of his family, his home, his motorbike; envy of the university place which was almost certainly his.

Clearly the boy had been hiding something during the interview, but the more he, Bowles, watched and listened, the more certain he became that he'd been wrong. 'I don't think he's our man,' he admitted reluctantly, 'or our boy, whatever you want to call him. He's only young but he's no fool; too intelligent, I'd say, to risk suspicion by concealing something unless he had an overpowering reason. He, uh, well – he seems a decent enough kid. Spoiled, like they all are these days if their parents have the dosh, but...'

This was an about turn. Channon shot him a look through the rain. 'But what?' he asked curiously.

'But I don't see him as a double murderer,' replied Bowles.

That hadn't been easy for him, acknowledged the older man, but it was the astute detective talking at last, not the deprived son of a layabout. 'Thanks for that, Bowles,' he said simply. 'Let's hope you're right.'

'Clothing under examination,' announced George Hunter by way of greeting. 'Pretty wet where it had been exposed to rain, but almost dry underneath. The footwear in particular might show where he'd been before he was dumped in the field.'

As always, Channon avoided looking at the face of the corpse, it was more bearable that way. Cameras whirred and Hunter continued to bend over the body. 'This little chap was pretty fit,' he said thoughtfully. 'Time of death about ten thirty last night as near as I can say at this stage.'

Channon recalled that with his clothes on Gribble had seemed saggy and shapeless and old; unclothed he was in surprisingly good shape. Lightweight, of course, but taut and wiry and muscular. 'Typical manual worker,' Hunter was saying. 'Not all that easy to overpower, except by surprise. No signs of preliminary stunning, no violence of any kind other than the strangulation. A fine, very strong cord, I'd say, twisted with some ferocity. We should get fibres for you from the weal around the neck.'

Hunter examined the hands. 'Fingernails none too clean so we'll get something there, but I suspect not from self-defence. As I say it was a surprise to him. Wrists and ankles were fastened pretty tightly to the wood, so maybe we'll get something for you there.'

And so it went on, with Hunter's running commentary accompanying his precise, practised movements.

Channon decided that there was no need to stay to the bitter end. 'We have to go, George,' he said. 'Will you ring through with your findings before you put it in writing? Stomach contents will be important, as always. I'll be glad to hear from you.'

Outside he and Bowles made silently for the car. You could always depend on a post-mortem to put the mockers on idle conversation, thought Channon, and tried to dismiss the neat little body from his mind. 'Going back to Luke Baxter,' he said, 'do you reckon he's protecting somebody?'

'It looks like it, but his pals are all in the clear. The only one who springs to mind is dear Papa.'

'I know, but we haven't a thing on him. Not a whisper of any kind of relationship with Samantha; no sign of his wife giving him an alibi on the night of the murder, not so much as a hair of his head from the scene of the crime or forensic.'

They headed through the morning traffic towards Curdower, while Channon's mind moved into the detached, analytical state which often preceded a piece of inspired thinking. Something was still nagging him about his visits to the roundhouse, something odd about one of the family. The mother? No – she was straight as they come. The daughter? Bright, of course, with a chip on her shoulder and not much time for policemen, but nothing about her that had struck him as odd. Young Ben? No – he was as soft and innocent as a babe newborn. Baxter senior, then? Edgy, unhelpful, verging on rude, but that was normal enough for somebody whose family were being interrogated...

That left Luke himself. He'd been hiding something all along, the interview had confirmed it, but it wasn't that, it was to do with his attitude. To his parents? *No!* Channon sat bolt upright – just to his father! Luke hadn't once looked at him, but whenever Robert Baxter spoke there'd been resentment in the boy's eyes, in his body language; there'd been wariness, and maybe some other emotion as well. That was what had been niggling him about the Baxters. Well, it wasn't exactly mind-blowing, was it? Lots of fathers were lacking in rapport with teenage sons; lots of sons didn't go overboard for their fathers.

From behind the wheel Bowles shot a glance at the older man. Evidently his remark about Papa Baxter had set off a chain of thought.

When they reached the incident room John Meade was talking to two uniformed men at the door. 'Where's Miller?' asked Channon.

Meade nodded towards the prefabricated building on the green. 'In there, cooling his heels with a constable for company. He is not a happy man, Bill.'

'Neither am I,' retorted Channon. 'Does he know details of why he's been brought in?'

'No – the lads were warned to give nothing away. He's had plenty of time to get edgy, so take the floor, he's all yours.'

Miller leapt to his feet as the two detectives entered. 'This is victimization,' he declared, baring the dazzling teeth in fury. 'I demand to know why I've been brought back here!'

Well, well, where was the calm self-possession of their last meeting, Channon asked himself. 'You can demand what you like,' he said evenly, 'but we won't necessarily grant it. We're dealing with you in accord with police regulations and the law of the land, so don't waste our time, Mr Miller.' He eyed the walker closely. Now he would ask for a solicitor.

But no such request was forthcoming. You never knew whether it was a sign of guilt or of innocence when they didn't ask. You never knew when they did ask, come to that. 'Take a seat here, if you please, Mr Miller.' He switched on the tape and with Bowles at his side faced Miller. 'Now, just try to relax.

240

The sooner you answer our questions, the sooner you'll be on your way back to Bristol. First – and think carefully before you answer – what do you know of a man called Gribble – George Gribble?'

'Nothing,' replied Miller stonily. 'Who is he?'

'We'll come to that later. Now, tell us how you spent your time after we took you home from here last evening.'

Resentment oozed from Miller like acid from an overfull carboy. 'I continued with what I'd had planned when I was interrupted. I went out for a stroll.'

'What, in the dark?'

'Yes. I like exercise.'

'How far did you go, Mr Miller?'

Tight-lipped, Miller answered. 'I think you've found out already that I hired a car.'

'It's our job to find things out,' agreed Channon. 'You'd hired a grey Vauxhall earlier in the evening. Is that correct?'

The restless green eyes gazed over Channon's shoulder. 'Why ask when you know?'

'I seem to recall you putting exactly that question at our last meeting, Mr Miller. The answer, as before, is that this is on the record, *for* the record. I say again, did you hire a grey Vauxhall?'

'Yes.'

'Where did you drive to?'

Bowles leaned forward. All at once he

knew – he just knew where Miller had been. Why hadn't he thought of it before? He opened his mouth and then closed it again. Let Channon stumble on and look a fool. What was it to him?

'Round about. Here and there. It was a nice evening,' replied Miller.

'Did you go back towards Curdower?' asked Channon.

'No.'

'You didn't go anywhere in the region of Curdower village?'

'What do you mean by "in the region of"?'

'A radius of five miles.'

'No, I did not.'

'Mr Miller,' said Channon, 'I asked you if you know a man called George Gribble. I have to tell you that Mr Gribble was murdered last night, in the vicinity of Curdower village. Now, let's not mess about. Where did you go?'

Miller's neat, unremarkable features had tightened. The skin around his nose was pale as wax and he was running his tongue across his lips. 'You couldn't pin the girl on me, so you think you'll try with a man?' he asked incredulously. 'Come *on*, chief inspector!'

He couldn't let this go on, thought Bowles, and looked enquiringly at Channon, who nodded. 'Listen, Miller,' he said, 'we already know you're a cross-dresser. To you it's a big deal, a great big secret, but to us it's merely an irritation. We have no interest in telling your wife about it, or in making it public knowledge. If you used your hire car to go somewhere in connection with your little hobby, for goodness' sake, say so.'

Channon kept silent. His hobby? In rural Cornwall? At ten o'clock at night? But Miller was eyeing Bowles with loathing. 'I don't see why I should discuss my personal affairs with you.'

'Don't you?' Bowles fixed his eyes on Miller. 'Not even when we're investigating two murders, and you just might be a suspect for either – or both? You didn't by any chance go to the back room of a pretty little restaurant called the Rosabelle?'

Miller didn't reply, and waved a silencing hand when Bowles said, 'We're waiting.'

'All right,' he said at last. 'I met a chap on the coastal path yesterday and we got talking. We found we had things in common and I went out to meet him at the Rosabelle.'

'Where the back room is used extensively by cross-dressers and transvestites,' said Bowles with a thin smile. 'Oh yes, we see a bit of the low life even in South Cornwall. Why the hell didn't you say so in the first place? What time were you there?'

'From just after ten until midnight,' answered Miller sullenly. 'Then I went back and dropped the car off. I'd paid in advance so I left it in the yard and put the keys through the door. Satisfied?'

Bowles couldn't resist a small, triumphant grin, directed at Channon, even though he was well aware he should have told him what he knew. 'Satisfied?' he repeated, leaning back in his chair. 'Not until forensic have finished with the Vauxhall.'

Channon was impressed. He should have known about the Rosabelle. He was the one who should know things, who was paid a DCI's salary. He jerked his head at Bowles and led him outside. 'Well done,' he said. 'I didn't know we'd got a transvestite haunt so near here.'

'You name it, we've got it,' answered Bowles, somewhat smugly. 'He could still have done Gribble, of course.'

'I know. Try and talk to the man he met and any witnesses at the Rosabelle.'

'Are we keeping him?'

'Oh, yes. We're doing no more chasing around after Mr Miller. He stays here till the Vauxhall's cleared with forensic.'

'Right,' agreed Bowles. And I'll make the poncey bastard sweat, he added silently.

It was lunch-time at Pencannon School and Tessa was looking for Ben. She spotted him at a table with some of his classmates, staring at a plateful of food as if he didn't know what to do with it. She went across and said quietly, 'Ben, listen. I've reported an upset stomach so I can have the afternoon off. I'm going home to see if things are OK. You've heard about Malachi's dad?'

'Everybody's talking about it,' he said miserably. 'Do you think that's why the police wanted to talk to Luke?'

'I don't know but I'll soon find out,' she said briskly. 'It's funny they should descend on him early this morning, but don't start worrying until there's something to worry *about*. I'm catching the bus back to Curdower in a minute, and I'll walk home.'

Ben was impressed by her decisiveness, but somewhat baffled. She'd never been concerned about the family before, she always sat back and found fault with everything. Still, she'd never been mixed up with murder before, had she? 'What will you do when you get there?' he asked.

'Give moral support,' she retorted, 'if anybody needs it!'

She turned to go but he grabbed her sleeve. 'Tess – Mum might decide to meet the bus at four o'clock if it's still raining. Tell her not to bother, will you? I want to go and see Malachi.'

Tessa decided that a visit to the Gribbles would reduce him to a wreck. 'I know he's your friend and everything, but he and his mum might be distraught,' she warned.

'Don't get all upset if they're in a bit of a state.'

'I expect they *will* be in a bit of a state if Mr Gribble's been murdered,' he said quietly.

It dawned on Tessa that there was silence round the table as the other boys tried to hear what they were saying. She turned her back on them. 'Have you told this lot that Luke's being questioned?'

'No, but somebody's already asked me if he's still the prime suspect.'

'Don't let them get to you,' she said, directing a cool glance at seven curious faces. 'It's hardly surprising if they're all agog, but just ignore it. I'm going, now. See you later.'

Ben stared after her. All at once he felt hungry, but when he put a chip in his mouth it was cold and felt like rubber between his teeth.

Chapter Fifteen

Sally faced her daughter across the kitchen table, knowing that if she hadn't been so worried she would have been overjoyed that Tessa had come home to see what was going on. It would be ironic, she thought, if murder should be the means of getting closer to this most difficult of her children. Having told her everything that had happened, she now said, 'He's keeping something back, Tessa, I'm sure of it. For goodness' sake tell me if you can think of anybody he might be protecting.'

Tessa shrugged. 'I can't think of anybody, Mum, but I don't think you need worry. You're always saying how clever he is so I can't see he'll put himself in jeopardy.'

'I didn't think I was always saying how clever he is,' protested Sally, taken aback. 'He's no cleverer in his line than you are in yours. You take after your dad in sciences – he takes after me in the arts; two sides of the same coin, sort of. Ben's got a bit of us both, but he lacks confidence – he's always needed support. Tessa, I've been telling myself that when this lot's over you and I will talk – really talk – but perhaps now's as good a time as any.'

Brown eyes stared into hers. Careful, Sally told herself, this is your chance, so don't mess it up. 'Things didn't seem half as bad once you walked in,' she said gently. 'You know, I've always wished that you and I were on the same wavelength, and now I think perhaps we're getting there. Maybe you've had the wrong slant on how I feel about you, Tess. The boys are the boys, but you are you. You're unique, you're special.'

Colour crept into Tessa's cheeks, but she merely pursed her lips without speaking. 'Why exactly have you come home in your lunch break?' asked Sally. To her astonishment tears welled in her daughter's eyes. The full lips that were so like her own stretched wide in a grimace, revealing teeth clenched in distress.

Sally reached across the table and grasped her hand. 'I love you, Tessa,' she said. 'Why did you ever doubt it? I've tried to show you again and again, but you always pushed me away. Tell me – why have you come home?'

'To see if you're OK,' muttered Tessa. 'I don't like seeing you so upset. I – I want to help, if I can.'

Sally's response wasn't that of a loving mother getting close to a difficult daughter; it was the response of a tense, strung-up woman. She burst into tears.

'Mum!' Tessa ran round the table and gathered her in her arms. 'It's all right,' she insisted, 'everything's going to be all right!'

They were holding each other close when the front door slammed and seconds later Rob stood in the doorway, eyeing the pair of them. 'God above!' he said irritably. 'What's going on, Sal?' He took in their closeness and his eyes widened, but he was too annoyed to pass comment. 'Look,' he said, 'I rushed to Truro police station like a maniac, only to be told that you and Luke had gone

248

home after "helping with enquiries". I might as well have stayed in London!'

It was Tessa who replied; quietly, but with clear rebuke. 'Mum needs you here. She's had a ghastly time and Channon says he might want to see Luke again. I'll leave you both to talk it over.' With great composure she wiped her eyes, planted a kiss on Sally's cheek, and walked out of the room.

Joy and relief chased each other round Sally's heart. Tessa cared, she really cared, but why was there always a down side to something good? Rob, her Rob, her lifeline, her safe anchor, was being awkward as hell. Again.

'Why didn't you ring me to say you'd left the police station?' he asked.

All at once she was furious. 'Because I wanted you here, you stupid moron! What's the matter with you? Your attitude to this whole affair is unbelievable. Your son's a murder suspect, for God's sake, he's been questioned by the police – and for your information they think he's concealing something. I happen to agree with them. I've tackled him about it and he won't discuss it. He simply says he won't put himself at risk.'

Rob stared at her, the blue eyes blinking rapidly behind his glasses. 'Look,' he said awkwardly, 'I told you the other day that I can't seem to get my head round all this. It's bugging me that we left Manchester to get away from drugs and shootings and the rest of it, and ended up being embroiled in murder. I'm truly sorry, Sal, if you think I've been letting you down.'

'I don't think,' she said bitterly, 'I know!'

He sighed and shook his head like a father dealing with a wayward child. It infuriated her so much she swung round to leave the kitchen, but he put up a hand to stop her. 'It won't help Luke if you go racing off in a paddy,' he said. 'Why do you and Channon think he's hiding something?'

'A witness overheard him arguing with Samantha outside the Martennis – almost threatening her, but Luke insists they were just talking. Channon doesn't believe him. Add to that the fact that he was out some-where on his bike at about the time George Gribble was being murdered at Blue Leaze, and even you must see he has problems.'

There was another of those unnerving silences. She fancied that Rob's broad shoulders drooped, and then told herself she'd imagined it when he said bracingly, 'You're getting in a real old state, aren't you? I'll go and talk to him. Maybe one of his pals has done something that could put him under suspicion, or something like that. But first how about a coffee, and you can tell me what's happened to poor old George.'

And because it was so much simpler to allow herself to be reassured, because it was what she needed, she made instant coffee and told him what she knew about George Gribble. Five minutes later he gave her a solemn little kiss on the forehead, paused for just a moment, then went upstairs to find Luke.

Two men in white overalls and boots were in the narrow road outside Blankett's Farm. One was Channon, pacing thoughtfully between the puddles; the other was the head SOCO, Fred Jordan, on hand to answer the DCI's questions.

Eyeing the taped-off area where Gribble's bike had been found, Channon tried to visualize the last half-hour of his life. 'Fred,' he asked, 'have you found out in which direction he was cycling? Or anything that suggests he stopped here to talk to somebody? Could he perhaps have been waylaid here and his bike thrown in the hedge?'

Jordan shook his head dubiously. 'This rain's a bugger,' he said. 'Dry as a bone everywhere last night and now the ground and vegetation turning to mush with the downpour. We've only just finished up at Trudgeon's, though, so we'll need several hours yet to get evidence from round here. An outdoor crime is always more difficult for us than an indoor one, and with the weather against us it'll be a long job. I'll get you on your mobile if I come across anything of use.'

'The shed where the barrow was stored, the barns, the yard,' Channon persisted, 'I should have thought our man would have left traces.'

'Oh, there'll be traces,' agreed the other. 'Traces of normal farm work and men tramping around. I've found before now that evidence isn't easy to come by on a farm, because even on a clean place there's straw and feathers and ropes, bits of animal excreta and God knows what else. Like I was telling you, we haven't even got a decent boot-print from Blue Leaze. The forensic boys will have to pull out all the stops on the wheelbarrow and the scarecrow set-up. Don't worry, we'll do our best for you.'

Channon shook his wet head like a dog emerging from water. 'Thanks, Fred, I'll leave you to it.' He headed for Blankett's main gate, where he found the farmer pacing the yard in wellingtons and black oilskins. She looked like a deep-sea fisherman on board ship, and came across to him through the downpour. 'Bad news, Mr Channon,' she said soberly. 'It's awful, isn't it, just awful?'

He nodded in agreement. 'We think your wheelbarrow was taken to transport George's body, so we'll have to examine the yard and the farm entrance here, as well as the road and the hedge where his bike was found. You see, we work on the assumption that nobody can pass through a given area without leaving

252

some trace, either of themselves, their clothes or their vehicle. Sometimes we're proved right, sometimes not.' He recalled his intention of asking her about the locals, and on impulse said, 'I wonder if you have a minute to spare?'

She pushed back her old-fashioned sou'wester and gave him the same sort of look as when she'd descended on the incident room and lectured him about 'catching the perpetrator'. All she said, though, was, 'You can come inside for a cup of tea, if you like.'

He followed her to a porch at the side of the house where they removed their outdoor clothes, then into a big, immaculate kitchen, where a middle-aged woman was at the sink, cleaning vegetables. 'This is my housekeeper, Mrs Voysey,' said the farmer. 'Will you make us a pot of tea, Hilda? We'll have it in the sitting room.' Once they were installed in easy chairs, she said, 'Can I help you with anything in particular, Mr Channon?'

'I don't know,' he admitted frankly. 'We have several lines of enquiry being followed by my scene-of-crime team, the forensic experts and a vast number of men. While those enquiries are proceeding I thought I should find out more about the local community, and I'm hoping you might help me. You're from a long-established family, and I see you as a woman of discernment.'

The merest curve of the lips showed that, as he'd intended, Maureen Blankett was pleased by the double compliment. 'Any comments I might make would be in confidence rather than in the form of a statement?' she asked.

'Of course.'

'Then fire away,' she said. 'The tea will be here shortly, so I can give you ten minutes.'

Channon concealed a smile. She was ready to help, but wanted it clear that she had little time to spare. 'First, Sam Deacon of Pengally,' he said, and noted her eyes widen slightly. 'I expect you know the gentleman, Miss Blankett?'

'Yes, of course I do. His family have owned Pengally for nearly as long as mine have been here, and I'm speaking hundreds of years. In fact I've traced my ancestors back to the Normans ... I don't think even Sam can match that. I can see his long meadow from my bedroom – prime grazing, it used to be. He has good arable land as well. I expect you'll have noticed that unlike many farming communities, most of the farms round here go in for both crops and livestock?'

He didn't want to get embroiled in the finer points of farming, but an unbiased opinion of Sam Deacon might possibly be useful. 'I have seen that,' he agreed. 'When you say Pengally used to have prime grazing, do I take it that it's been allowed to get run down?'

'If you've been there you should know the answer to that one,' she said ruefully. 'Ever since his divorce old Sam's been slacking. He's a bit of a lad, of course.'

'Really? In what way?'

'Well, you'll have found in police records that he was charged with being drunk and disorderly some time ago?'

'Yes, we did manage to come up with that.'

She smiled and shook her head in the manner of a mother defending a wayward small boy. 'He's an individualist, you know – a true eccentric, but to succeed in farming you have to conform to certain rules of business, the same as in any other type of selling. I think he was always a bit put out when other farms in the area seemed to do better than him.'

Channon recalled Sam Deacon's comments about Jim Trudgeon, and decided to think about that aspect later. 'Was Mr Deacon ever "a bit of a lad" with the opposite sex?'

'Not that I know of – at least, not in the last thirty years,' she said drily, 'though I did hear that a suggestion of indecent exposure was set aside by the drunk and disorderly charge.'

'Yes. How did that strike you, Miss Blankett? Did it tie in with what you knew of him over the years, or would you say it was completely out of character?'

'I'd suggest you asked his ex-wife about it, rather than me,' she said briskly, 'except that she died a couple of years ago. There were rumours that his marriage wasn't happy, but I never heard he was unfaithful. They didn't have any children, though I got the impression he was fond of them. It was rather sad, really; when Samantha was little I used to see him watching her for hours on end when she was on the tractor with her father. You haven't found out any more about who killed her, have you?'

'We have leads,' he replied carefully, 'but we're still checking. You've known Samantha for years, I take it? Is there anything you can help me with about her, or her parents? Just the merest snippet of information can sometimes slot in with what we already know and give us a lead, you see.'

Maureen Blankett poured tea as graciously as if she was holding an afternoon tea party. 'I'm not – what do they call it – not "with it" when it comes to the behaviour of teenagers,' she told him, 'but I do know that her parents doted on her and that she had an eye for the boys, or you might say the men. She was so pretty and outgoing there was always somebody after her. Let me see ... a year or so ago I heard she was involved with a young farmer – in his thirties, I should think – from the other side of St Austell. A son of the

Tredize family who own great stretches of coastal land, but no doubt you know all about him. It came to nothing anyway – he was far too old for her. As far as I understood it she was a normal, happy young woman.'

Channon mentally reviewed the names of Samantha's friends on her parents' list. Tredize had been among them so the man in question would have been investigated already, though at his age he could hardly be termed one of the 'young lads' mentioned so dismissively by Jim Trudgeon.

China teacup in hand, Maureen Blankett was eyeing him with the razor-sharp blue gaze. 'What about that walker I told you about, Mr Channon? Surely that was a lead?'

'It certainly was. We've had the man in for questioning more than once. In fact, Sergeant Bowles is busy at this very moment on investigations connected with him. So far, though, he's in the clear.'

She frowned. 'The man admits meeting her on my path?'

'Oh yes, but a chance meeting with Samantha doesn't necessarily put him under serious suspicion. When the weather clears, Miss Blankett, just for interest I'd like to walk the path for myself – follow her trail right along to where she reached her father's land.'

She surveyed him with an odd expression: pity, mingled with a hint of ridicule. 'With your magnifying glass at the ready?' she asked, then at once wafted a hand in self-reproof. 'I'm sorry, that was uncalled for. It's so difficult to accept what's been going on in a place like this. If you think it will help, you must feel free to walk over every inch of my land. Now I don't want to rush you, but is there anything else?'

'I wonder if you know the Baxter family from the roundhouse?'

'I pass the time of day with them, as one does. The mother seems pleasant enough. We chatted for a minute or two in the dry-cleaners on Saturday morning.'

'The dry-cleaners in Truro? Taking in or collecting?' The question came as naturally as breathing.

'Taking in, and what a pile! It must be expensive, these days, to rear a family, though the Baxters are regarded as well-off outsiders by the village folk.'

'How long would they have to live in Curdower before being accepted as locals, then?'

She attempted a smile, but didn't quite manage it. 'Locals? They'd never be accepted as locals, how could they be? As residents, perhaps, after, say, ten years or so. They've bought one of our most treasured dwellings as a mere business proposition and we're

258

expected to be grateful. The roundhouse is unique to Curdower, though there are smaller versions elsewhere – four in one village just along the coast. But the Baxters – I know very little about them.'

'I see, thank you. Now, to George Gribble. How long had he worked for you?'

'Oh, six, maybe seven years, on a casual basis. When they first came to Curdower he cycled up here asking for work with Malachi on a little seat behind him. Poor George, I can't believe it.'

'He also worked for Sam Deacon, I believe?'

'Yes, though he did fewer hours over there than for me. I'd have taken him on full-time, but my present staff are satisfactory and they've been with me since long before the Gribbles arrived in Curdower. I've already given details of his working hours to one of your men, by the way.'

'So I understand. Do you know his wife?'

'Everybody knows Zennie, though as far as I'm aware she hasn't a real friend in Curdower. It's her looks, I suppose – she makes other women jealous. Again, talk has it that theirs isn't – wasn't – a happy marriage. Perhaps it was an attraction of opposites.'

'Do you know if Zennie was faithful to George?'

Maureen Blankett curled her lip slightly. 'This is tittle-tattle, isn't it, but if it helps I suppose it's justified. No, I've never heard of her having an affair or anything of that sort, which is all credit to her, I suppose, because she must have had offers. She's so very striking – beautiful, really, if you like the obvious rather than the subtle, but I used to feel sorry for George. I never ever saw her being nice to him, let alone anybody else. It came to my hearing once that the men in the village had a rather vulgar name for her, one that I couldn't possibly repeat. I presumed it meant that she led men on and then rejected them.'

Channon could guess what the name had been, but he merely nodded thoughtfully and got to his feet. 'I won't keep you any longer, Miss Blankett, but if anything occurs to you that you think might be of use to me, would you give me a ring? The incident room will either put you through to me or pass on your message. Thanks for the tea – it was more than welcome.'

Once again in her black waterproofs she saw him off at the gate and he made for Curdower, considering the few snippets he'd gleaned over the teacups. Not much of significance, it was true, except of course that Sally Baxter had been in the dry-cleaners the morning after Samantha had been killed. He was shaken by his own dismay at the information. It couldn't mean anything – could it? He hadn't asked which shop it had been, but

that information would be coming in anyway. After a murder with blood loss the routine enquiries always included dry-cleaners.

At least, though, he'd dealt with one of
George's employers. Blamey and Yates were
talking to Sam Deacon and any other
farmers who had used him from time to
time, and as for poor old Trudgeon, he'd
already made a brief statement. If no more
leads had come in by tomorrow that would
be soon enough to put him to more detailed
questioning. Another meeting with the
traumatized, trivia-talking wife didn't much
appeal, but if duty called ... and speaking of
duty, Zennie Gribble would be demanding
another visit from him before long, and he
couldn't blame her for that.

Who'd have the job?

Malachi stared in dismay at his friend and
closed the door behind him. 'She might not
want you here. She's sitting in a chair
staring at nothing and we haven't had any
dinner.'

'I won't come in,' Ben assured him. 'I – I
just wanted to see if you're all right.'

Malachi didn't look all right, he looked
terrible. His eyes were pink and puffed up
and he was still wearing his pyjama top over
his jeans. 'How can I be all right?' he whispered angrily. 'Me dad's been murdered.'

'I know,' said Ben, shuffling his feet. 'You

say she might not want me here – you mean because she wants to be on her own?'

'No – because she thinks your brother might have done it!'

Ben gaped at him. 'My brother? You mean Luke?'

'You've only got one brother,' Malachi pointed out, rolling his eyes. 'She's told the police about him.'

All at once Ben's knees felt weak and he put a hand against the doorpost. There was a gurgly sort of feeling in the pit of his stomach, like the time he'd caught a bug and started with diarrhoea. 'What was there to tell?' he demanded. 'Luke wouldn't hurt anybody.'

Malachi's lip quivered. 'He knew where me dad was going last night – because I told him! The police'll have arrested him by now.'

The door behind him opened and a quiet little voice said, 'Who're you talking to, Malachi?' It was his mum. She looked down at Ben and flapped her hand at him. 'Go home,' she said wearily, 'you're not to come here again.'

Ben looked up at her. He knew you shouldn't say anything to upset somebody whose husband had just been murdered, but he felt the words rising up and he knew he wasn't going to say them politely, like he usually did. 'I've come out of school to say

I'm sorry about Mr Gribble,' he shouted, 'and if you think my brother's got anything to do with it you're wrong!'

Zennie didn't reply. What was there to say to a child whose brother had worn black leathers and a black helmet and had looked like the devil himself only an hour before Georgie was murdered? Black clothes for a black deed on a black night. Her life was black, the future was black, the hole where her heart should be was black. Malachi must have thought the same, because he was crying again. She put a hand behind his shoulders and without so much as a glance at the boy on the step pushed her son inside and closed the door.

Ben went down the path. He would have liked to kiss Malachi goodbye, he told himself miserably, but boys didn't kiss other boys – not ever. In any case he knew he must get home in a hurry or he would dirty his pants. With one hand against his abdomen he started to run home.

Chapter Sixteen

'He was in such a state we bundled him in the car and turned right round to bring him home! Wheezing like mad he was, and though he's a big lad I think he's messed himself.' Jane Bingham of Starfish Cottage was all sympathy as she helped Ben out of the car, but her eyes were bright with curiosity. 'We were a bit surprised to see him out on his own with a murderer on the loose, but you're so busy, aren't you, with the police coming and going all day long? Is there anything we can do, Kenny and me?'

Sally almost groaned. She could have done without the Binghams breathing down her neck at a time like this, but no doubt she should be thankful that only one of the four cottages was occupied. 'I'll let you know,' she said, 'and thanks ever so much for bringing him home, it'll be his asthma that's making him breathless.' Tessa was hovering, and to her she said, 'Find his inhaler, Tess, while I get him to the bathroom. Then go and tell your dad.'

The inhaler eased Ben's breathing, but not his humiliation. 'I can see to myself, Mum,' he said, and pushed her away when she'd turned on the shower.

Minutes later he was fastening his jeans when Sally went to talk to him. 'Ben, I know you sent word not to pick you up, but I'd have been waiting for you at the end of Malachi's lane if you'd come out of school at the usual time. We've told you we don't want you going around on your own at present, so why did you leave school early?'

Naturally co-operative, he hated to be told off. 'I was worried about Malachi,' he muttered, still wheezing slightly. 'Tessa told them at school that she'd got an upset stomach, so I thought I'd do the same. I'm sorry, Mum.'

She patted the bed next to her. 'Sit down for a minute, love. Was it very awful at Malachi's?'

He nodded, remembering how he'd bellowed at Mrs Gribble, though somehow that didn't seem to matter now. 'Mum,' he said desperately, '*has* Luke been arrested?'

So that was it! Sally's lips tightened with pain for her earnest, gentle son. 'No, of course he hasn't,' she said calmly. 'We've both been to Truro police station, that's all. They asked him lots of questions and then said he could come home. They check on everybody, you see – it's routine, and they knew that Luke had been out and about on his bike. Who told you he'd been arrested?'

'Malachi said his mum thinks Luke killed

his dad, and so he thought he'd have been arrested.' It sounded so far-fetched that Ben gave a sickly little smile, as if telling a weak joke. 'It was horrible there,' he told her. 'His mum's all quiet and staring, sort of, and they'd had nothing to eat since their breakfast. He's still wearing his pyjama top over his jeans.'

'Who's looking after them, then? A policewoman?'

'No, they're on their own.'

Sally let out breath in a long, weary sigh. What next? Zennie never saw her family in Falmouth and she'd actually boasted that she had no time for the women of the village; so unless she had a friend at work she, Sally, was probably closer to her than anybody. It disturbed her to think of strange, beautiful Zennie and her son being all on their own. 'I'll go over later on with something to eat,' she promised. 'What about you, Ben – do you think you've picked up a tummy bug or something?'

'I don't know. My inside started gurgling when I thought Luke had been arrested.'

She gave him a hug and looked over his shoulder to where the rest of the family were all standing together in the doorway. 'Well, Luke's here now,' she said, 'so you can stop worrying. Let's all go downstairs for a bit – I've got a casserole in the oven for this evening and I'll make you something nice for afters.' And as if it were no different than any other day, the three young ones scuffled their way downstairs, school work forgotten, arguing whether they should play snooker or Monopoly.

Between her and Rob, however, things were more restrained. Earlier, he had come down from talking to Luke, whistling tunelessly and trying to look unconcerned. 'Cut out the bad acting,' she told him impatiently. 'What did he say?'

'The same as he said to you,' he retorted. 'He won't do anything to put himself at risk, and to stop worrying.'

She grabbed the front of his shirt. 'But don't you think he's hiding something?'

He avoided her gaze. 'You're the one with the intuition, not me! For goodness' sake, Sal, the police will be checking on everybody, not just Luke.' And with that she had to be content.

Funding, budgets, costing, Channon didn't want to know. The rain had stopped at last and he wanted the rest of the daylight to be used to the best advantage. He waved a dismissive hand at John Meade's list of figures and said briskly, 'Tell those cretins in Finance to take a walk! It's less than twelve hours since they gave us major incident status and already they're beefing. Costs will go down when we catch the killer – if we don't catch him and he kills again they'll go through the roof!'

'All right, Bill, keep your cool!' Meade was calm water in the maelstrom that was the incident room: phones ringing, computers bleeping, men coming in, going out, pacing the floor, drinking tea, wolfing snacks. The place reeked of burgers and chips and cigarette smoke, so Channon grunted in distaste and retreated to the pre-fab on the village green.

Following him to his new office there, Meade related what was happening. 'Bowles and his men are still checking on Miller through witnesses from the Rosabelle. He says it's slow going because the nature of the place makes fellas unwilling to use names or even to admit they were there – except for a few exhibitionists. You know what he's like, though; he'll get results if anybody can, and he doesn't like our friend Miller.'

'Neither do I,' said Channon. 'What else?'

'There's a report on your desk from Blamey and Yates – their interview with Sam Deacon. Says he was on his own at Pengally all evening, but has no witnesses after 8 p.m. He gave them more background info on George, but nothing new. It's a lengthy report, but thorough – they haven't missed a trick.'

'I'll read every word,' Channon promised. 'What's come in from routine enquiries?

The sightings of George on his bike and vehicles in the vicinity? Young Baxter saw a tractor going into one of Trudgeon's fields just before ten. Anything on that?'

'Yes, we've got details and it was all in order. The regular farmhand confirmed he was working late. He saw nothing, heard nothing, the same as everybody else at Blue Leaze – until Jim found George's body, that is. Something else has just come in, though, that'll interest you. We had two reports of vehicles seen near Blue Leaze and also near the Becky. One witness said he thought he saw a black Shogun, the other a black Discovery. The guy who said it was a Discovery remembered most of the number. We're pretty sure they're one and the same vehicle, and – wait for it – it's Robert Baxter's.'

Channon was pouring a glass of water. He filled it carefully and screwed the top back on the bottle. Then he sat down. So the barely civil father had been out near Blue Leaze. Had Sally Baxter known? Had she known it when her son was being questioned about where he'd been on his motorbike? If so she'd kept quiet about it when she was well aware they'd be checking every single vehicle that had been on the roads and that he was desperate to eliminate anybody not connected with the killing.

'Details,' he demanded. 'Exact times. Did they see who was driving and which way he was heading? Who's available to go to the roundhouse to talk to Baxter? No, no – I'll go myself, with Yates or Hallows if they're around.' He was a fool, he told himself. Hadn't he done enough to spare her feelings for one day? Yes, maybe he had, but if her family had to answer more questions, he was going to be the one who asked them, and that was that.

Malachi answered the door eating a piece of cheese. 'Hello,' said Sally gently. 'I've brought a meal in case your mum doesn't feel up to cooking. Can I bring it in?'

He eyed her warily, but allowed her over the doorstep. Then he whispered, 'Will you wait here, Mrs Baxter, while I tell her?'

Clutching her basket of hot dishes, Sally waited obediently, her heart wrenched with pity when Zennie appeared from the sitting room. Her face was paper-white but her hair had a life of its own, standing out from her head in a wild, tangled mane. Without lipstick her lips were white as well; it was as if the blood had been sucked out of her.

Arms crossed, she stared silently at Sally, who cleared her throat and said, 'Zennie, I've come to say we're all so very, very sorry about Georgie. Is there anybody we can get in touch with who could come to stay with you for a while? It seems all wrong that you and Malachi are here on your own.'

The tiger-like eyes stared out from their circles of smudged mascara. 'Two women called earlier on,' she said quietly. 'They said they were concerned about us, but I told 'em to sod off. They didn't want to know me when he was alive, so why come now he's dead? The vicar's been as well, to ask if I want a service for Georgie, like the one they had for Samantha.'

Sally's gaze strayed uneasily to Malachi, who had finished his cheese and was listening intently. 'And what did you tell him?'

'That I'd think about it. I'm tired, Sally, I'll have to go and sit down.' At the door she turned, the eyes suddenly alive. 'They haven't charged him, then?'

This couldn't be happening, thought Sally. It was too bizarre – and too sad. 'You mean have they charged Luke? He didn't do it, Zennie – he didn't kill Georgie – how could you think it? Channon questioned him for ages and then sent him home. I was there – I heard it all. The police will find out in the end who did it.'

Zennie fluttered her hands and they looked like white moths beneath the wine-red nails. 'I've been trying to decide whether I was a bit hasty,' she admitted, 'but it's all so black I can't seem to see what's true an' what's not. Everything's black, you see.' She thumped her chest despairingly. 'It's black inside here! There's a big black hole in here, an' it's black as pitch.'

Sally's instinct was to hold Zennie close in the hope that she would cry. Such a thing would have been difficult enough when they'd been on the old terms of her dropping in at the roundhouse now and again for a coffee and a chat, but now, with the other woman unsure of Luke's innocence, it was impossible.

'Look, Zennie,' she said at last. 'Even if you aren't hungry I expect Malachi could manage to eat something. I've brought you some beef stew and vegetables and baked potatoes. Would you like me to dish it up for you?'

'Yes, please,' said Malachi. 'I'm sorry, Mum, but I am a bit hungry.'

Sally unloaded her basket on the kitchen table. Zennie stared at the stew and her pale lips twitched in what might have been a very small smile. 'Thanks, Sally,' she said, 'I – I appreciate it, but will you go now? I can't talk any more.'

The air smelled damp and earthy as Channon set off for the roundhouse with DC Hallows. To the west of the village glowed a spectacular, cloud-streaked sunset, but he was in no mood to dwell on the glories of nature.

They were passing the end of the lane behind the church when he spotted a familiar car. 'Stop here!' he said sharply. Sally Baxter's red Fiat was parked outside the Gribbles' house, and at that moment she was saying goodbye to the boy Malachi. 'We'll have a word with her before she goes home and talks to her husband,' he told Hallows.

Feeling worn out after dealing with Zennie, Sally was about to switch on the engine when she saw the two men heading towards her. It came as a shock to find she was pleased to see Channon. That dark level gaze, she thought, that air of calm authority would act like balm on her tattered nerves. He would be on his way to see the Gribbles, so she would tackle him about them being on their own. She wound down the window and waited.

'Could we have a word, Mrs Baxter?' he asked.

'What, here?'

'Yes, if you please.'

She sensed at once that balm for her nerves would be in short supply. 'I thought you were on your way to see Zennie Gribble,' she said in puzzlement.

His glance flickered to the cottage. 'Not at the moment.'

'But Mr Channon – she's in a bad way. Surely you have welfare people or somebody who could give her some support?'

'She's got you, apparently.'

'No, she hasn't! I've just taken them a

meal, that's all. I can't get close to her because – because of Luke. Surely the police don't just leave a murdered man's family to cope on their own?'

Channon sighed. 'We did ask Mrs Gribble if we could notify anybody, and she insisted they'd be all right on their own. A Victim Support volunteer will be seeing them very soon, but if you're seriously worried I'll inform the welfare people as well.'

Mollified, Sally nodded. 'Thank you.'

'So I'd still like a word. We were on our way to the roundhouse when I happened to notice your car.'

'What's the matter?' she asked. 'Not Luke again?'

'No, this time I need to talk to your husband. Is he back from London yet?'

'Yes, he's been back since mid-afternoon.'

'Please think carefully before you answer this, Mrs Baxter. Did he leave the house last evening?'

Mortification hit her. In the turmoil surrounding Luke she'd forgotten that Rob had been out at the same time. She wouldn't have forgotten if she'd been asked about it, though. 'I'm sorry,' she said sincerely, 'there was so much going on it went straight out of my head. Yes, he went out at about a quarter to ten – he was gone for about an hour, I think, maybe a bit longer.'

'Do you know where he went?'

'To Pencannon School. He'd left his smallest laptop in the computer room and he wanted it to take to London.'

Channon looked her in the eye. 'It didn't occur to you to mention it when I was questioning Luke?'

Still on edge, she retorted, 'It didn't occur to you to ask me, come to that.'

'No, it didn't,' he agreed, 'why should it? Witnesses saw your husband's Discovery and if I'd known he'd been out at that time it would have saved us tracing the owner.'

'No doubt it would,' she agreed stiffly. 'I've said I'm sorry.'

Channon told himself he was insane to feel put out that they were at odds with each other. 'It's all right, don't worry about it,' he said quietly. 'We'll carry on to the round-house and see you there.'

'You mean you still need to talk to Rob? Oh – you want to see if our versions tally, is that it?'

'Yes, it is. Your husband was seen near Blue Leaze within an hour of a brutal murder, so naturally I'll need a statement from him.' With a nod he turned to go back to the car with Hallows and on the way took out his mobile. Men would be setting out to question the caretaker of Pencannon School by the time he saw Rob Baxter.

Sally drove behind the police car with the sun laying bands of gold and copper across her arms. She must prepare herself to be a buffer between Rob and Channon, she thought, or Rob might get a bit uptight.

Behind her a police motorbike flashed its lights and she pulled in closer to the hedge. Clearly the rider wanted to speak to Channon urgently, because at the next passing place the police car pulled in and the motorbike stopped next to it. Thankfully she surged past them. Now she would be able to warn Rob that this time they were coming to question him, rather than his son. It would do him good to be on the receiving end for a change, even if it was a mere formality.

'What's this, Steve? Good news or bad?' Channon got out of the car to talk to Steve Soker, who was still astride the bike and lifting the visor of his helmet.

Soker leapt from the bike. 'I never thought I'd catch you, sir! I was dashing around looking for you and they said you'd gone to the Baxters, so I thought – well – I thought I'd better come after you, and – I forgot to tell Inspector Meade I was coming.'

'Relax,' said Channon calmly. 'I'll fix it with him. Now – what is it?'

'Samantha's computer, sir. You remember you told me to do some more on it whenever I could?'

'Yes, yes, have you found something?'

'Yes, an e-mail, sent at 6 p.m. on the day

she was killed.'

Soker couldn't conceal a satisfied little grin. 'It was under a separate password from all her other stuff. I've done you a printout of it, sir.'

Channon took it from him and read it. 'You did right to chase me with this,' he said heavily, and faced the other two in silence, his mind analysing and assessing. It was very quiet on the narrow road that led down to the sea, and behind Soker's helmeted head the sky was splashed with rose and turquoise and amber. Channon thought it highly coloured and dramatic, just like this latest development. He tapped the e-mail. 'Was this on her mail file for anybody to see if they knew the password?'

'No, sir, it had been deleted to her mail-trash. I retrieved it from there.'

'Well done, Steve – this will be vital evidence. You can come with us, now, you've earned it. Did you simply make a guess at the password?'

Soker grinned. 'Lots of guesses.'

'So what was it?'

'"Rainbow", sir.'

'Rainbow?' echoed Channon. 'Oh, I see! Very good.' That showed deduction as well as hard work. 'Look – I want you to search for anything else that Samantha sent – or received, or looked at – anything at all. Rest assured that all this will go on your record.'

Briefly his mind turned to Bowles, scraping around for witnesses at the Rosabelle; he'd be sick at not being in on this. He, Channon, couldn't let him miss it; he would tell John Meade to contact him and bring him back to Truro.

He looked at the distant sea and breathed salt-laden air into his lungs. He felt no excitement at the prospect of what lay ahead, in fact distaste and reluctance were closing in on him like fog in winter. He turned to Hallows and said grimly, 'Let's go.'

Chapter Seventeen

Sally knew at once that something was wrong. There were three of them at the door and one was the speeding motorcyclist. Not only that, Channon was avoiding eye contact with her and his mouth was set in a grim, uncompromising line. She asked them in and shot a look at Rob, who had seemed merely irritated when she dashed in and told him the police were on their way. Now, his glasses flashed with reflected lamplight as he observed each of them in turn.

Channon was politeness personified. 'If we might speak to you and your wife in private, Mr Baxter?'

Warily, Rob nodded. 'Excuse us, will you?' he said to the young ones. Ben left the room promptly; Luke gave an edgy shrug and followed him, while Tessa directed an apprehensive little smile at her mother and trailed behind her brothers.

'Mr Baxter,' began Channon, 'we have reports that your Discovery was seen in the vicinity of Blue Leaze just after ten last night. Your wife has told me that you went to Pencannon School, and of course we're verifying that with the caretaker. Did you see anything suspicious when you passed Blue Leaze and the other farms up there?'

Rob had breathed out visibly when Channon started. Now he shook his head. 'It's pretty quiet on the roads round here at that time in the evening. I think I saw a tractor heading up the slope towards Trudgeon's place, and a big cream Honda flashed to get past me as I approached the Becky. I can't remember anything much on the way back.'

'You didn't see anybody on foot?'

Rob shook his head. 'No, I would have noticed that, I think.'

'We'll take a detailed statement later about your trip to the school. Now, to my next question...' The dark eyes met Sally's for the first time, but she could read no messages in them; his tone, though, was gentle as he suggested, 'Perhaps you and your husband could take a seat?'

Obediently Sally sank down on a settee, but Rob and the others continued to stand. The detective continued, 'In your statement made after the death of Samantha Trudgeon, Mr Baxter, you said that on Friday night you didn't leave the house after 11 p.m. Do you still hold to that?'

'Not exactly,' Rob admitted carefully. 'As a matter of fact I walked in the garden for a few minutes, thinking about some work I was doing for a client. It sometimes clears my mind to get a breath of air. I didn't mention it before because I couldn't see how it would help you and it certainly wouldn't have helped me – it might have put me under suspicion.'

'But Mr Baxter,' pointed out Channon silkily, 'you're under suspicion now. Why didn't you tell us in the first place? If everybody would just tell the truth during an investigation, we might conceivably solve the odd crime before it becomes ancient history.'

Sally opened her mouth to speak and closed it, telling herself that she wouldn't interrupt, she wouldn't interrupt if it killed her. She would watch Rob's familiar face, watch his mouth to see if any more surprising admissions came out of it. Channon would get to the point of his visit before long – because there was more to come, she was certain of it.

Once again the detective glanced at her. 'I'm sorry about this, Mrs Baxter,' he said, then turned to Rob. 'Mr Baxter, I have to tell you that we have here a printout of an e-mail sent to you by Samantha Trudgeon at 6 p.m. on the day she was murdered – the day you said you never saw her.'

Sally went rigid with dread. He'd had an e-mail from Samantha? On the day she was killed? What about? Why hadn't he told her? She didn't like his expression, it held too many emotions, though the only one she could decipher was fear.

Channon was saying, 'Mr Baxter, please listen to this email, then tell me if you received it on Friday.' Tonelessly he read out:

'"Hey, Mr Greenpeace, that last time was the best ever, but when's the next one? Talk about the difference between the man and the boys! You didn't send me our special signal in class yesterday, or if you did I missed it. I'll be on the cliff path outside your house at eleven thirty tonight – whoa, steady, not just for that – something's come up and I need your advice. I need it urgently, so be there, Mr G, or I might, I just might have to knock on your door like a damsel in distress."'

There was silence in the room apart from the steady tick of the grandfather clock. Rob Baxter's face was grey, with two red blotches high on his cheeks; his hands were clutched together at waist level and he was staring at the curving wall behind Channon. DC Hallows, observing both him and his wife as the DCI had ordered, was asking himself whether he'd have been better off staying in uniform on transport control. Soker, still euphoric about his success in recovering the e-mail, was wondering why the DCI was letting the wife in for all this and Channon was telling himself that he was right to follow this particular method rather than his own personal preference.

As for Sally, after one stupefied moment her mind began to race, clocking up questions and answers so fast it felt as if she had the world's most powerful computer inside her head.

This was *it!* This was what Luke had been talking about with Samantha outside the Martennis. He'd *known* – this was what he'd been hiding because he didn't want her to be hurt. This was why Rob had been so uptight when his own son found Samantha dead; why he'd made love in that mad frenzy on Saturday night, why he'd been as awkward as hell for four solid days. Black rage struggled with disbelief that the man she'd loved for twenty-one years had been embroiled with a seventeen-year-old. God above – he had a son the same age! It didn't bear thinking about that the dead girl might have been pregnant. It was a nightmare –

the vilest nightmare she could ever have imagined. But wait, it would be more vile still if he'd – no, he couldn't have – he could not have killed Samantha.

She became aware that Channon was watching her closely. All at once she realized why he'd stage-managed the confrontation in her presence; he'd wanted to see her reaction – to see if she already knew. Well, he'd have received the answer to that one. Now he was speaking again. 'The e-mail had been sent from Samantha's computer under a different password than her usual one. Then it was deleted, but my man here extracted it and did this print-out. Mr Baxter, did you receive the e-mail?'

'Yes,' answered Rob woodenly.

'Did you have a relationship with Samantha Trudgeon?'

'Yes,' he said again, still staring at the wall, 'a brief one, but I didn't kill her.'

'That's what we'll investigate,' answered Channon. 'Mr Baxter, my men will be here soon to search the house and take away your computers. It will save time if you tell us now whether you too work under a password for correspondence with Samantha. We've discovered, and of course you know, that for individual mails to you hers was the word, "Rainbow".'

'I know it,' agreed Rob.

'And yours was...?'

'Pretty obvious, isn't it? Mine was "Warrior".'

'Yes,' said Channon soberly, 'I thought it might be.' He turned to Hallows. 'Right, go ahead.'

Hallows cleared his throat and said firmly, 'Robert Baxter, you are under arrest on suspicion of the murder of Samantha Ellen Trudgeon. You do not have to say anything, but it may harm your defence if you do not mention, when questioned, something which you later rely on in court. Anything you do say may be given in evidence.'

Rob stood there, neither moving nor looking at anyone. 'Take him in,' ordered Channon, and without a word Rob allowed himself to be led outside.

As if compelled to see him driven away, Sally forced herself to head for the door, but stopped as Channon put a hand on her arm. 'Small comfort perhaps,' he said quietly, 'but I can tell you that Samantha wasn't pregnant.' He ran a hand through the thick, grey-streaked hair and said heavily, 'I'm sorry, I'm really sorry. Do you want to come with us to the station in Truro?'

'No,' she replied, 'oh, no. I have to talk to my children – to Luke in particular. You were right in thinking he was shielding somebody.'

'We were both right,' he agreed, 'but we didn't know who it was, did we?' With a shake of the head he walked out into the damp-smelling twilight.

They were packing up at last. Jim Trudgeon was watching from an upstairs window as the police removed their equipment from his top field.

What a day! He'd felt so ill after finding Georgie's body that bed had seemed the only possible refuge, but he couldn't stay there wide awake and leave the work to his dad and the paid help. He needed sleep, he needed oblivion, but there was something he needed more – to have Ellie weeping in his arms so they could comfort each other. At that moment she was downstairs talking trivia and his mother was listening, listening, listening.

Earlier in the day he'd wondered if Ellie was about to return to the real world, because for the first time in four days her eyes had shown a glint of awareness. Then it had faded and she'd baked a fancy iced cake as if there was a party in the offing. So for his own sake as well as hers he'd followed the inspector's advice and rung the incident room to ask for a psychotherapist.

Now he watched as men loaded duck-boards and spotlights and waterproof covers on to a lorry. Had they found clues as to who'd killed Georgie? He hoped so, he really did, but in his heart he saw all that as a side issue compared to the murder of his daughter. Georgie, after all, was grey-haired, he was past his prime; while Samantha hadn't even reached her eighteenth birthday.

Reluctant to go down to witness his wife's delusions, he lingered by the window and watched the last coppery strands of the sunset. Then in the fading light he saw a man's figure approaching the house. There was no mistaking that shoulder-shrugging walk and the wide-brimmed hat – it was Sam Deacon, come over from Pengally. If he was making a visit of condolence he must be kept away from Ellie, or he'd be dumbfounded by her attitude.

Trudgeon went downstairs but as he opened the front door Ellie appeared from the sitting room. 'Why, Mr Deacon,' she said graciously, 'do come in. Can I offer you a cup of tea or a glass of my husband's home-made beer?'

Deacon removed his hat. 'Thank you, no, Mrs Trudgeon. This is just a brief visit to bring you both my deep sympathy and to make a small offering as a tribute to your daughter – the Little Miss, as I used to call her.'

Ellie's eyes swivelled uneasily from side to side. 'Oh?' she said.

'You might not know I have an interest in photography,' went on Deacon, 'doing my own printing and enlarging and so forth.'

He eyed the silent couple uncertainly, then laid the parcel he was carrying on the hall table and unwrapped it. 'It isn't my intention to intrude,' he assured them, 'nor to add to your grief. The fact is – well – I had the idea you might like to have this.'

He gave Ellie a picture, beautifully mounted in a broad gold frame. It was an enlarged snapshot of Samantha at about six years of age, wearing shorts and a pink suntop, perched on the seat of her father's tractor. She was laughing, her blonde hair swirling around her head against a backdrop of trees that bordered a field of yellow wheat. Hand in hand, looking up at her, were her parents.

Nobody spoke, nobody moved until Ellie laid the picture against her chest and folded her arms across it. Sam Deacon cleared his throat. 'She was such a happy little soul I couldn't resist taking a shot of her every now and again. I always reckoned this was the best of the lot, so I've worked on making it special for you.' He tried to shake Ellie's hand, but she was clutching the picture, so with an odd theatrical flourish he leaned forward and kissed her wrist. Then he opened the door and left them.

Slowly Ellie handed the picture to her husband, who propped it up on the table so they could look at it together. All at once a harsh grating sound issued from Ellie's throat; not a cough, more a strangled howl. Eyes wide, mouth agape, she turned to Jim and let out the first agonized sounds of her grief, while next to them the little girl on the tractor continued to smile.

Bowles was far from happy as he drove to Truro. The message from Channon had dragged him away from a three-man check-up on Miller, when another couple of hours' work might have confirmed that nobody – not even the man who'd told him about the place – could with certainty back the little runt's tale of being in the Rosabelle at the time of Gribble's death. Of course the hire car might show something, but forensic were dragging their feet on it.

Reluctantly he acknowledged Channon's fairness in sending for him; but what, he asked himself sourly, could there be to pin on dear Papa? Channon had admitted that not a hair of the man's head had been found at the scene of the crime, so what had led to his arrest?

Lukey-dukey had been hiding something, of course, but it was hardly likely he'd been keeping quiet about seeing his old man knifing Samantha, or trying to throttle her, or even chucking her over the cliff. It could only be connected with the reports that had come in – two of which had said that a black Discovery and possibly a Shogun had been spotted near Blue Leaze. Papa B. had a Discovery and Mama B. had her own Fiat Brava. Lucky pair, weren't they? Or maybe not so lucky ... not now.

Oh, what the hell – he'd be at the station in ten minutes to get the full story, and then he'd join in grilling dear Papa.

Sally found she didn't want to watch Rob being driven away, after all. She simply closed the door behind Channon and turned to look at the familiar pieces of furniture, the pictures, the huge glass bowl of garden flowers, the circular fringed carpet that had given her such pleasure when she found it. It seemed unbelievable that she'd been happy in this round, beautiful house until – when? She realized that she hadn't been truly happy, truly at ease, since she got back from shopping on Saturday morning. With her feet feeling heavy as lead she headed towards the stairs, but Luke slipped into the room and closed the door behind him.

'I've asked Tess and Ben to give me a minute with you before they come down,' he said quietly. 'We saw them take Dad away. What's happened, Mum?'

She didn't answer, but went to him and put her hands on either side of his face. 'Thank you,' she said, kissing his cheek. 'Thanks, love, for trying.'

He wriggled his shoulders and flipped back the ponytail. 'What do you mean, Mum? What have you found out?'

'That...' Oh, how could she put it into words? She wet her lips and tried again, 'That your dad received an e-mail from Samantha on Friday evening, asking him to meet her on the cliff path, and that–'

'Good grief!' He was clearly astounded. 'Go on – what else?'

'You know what else, Luke. The e-mail more or less spelled out what's been going on between him and Samantha. He admitted it. The police are coming here with a search warrant, and Luke – Channon's arrested him on suspicion of murder.'

Her son's bright eyes were wide and staring. 'What? He can't think that! Do *you* think that, Mum?'

'No,' she said bitterly, 'but I didn't think he was involved with a girl the same age as you, did I – or any girl at all, come to that. He admits to a relationship, but he denies killing her. Luke – how did you get to know about him and Samantha?'

He writhed with reluctance to answer her. 'Look, Mum, we'll have to be quick. Tessa wants to come down to see if you're OK.'

'Yes, yes,' she agreed hurriedly. 'Tell me – how did you know?'

'Well – at first it just seemed like a mad suspicion– I thought she had a crush on him or something. Whenever we talked she brought him into the conversation – it seemed a bit over the top, somehow, though I don't think she mentioned him to anyone else. Then one day I'd stayed late to finish my big rainfall map, and when I was ready to go home my bike wouldn't start – it was really playing up. I went to see if Dad was still in the computer room to give me a lift and I – I saw them together in a little cubby-hole sort of place they have there. He wasn't kissing her or anything, just – uh – holding her, but there was something about it – I just knew. They hadn't seen me so I went away and eventually got my bike going.'

A dark implacable rage was building up inside Sally. 'Did you speak to him about it?'

'No, I thought he'd deny it, and, well, I couldn't face him being a liar as well as an adulterous pig.' Luke almost smiled on coming out with that, as if it gave him satisfaction to say it out loud rather than merely thinking it. 'I spoke to Sammy instead, but she just laughed and said it was a bit of fun and why didn't I grow up. That's what we were talking about outside the Martennis – it was then I told her to keep away from Dad. That's why I couldn't tell you or Channon. I knew I was bringing suspicion on myself, but I simply couldn't stand the thought of you finding out. I'm sorry I messed it up, Mum.'

'You didn't,' she assured him, 'you were brilliant. I'll never forget what you did to prevent me being hurt – never. But listen, did you tell your dad what you knew when you talked to each other this afternoon?'

Luke's lips tightened. 'Yes. He said not to worry as it had been all over between them and he thanked me for trying to keep it from you. He asked me not to tell you or anybody else unless I was arrested.'

'Oh. You'd be allowed to spill the beans if you were accused of murder, was that it?'

'Well, sort of. Mum – Tessa and Ben will be down in a minute–'

'Do they know about it?'

'No, of course they don't!'

'Thank God! We'll tell them that Channon has taken him in for questioning because he was seen near Blue Leaze last night. It'll let them down lightly for the time being.'

But Luke was eyeing her in bafflement. 'I thought you'd be crying and everything,' he said with a touch of resentment.

'I don't want to cry,' she told him. 'I want to shout and scream and break everything in the house, but I'll do it later, when I'm on my–'

The door opened. 'What's happened?' demanded Tessa. Ben, wide-eyed, was behind her.

'Your dad's been taken to the station for questioning,' Sally told them, 'because at the time Mr Gribble was murdered he was out in the car, getting his laptop from school. In a few minutes the police will be here to examine his computers.'

'Why?' asked Tessa promptly.

'To see if there's any of Samantha's work on them,' Sally replied. It was quite easy to lie, she thought, when you were desperate. 'Then I'm going over to Truro to see if he's ready to come home.' They'd get to know sooner or later, but they needed a bit longer to adjust to what had happened so far. With luck – a great deal of it – they might never have to know about their father and Samantha.

Above Ben's head her eyes met Luke's and she almost groaned aloud. She was treating him like an adult accomplice rather than a seventeen-year-old boy. It couldn't be happening – it couldn't! But it was.

Chapter Eighteen

Bowles was taken aback to find Channon sitting in his office gazing into space. 'Sir? I thought you'd brought Baxter in?'

'I have, but he'll say no more until he gets a legal rep. Here – read this e-mail, and note the date and the time.'

293

Bowles was stunned by the letter. 'The devious swine! He kept that dark, didn't he? Why was Samantha in such a hurry to see him, d'you reckon? She wasn't pregnant, so it can't have been that.'

'We don't know,' said Channon, 'yet.'

'But d'you think Lukey-dukey was aware of all this? Maybe that was what he was arguing about with her.'

'I suspect his mother thinks it was, and so do I.'

'But Baxter must have sussed that out.'

Channon sighed. 'If he did, he wasn't in a hurry to get the boy off the hook, was he? There's been progress, though – he's admitted going to the cliff top just after eleven thirty but says she wasn't there. He waited for ten minutes or so and then went back indoors.'

Bowles rolled his eyes. 'I'm sure he did!'

'Exactly, but don't forget we haven't a scrap of forensic on him,' warned Channon. 'I put a check on a pile of stuff taken to the cleaners by his wife on Saturday morning, and I've just had word it was free of blood, free of anything suspicious at all, come to that. Men are over at the roundhouse now, going over the place, searching his computer room and bringing away his base units and modems. I've arranged for somebody in a more official capacity than Soker to check on those, by the way. Another thing – the caretaker of the school has confirmed that Baxter did call to pick up his laptop at about ten past ten last evening.'

The DCI leaned back in his chair. 'Now, while we're waiting here, let's clear up a few loose ends so we'll be able to concentrate on Baxter – he's our best bet yet, evidence or no evidence. He's also Samantha's only current partner as far as we know. So, the first loose end – anything on Miller from the Rosabelle?'

'No actual confirmation he was there,' admitted Bowles. 'Appearances, as you'd expect in that sort of set-up, are deceptive, names aren't used much and the proprietor was less than helpful. No news from forensic on the hired Vauxhall, is there?'

'Not yet. Regarding Miller's possible involvement with Samantha – you did check with his landlady for the Friday night?'

'Not personally, no. To be frank I saw it as a routine timewaster. I did ask for a report from the two DCs who took her statement, though. Let me think ... it was a Mrs Trelewyn at a house just along the road from Curdower village, about half a mile inland. She confirmed that Miller had an evening meal there and then went to his room. He'd already told me that he went to bed for a read.'

'Well, in the morning we'll be at the stage where we can't hold him any longer without new evidence. If we do he'll be justified in making a complaint, and so I–'

The telephone rang as a call was put through from Curdower, where a policewoman said hesitantly, 'I'm sorry to bother you, sir, but we've just heard from Blue Leaze. Mr Trudgeon asked me to be sure to give you a message.'

'Yes, yes, go ahead.'

Puzzlement echoed down the line. 'He says his wife is much better now she's distraught, so he's cancelled his request for a psychotherapist to see her. Does that make sense, sir?'

'Perfect sense,' Channon assured her. Then because he remembered the frustrations of being a young officer who never knew exactly what was going on, he explained: 'Mrs Trudgeon's mind refused to accept her daughter's death, so she pretended it hadn't happened. If she's distraught now it means that at last it's registering with her. Do you follow?'

'Yes, sir – thanks. Oh – he said to tell you it was Mr Deacon who helped her.'

Channon turned to Bowles. 'You heard my end of that? Apparently Sam Deacon had a hand in helping her, which is odd, considering that they weren't exactly the best of friends. You and Yates went to see him, didn't you? What did you make of him and his farm?'

Bowles shrugged. 'A decent enough old guy, I suppose, though his sidekick Baldwin would back him whatever his story. Deacon was a bit like an out-of-work actor.'

'Huh?' Channon recalled Maureen Blankett's comments about the man who farmed Pengally. 'Acting hasn't all that much in common with running a farm.'

'It was his looks as much as anything, and his clothes – they weren't exactly faded cords and a shrunken pullover. As for his farm, it can't be doing so well because he's selling old junk to make a bob or two. Otherwise, nothing suspicious.'

'We'll have to keep an eye on him, though,' reflected Channon. 'Now, what do we know about the little scarecrow? First, the SOCOs didn't get much from the field, mainly due to the weather. They've managed a couple of casts of bootprints that are probably Trudgeon's, and they found the wheelbarrow tipped in the hedge near the body.'

'What about the wooden crossbrace?'

'It belongs to Trudgeon. He says it's there permanently – it simply sits in one of two metal sockets at either end of the field. He uses them from time to time because it's his best cropping field and a scarecrow's in keeping with the type of farming he practises. No prints from that or the barrow. They think the crosspiece was laid flat next to the socket and Gribble's wrists and ankles tied to it with rope; then the whole thing was levered upright. They haven't yet found a match for the rope.'

'Has Hunter come up with an exact time of death?'

'He's confirmed the first estimate of between ten fifteen and eleven last night. We've got to take it that George was killed to shut him up. If that's the case, he knew something – but what? Maybe we'll find out from Baxter.'

And maybe we won't, thought Bowles. Baxter struck him as one of the heavy brigade when it came to brains. You didn't get his kind of lifestyle and his kind of wheels without real ability. Bring on the legal eagle, the sergeant told himself impatiently, and let's get moving...

Zennie eased herself from the sanctuary of the armchair. Bed, she thought with longing, bed ... she needed to lie flat. Her back was aching; her head, her shoulders were aching, and so was the black hole where her heart should be. Tomorrow would be soon enough to think of the future. Maybe she would take Malachi and go to see Sally, so she could tell her she was sorry for accusing Luke; she'd be able to talk to her, which was more than she'd felt like doing with her own sister Eugenie.

There'd been a phone call from her earlier

on, curiosity battling with reluctance in her sister's voice. The family had seen about Georgie on the telly, and they'd wanted to know if she needed anything. Memories of the grubby little house near the pig farm had started coming back into Zennie's head and she didn't want them there. 'If I do need anything,' she'd replied, 'I won't ask you lot.' That should have been the end of it, except that Eugie had insisted on telling her that her ma was in hospital with liver disease, Great-uncle Ishmael was dead, two of the cousins were pregnant, one was married, one on remand and another had gone to Australia. It had been like listening to somebody reading the local paper rather than receiving the sympathy that should have been on offer.

In the bathroom Zennie examined her face, repelled by the remnants of make-up and the ravages of tearless grief. Slowly she cleaned her skin and brushed through the tangled mass of her hair; she was heading stiffly to her bed when she heard despairing little snuffles from the next room. Oh, no, Malachi was still awake and it was past ten o'clock; she sighed and pushed open his door.

Wet dark eyes stared at her as he wiped his nose on the sleeve of his pyjamas. Zennie breathed out wearily, then heard herself say, 'You can come an' sleep with me, if you want.'

Still snuffling, Malachi padded after her to her bed, where for the first time since he was a toddler she lifted the covers and lay down next to her son. It felt funny doing it, it felt awkward, but there was a kind of comfort in having him there.

Baxter's solicitor was one of those on call at the station. Wallman by name, he was forty-ish, balding, sure of his ability, but even so somewhat daunted at being brought in to represent a man under suspicion of two murders that were national news.

The preliminaries over, Channon began in his customary gentle manner. 'Mr Baxter, I'd like to begin with your e-mail correspondence with Samantha Trudgeon. You've already said that you communicated with each other by that method, and as I told you earlier, anything we can find in your computer records will be examined in detail. Did you receive and read the e-mail she sent at 6 p.m. on the day she was killed, asking you to meet her at eleven thirty that night?'

'Yes.'

'And have you any idea why she wanted your advice?'

'No.'

Channon knew there was no justification for his next question, but some perverse impulse made him ask it. 'You don't think she might have wanted to tell you she was pregnant?'

'No, I don't. I'm not that much of a fool.'

'Really? You'd been having sexual relations with her, though?'

Rob Baxter's lips twisted. 'Yes.'

'For how long?'

'A couple of months.'

'You didn't see anything wrong in having sex with a seventeen-year-old pupil?'

Tight-lipped, Baxter shot a glance at Wallman, who merely nodded his permission to answer. 'I thought I was being questioned about my possible connection with a murder,' he said, 'not about my morals.'

Here we go, thought Bowles, another awkward squad. 'Answer the question, Baxter,' he said sourly.

'Samantha was within weeks of her eighteenth birthday. I was a voluntary tutor, not a paid member of staff at the school. In those two respects, I saw nothing wrong. In other respects, I'm not particularly proud of myself.'

Thank the Lord for that, thought Channon grimly, and couldn't help asking, though again he knew the answer, 'Did your wife know about the relationship?'

Baxter looked down at his hands. 'No.'

'What about your son Luke?' The reason for the boy's resentment of his father was now all too clear.

'He knew. I found that out earlier today, and to save you asking, he was trying to persuade Samantha to finish with me when they talked outside the Martennis. She refused. She was a nice kid, you know, just a bit – a bit uninhibited. Life was a laugh, life was for living, so go for it – that was her attitude.'

'A pity, then, that in her case life wasn't for living after the age of seventeen,' retorted Channon acidly. 'Did anybody else know what was going on between you?'

'No. I'd insisted that she told nobody.'

'I bet you did!' interjected Bowles.

Channon silenced him with a look, and continued, 'Did you think it could last?'

'Of course I didn't! Neither of us expected it to. It was – an interlude.'

'I see. Now to the night in question. Do you still maintain that Luke was in by eleven o'clock and didn't go out again?'

'Yes, I can confirm that.'

'And what time exactly did you yourself leave the house for the cliff path?'

'I've already told you – just after eleven thirty.'

'You told us earlier about having a stroll in the garden to clear your head – do you still say that happened?'

'Yes, it did.'

'Mr Baxter, had you looked out at the cliff top before eleven thirty and seen Samantha waiting there?'

'No, but I knew she wouldn't keep her threat of knocking at the door. I simply delayed going out for a minute or two after that time because I didn't want to see her – I wanted to finish it. She was nowhere in sight.'

'Did you look around? Did you walk along the path?'

'Only for a few yards. It was moonlight, you know. I could see she wasn't there.'

'Did you see anyone else?'

'No. If there'd been anybody else there I'd have made myself scarce, wouldn't I, and once I knew she'd been killed I think I might possibly have forced myself to tell you I'd seen them.'

Bowles was watching him carefully. So far he hadn't put a foot wrong, but of course he'd had plenty of time to prepare his story. He was cool though, self-contained, and if he felt shame he was keeping it well hidden.

'Did you see any signs of a struggle?' asked Channon.

'Where, on the path?'

'Anywhere on top of the cliffs.'

'No, but I wasn't looking for anything, and in any case, she was killed down on the beach, wasn't she?'

'We are asking you the questions, Mr Baxter,' said Channon coolly, 'not the other way round. So you couldn't see her and you saw no signs of a struggle. What happened next?'

'I hung about for a few minutes, then I went back indoors. I watched from the window for a while, to make sure Samantha hadn't arrived late. Then I went to bed.'

To sleep with your wife, thought Channon bitterly. He'd believed himself hardened to all aspects of human nature, but he found he was shocked by this man's cool attitude to his adultery. A picture dropped into his mind of Sally Baxter with a dishcloth in her hand, crying when he'd told her about losing Claire and Danny. Was this man right in the head to cheat on such a woman?

Deceptively gentle, he continued. 'That all sounds remarkably innocent, Mr Baxter, but I put it to you that Samantha told you something that you didn't want to hear, such as she was going to tell your wife, or that she wanted you to go in for a divorce, or that she was going to report you to the head of Pencannon School. I suggest that you lost your cool and strangled her with a belt, then threw her over the cliff, where you left her, hoping that the tide would do you the favour of removing the body.'

Baxter wet his lips but stayed remarkably calm. 'I didn't strangle her,' he said, 'and as far as I remember, I wasn't even wearing a belt.'

'Only answer the questions, Mr Baxter,'

advised Wallman. 'Don't volunteer information.'

Baxter looked at him in irritation. 'I don't see what harm it can do if I volunteer information that happens to be true. I'm pretty sure I was wearing my black jeans and I don't use a belt with them.'

Bowles kept silent. Channon was a wily devil with all this guff about the manner of death; clever, too, not to give out anything false as actual information. Of course he couldn't reveal that there'd been three different methods used before the killer hit on one that worked. He weighed up the man across the table and decided he was a bit of a hunk, as the women called it these days, not to mention big enough to kill a size ten girl – even a very fit one – at the first attempt.

The questions continued. Wallman was vigilant but he knew Channon had a reputation for playing it by the book. There'd be no intimidation from him, no coercion, he thought. As for Baxter, he appeared to be innocent. He also appeared to be loaded, which in the end would compensate for his, Wallman's, loss of sleep if this went on much longer. He wondered how the man had the nerve to admit to having it away with that lovely young kid. How did some guys do it? The odd times he himself had managed it, the women had all been well-worn old boots and he'd ended up a nervous wreck in case his wife found out.

After half an hour Channon nodded to Bowles and switched off the tape. Once outside the room he said, 'We're getting nowhere fast and it's been a long day. I'm going to let him stew in a cell overnight and we'll take it up again in the morning, by which time we'll know if they've found anything at his house. I'm going to see that everything's in order with the custody sergeant, and at the same time I'll have a word about Miller. He'll probably be getting bedded down by now, so I reckon we'll keep him till morning. You get off home and I'll see you first thing.'

Bowles had been scanning the waiting area. 'Baxter's wife's here,' he said. 'Will you let her see him?'

Channon thought about it and sighed. 'She's given him no alibi and there's no hint of collusion. She didn't know about him and the girl, she didn't know he'd left the house that night. I think we can let her see him.' And the best of luck, Mrs Baxter, he added silently.

Sally found it unnerving that Rob looked much the same as usual when their life would never be the same again. He was tense, of course, but he still looked big and fair and infinitely capable, in spite of being in custody.

At his side a smooth-looking individual was closing a briefcase. The solicitor, she thought; Channon had explained about him. Politely the man handed her his card. 'I'm available at this number and at your service, Mrs Baxter,' he said as he left.

Soon, she thought, she might feel sadness. She might feel pain, loss, fear, guilt, regret; but for now one emotion outweighed all others. It was anger. It didn't occur to her that she was taking the chair that Channon had been using; she simply sat down, faced her husband, and said coolly, 'I see you've got yourself a solicitor.'

'Yes,' he agreed carefully. 'Look, Sal—'

She interrupted. 'You wouldn't have to use your mobile to get hold of him, of course.'

'My mobile?'

'Your mobile that went dead on me when I needed you. Your mobile that you *switched off* to give yourself time to think! And when you'd had your thinking time you *didn't want to know* when I asked you about a solicitor for Luke!'

He stared at her and the blue eyes seemed very dark. 'That's all true,' he said hoarsely. She wouldn't have known it was Rob's voice if he hadn't been facing her. 'Sal, can't you see that I could sense what was coming? Can you try to understand why I was behaving like a swine?'

'A swine? You mean a pig? You and your eldest son think alike on that if on nothing else. He thinks you're an adulterous pig. I agree with him.'

Rob sank lower in his chair. 'That's clear enough, anyway. Look, will you tell me what's happening at home?'

'Oh, nothing too drastic. The Binghams have decided to leave first thing in the morning. Police are swarming all over the house but you'll be glad to know they're being ever so careful. They've removed your base units and modems and taken the Discovery away for forensic examination. Tessa is uptight because she can't organize things or do anything to help, and Ben's a nervous wreck – he's been sick and his asthma's bad. The other two are keeping an eye on him and I left them all together in Luke's room. Apart from that, things are ticking over quite pleasantly.'

'Don't, Sal,' he begged, 'please don't. Do Tessa and Ben know about – about me and Samantha?'

'No. Luke hasn't told them and neither have I. I'm hoping they won't find out.'

'Sally,' he groaned, 'Sally. I can't tell you how ashamed I am.' He reached across the table and for one weak moment she let him hold her hand.

'Rob,' she whispered, 'how could you?

How could you *do* it?'

'I don't know. She was there. She was very available. I was tempted. I must have been–'

She snatched her hand away and jumped to her feet. 'I don't mean *that!* I'll think about that later. I mean how could you let Luke in for all this?' She waved both hands in the air to encompass the room, the tape recorder, the police notice on the wall. 'He's only seventeen but he was at this very table, being questioned about a murder! He put himself under suspicion to shield you and so I wouldn't be hurt. You could have prevented it, given him support. You could have acted like a *man* – like a *father!*'

'If I'd told Channon about Samantha and me I don't see how it would have helped Luke,' he said doggedly. 'I told you before, I couldn't think straight because I was petrified you'd get to know. I couldn't seem to get my head round it. It's been a nightmare from the moment Ben found her body – Ben, of all people!'

'Yes, Ben, of all people – and a fat lot of support he got from his father!'

He stared at her. 'Nothing that you or anybody else can say will make me feel any worse than I do at this moment.'

'Not even being charged with murder? With two murders?'

The skin around his nose and upper lip changed colour until it looked like grey wax.

'You don't believe I've killed them? Sally – say you don't believe it!'

'I don't think I do,' she said, leaning with her hands flat on the table. 'On the other hand, it's obvious I don't know you as well as I thought I did. You're staying here the night, Channon tells me, so sleep well, Rob, and sweet dreams.'

Without a backward look she walked out and made for the main door, but Channon appeared from a side room and blocked her way. 'A brief word, Mrs Baxter,' he said awkwardly, 'I just want to tell you I'm sorry about all this.'

She nodded. 'I know that.'

'Look, I was wondering if you're planning to send your two younger children away for a few days? We've had to give a statement to the media, I'm afraid, saying that a local man is helping with our enquiries, and it's likely that word will get out who it is. Are there grandparents or other relations they could go to? Friends, perhaps?'

'We have no relations apart from my brother in Canada and my husband's two elderly aunts in residential care back in Lancashire. We do have friends, though, in the Manchester area. I'll think about it. Thank you.'

'Are you fit to drive home?' he persisted. 'I can send you in a car, if you like.'

'Thank you, no, Mr Channon, I'll need

my car tomorrow. What do you think I should do next? Should I come again in the morning?'

'You're free to come at any time. You might find us interviewing your husband, of course, but if so you can wait – in private, if you like.'

There was no point in saying that she didn't want to see Rob. What she did want was to know what was happening at any given time so that she could tell the children in her own way. This horror, she told herself, this utter horror couldn't last. Sooner or later it would end, and life, such as it was, would go on. Too tired to say thank you, or goodnight, or anything else, she bent her head and walked past Channon into the darkness.

Chapter Nineteen

It was 6 a.m. and sunbeams were slanting across the garden beneath a clear, pink-pearl sky. Channon was eating breakfast at the table by the window, staring at the silent green fields that sloped away from the house. Remnants of mist were clearing over the distant sea, and a red-sailed yacht was tacking across the bay in search of a breeze.

It seemed to him that the tranquillity out there was at odds with the activity going on inside his head; he was thinking about his next session with Baxter, the imminent release of Miller, the forensic reports on the hired Vauxhall and those on Baxter's Discovery. And possibly worst of all – a visit to Mrs Gribble and her son.

Steadily he ate; not solely for enjoyment but as a measure to avoid wasting time eating during the day ahead. He was clearing away his crockery when the phone rang. 'Morning!' boomed Eddie Platt from forensic. 'I hope you're not still in bed, Bill, because I've been hard at it all night. They tell me you want to hear from us at the double.'

'Don't I always?' replied Channon. 'Anything about anything?'

'Not much, I'm afraid. Nothing inside the Vauxhall that couldn't be accounted for by general use in a country area, except for fibres matching those of Miller's sweater. It doesn't prove anything of course except that he was in the car – which you already know. Traces of vegetation from the wheel treads are similar to samples from the road outside Blue Leaze, but not unique to that particular stretch. In short, we'll carry on giving it the once over but nothing significant so far.'

'And the Discovery?'

'Again, traces of road surface matching

that near Blue Leaze and half a dozen other places. How about this, though? Vestiges of a seaweed pod and traces of sand in the footspace of the back passenger seat. Not mindblowing, I admit, as he lives practically on the beach.'

'Is it actually from Curdower?'

'We don't know yet. Hunter's getting his tame botanist or whatever on to it. We'll know by about ten o'clock and I'll give you a ring. Oh, one final thing. We've matched the rope that tied your little man to his cross with a length found behind the door of the small barn at Blankett's Farm. Not surprising, I suppose, as the wheelbarrow came from there. It'll be put away as evidence in the usual way, of course. Now, can I take time off for a bacon sarnie?'

'If you were here I'd make you one myself,' said Channon. 'Thanks, Eddie.'

Ten miles away in his Truro flat Bowles was still in bed but wide awake. He was in a foul mood; it had been past midnight by the time he got to bed, but instead of going out like a light as he usually did he'd noticed that his bed seemed a bit grotty. He'd sniffed it and decided it smelled. It had shaken him because he had a woman in to clean the place. She didn't change the bed, though; that, like his personal laundry, was his own responsibility. He hadn't the faintest idea how often Sue used to change the bed linen, but he reckoned it must be four or five months since he'd had a rush of blood to the head and done it himself. By the smell of it, that was too long.

Then he'd started with pointless imaginings of Sue in bed with her new partner, the supermarketeer. It was bliss being without her, of course; in fact it was heaven to arrive home late and not have her moaning about his meal being spoiled, but he might as well admit it ... he missed her.

After that he'd found himself thinking about the case – the case in general and Channon in particular. The DCI was soft, he'd always said as much, but there was something about the way Channon worked that was getting to him. He kept finding himself evaluating the senior man's methods, his – for want of a better word – his ethics. He'd have to watch it or he'd be turning soft, as well.

As for Papa Baxter, he was a cool one: the product of a good education, a good job and a keen, astute mind. Could they hold him solely on the girl's e-mail? Yes, but unless forensic came up with something good they couldn't charge him, they couldn't even begin to make a case against him.

Now if they could get something on that other cool customer, Miller... Mentally, Bowles re-examined the report from the

DCS who had interviewed the landlady. There'd been a clear statement from her and a good background report on the B&B routine, the position of the house, etc.

Wait! Bowles shot out of bed and grabbed the folder where he kept his own notes on the case and his copy of the report. He scanned the typed pages and let out a curse. He'd missed that right enough, but it wasn't too late to do something about it. Hey, hey! His bad humour evaporated and he told himself that life as a detective sergeant had its brighter moments. Whistling, he went for a shave. There was a little something he needed to check before he joined Channon at the station.

The bedroom door opened quietly. 'Oh, good, you're awake, Mum.' Tessa came in with a beautifully laid tray. 'I thought you could relax over your breakfast before you face the day.' She put the tray on the bed and went to each window in turn, swishing back the curtains.

'My goodness,' Sally said faintly, 'what a lovely surprise!' After a sleepless night her appetite was nonexistent, but she would have to eat and drink or risk upsetting Tessa. She took a sip of orange juice. 'Are the boys awake, love?'

'Luke's still flat out, but I didn't open Ben's door in case I disturbed him. I'm going to leave you to have your brekkie in peace, Mum, but can I come back – to talk?'

Their eyes met and Sally's heart sank. 'Of course you can. Just give me quarter of an hour to gather my wits, will you?'

When she was alone Sally poured a cup of coffee and leaned back against the pillows. Tessa was changing with each passing hour; was it in spite of what was happening, or because of it? She didn't know, but she'd better decide how much to tell her because that single glance had said as clearly as words that her daughter needed to know what was going on.

She had always doted on Rob. Would she be able to face the fact that he'd been having a sexual relationship with a girl the same age as her brother? Could she deal with him being arrested on suspicion of murder? Forcing down a mouthful of toast, Sally warned herself to give honest answers, but not to tell her anything she didn't ask about. Tensely, she waited for Tessa to come back.

Her opening words were typically direct. 'Mum – I thought we were trying to start afresh, but you've told Luke more than you've told me. I can tell he knows something awful but he won't say a word. What's going on?'

Sally squirmed under the bedclothes. Tessa's unplaited hair wasn't helping. It was swinging in heavy brown waves around her face and she looked younger and softer than she did with it taken back in the plait. 'Mum!' she protested impatiently.

Sally took a breath. She couldn't – she wouldn't destroy Tessa's newly won trust in her. 'First of all,' she said carefully, 'I haven't told Luke anything. Whatever he knows, he's found out for himself.' Lord, that wasn't strictly true! She'd better be more careful. 'What do *you* want to know, Tess?'

'Whether they've arrested Dad.'

'Yes, they have,' she confirmed heavily, 'they've arrested him.'

'What for?'

'On suspicion of murder.'

'But why?'

'He was out in the car near where George Gribble was murdered.' That was stretching it, and the brown eyes were narrowed.

'Why did they search the house, then? Why have they taken his computers? You said it was because something of Samantha's might be on them.'

'Well, it might. They're investigating both murders, Tess.'

'Mum, I don't see why they've kept him all night just for being out in the car when he went to the school to pick up his laptop. Is there something else? You've got to tell me if there is. Luke knows, doesn't he? He's holding his mouth all funny.'

Playing for time, Sally patted the bed.

'Come and sit here, love. The police found an e-mail that Samantha had sent to your dad asking him to advise her about something. They thought it was suspicious.'

'But why? He's getting e-mails all the time, from work and from his students – they think it's good fun.' Tessa put up a hand to twirl her plait, but finding it wasn't there, fiddled with the ends of her hair, instead. 'This e-mail,' she said, 'it has something to do with what's happened to her, hasn't it? Mum – do they think he's murdered Samantha?'

With deep reluctance Sally admitted it. 'Yes. That's why they're questioning him.'

'But can't they see he wouldn't do it?'

'I expect they can see it only too well, but they have to investigate everything.'

Tessa considered that. 'Has he got a solicitor?'

'Yes, love, of course he has.'

'So what's happening today?'

'I don't know yet. I'll find out when I go over there.'

'Last night on television they said that a local man had been arrested. That wasn't Dad, though, was it?'

Sally was starting to feel sick. 'Yes, I think they were talking about Dad. They have to give updates to the media all the time, you see.'

Tessa twisted her hands together and Sally

remembered how only hours ago she'd told herself that people did actually do that in moments of anguish. 'Mum,' she said now, her voice trembling, 'it's all so awful I can't see there can be anything any worse, but I have a horrible feeling about it. *Is* there anything else?'

Sally almost groaned. God in heaven, what should she say? She couldn't do it – she could *not* tell her about Samantha. In the end she resorted to compromise. 'Listen, love, there is something else, but for a very good reason I don't want to tell you about it. Luke only found out by accident or he wouldn't know either. Can we leave it at that for the moment? Please, Tess.'

There was no shadow of knowledge in Tessa's eyes, no realization. She was simply baffled, bewildered and frightened. 'All right,' she agreed, 'but you might *have* to tell me in the end, mightn't you? And what about school? I don't fancy everybody knowing about Dad. They'll either drive me mad asking questions or by being tactful and saying nothing.'

'You'd all better stay at home for a few days,' Sally told her. 'I'll ring the head later on, and I expect Luke will have a word with Bammo. If you and Ben want to talk to anybody you'd better ring them before school, but first we'll all have to decide how much we want to tell people.' She gave a sigh of sheer exhaustion. 'I'll get up in a minute and have my shower.'

Tessa merely shrugged and stalked out, her chin in the air. The gulf between them was widening again, Sally thought in despair, and she didn't know what on earth to do about it.

'He's some wizard on finance, sir – talk about big business! But as for mail to and from Samantha – there's nothing.'

Channon faced the senior of two men who had spent the night hours working on Rob Baxter's computer records. 'Nothing?' he echoed. 'You mean nothing at all or nothing of any significance?'

'Nothing to connect Baxter with Samantha apart from financial e-mails received during exercises that were set for all the students in his group at school. We can find no private mail between them. I reckon they were both extremely careful with all their Rainbow and Warrior stuff. Once sent or received they didn't just shift them to their mail-trash, they deleted them from there as well.'

'Except in the case of the one sent on the day she was killed, eh? I suppose that would have gone the same way as soon as she got round to it. Have you searched through everything?'

'Not quite, sir. His files are in good order,

as you'd expect, but they're absolutely massive. I'll let you know right away if we find anything else.'

'You're bearing in mind the rules about confidentiality and the safeguarding of data?'

'Yes, but sir – haven't you got enough on him without the computer stuff?'

Channon shook his head. 'Not by a long way – that's why I was hoping for something from you. So get off home for a sleep, both of you, and then carry on looking.' The man turned to go and stood to one side to admit the station's custody sergeant. 'We'll start questioning Baxter again at eight thirty,' Channon told the new arrival. 'Anything to report?'

'Not on Baxter, except that he's in the depths of despair – so low he can hardly speak, let alone eat. He's had a cup of tea but that's all, so to be on the safe side I've put him down for regular checks. Barry Miller, though, is a different matter. Breathing fire and brimstone, he is. He says if he isn't out of here by nine thirty when his twenty-four hours is up we can send for the best solicitor in Cornwall and he'll instruct him to fasten your reputation to the urinal wall and, er, deal with it appropriately, if you get my meaning.'

Channon nodded. 'Yes, yes. I'll be giving you the order to let him go as soon as I've had one last look through his statements.'

When Bowles finally arrived he was wearing a satisfied smile which he changed to an expression of dutiful solemnity when he saw Channon about to enter the interview room. The DCI greeted him irritably. 'I thought I said I'd see you first thing? It's almost half past eight, in case your watch has stopped.'

'I know,' said Bowles coolly. 'I've been otherwise engaged. I've been to see a Mrs Trelewyn – Miller's landlady for Friday night.'

Channon removed his hand from the door handle. 'What prompted that?'

'Well, early this morning something occurred to me so I reread the background notes on her statement. They mentioned that her place is a bungalow.'

'So?'

'So I went and asked to see the room Miller had stayed in. Fortunately it was empty, but the thing is, sir, it's a sort of bedsitter overlooking the back garden and the fields.'

Channon eyed him keenly. 'Yes?'

'It has patio doors that can be opened from inside or out. Miller could have gone to bed early, but later on he could have gone out through the doors and returned the same way, without the landlady knowing.'

Channon didn't say anything for a minute. Bowles had delegated the taking of Mrs

Trelewyn's statement, but at least he'd read it, and much later read it again. How many officers, Channon asked himself, would then have decided to check the house itself? Not, he thought, very many.

'Well done,' he said, 'well done. I was just about to have another session with Baxter, but considering no new evidence has come up I'll postpone it and have a word with our friend Mr Miller. There are possibilities here, sergeant. Put Baxter back in his cell and bring out Miller.'

Dispensing with the dutiful expression and letting a triumphant grin take over, Bowles hastened to oblige.

'I hope this is going to be a farewell apology,' was Miller's greeting. 'I'm due back in Bristol this afternoon.'

Channon ignored the remark, switched on, and started. 'Mr Miller, you've told us that you stayed with a Mrs Trelewyn on Friday night, and that you went to bed early. Mrs Trelewyn has confirmed it. Now I want to know if you left your room later that evening?'

'My God!' Miller was so incensed he actually bared his teeth. 'You won't rest, will you, till you've pinned your bloody murder on me?'

'The murder *was* bloody,' agreed Channon, 'bloody and brutal, so you can forget going back to Bristol until I say so. The sergeant here has confirmed that your room at Mrs Trelewyn's had patio doors which could be opened from either side. Now – and think carefully before you answer – did you leave your room late on Friday evening?'

There was complete silence apart from the sound of Miller's breathing and the faint hiss of the recorder. 'Mr Miller?' prompted Channon.

Miller shot a venomous look at Bowles, wet his lips and said quietly, 'I did.'

Channon swallowed a surprised grunt. That had been easy, but how about the next one? 'Where did you go?'

Miller sat bolt upright in his seat. 'I'm sure you've got a convenient witness. I went down to Curdower beach.'

Well, well, well. They were getting somewhere at last. 'What time was this?'

'About eleven fifteen, maybe eleven thirty, I can't remember exactly.'

'Why did you go there, Mr Miller?'

'This sounds weak, but it's true. I wanted to see the moonlight on the sea.'

'Had you, perhaps, arranged to meet somebody?'

'At that time? I'm a happily married man with just one tawdry little secret and you know what that is. I simply felt like going out. I went. I saw the sea in the moonlight.

It was beautiful. I went back to the house.'

'You just happened to be looking at the beauty of the night within minutes of a girl being murdered – a girl you'd met earlier that day.'

Miller's eyes glittered with rage and the noise of his breathing filled the room. 'I don't know anything about any murder! I just happened to be there, and so did somebody else.'

Channon was very still. 'What? You saw somebody else?'

'Yes, I did. Why don't you get after them instead of persecuting me?'

'Them? More than one?'

'Oh, yes, it was like Piccadilly Circus out there. Two men. One I saw clearly, the other from a distance.'

'They weren't together?'

'No, one was at the edge of that pebbled slipway as I arrived – he was in a hurry. The other I saw a few minutes later. I was sitting facing the sea near that jumble of gorse and bracken. He simply appeared from nowhere and walked along the path for a minute or two – a big fella, fair, with glasses. Tell me, Mr Chief Inspector – have you had *him* in for questioning?'

'As a matter of fact, we have,' said Channon with satisfaction. 'He's here at this very moment. Now – did you see this man speak to anybody?'

'No, and he didn't see me. When I came away he was gazing out to sea.'

'And what about the other one – the one in a hurry? Where did he go?'

Miller let out a noisy sigh. 'Look – the only reason I noticed either of them was because I'd expected to have the place to myself at that hour. As I say, he was at the edge of the slipway when I arrived. He didn't go up the road, he crossed to the trees at the front of the cottages in the grounds of that round house and then disappeared, as if he was either going inside one of them or making for that other narrow road going up from the beach.'

Miller glanced at the tape. 'I don't know where he went. What I do know is I wasn't the only one there, so why don't you go after the other two? I'll swear to seeing them if you can bring yourself to believe a single word I say.'

'We'd have been more likely to believe you if you'd told us all this before,' interrupted Bowles. 'Why didn't you?'

'Because you were so bloody eager to pin something on me, that's why. I decided you could whistle for any help I could give you.'

Channon exchanged a look with the sergeant. Miller's rage, his sighting of Baxter, the very implausibility of his story all gave it an uncanny ring of truth. 'We can't release you until we've investigated what you've just told us,' he told him, 'and I assure you we can soon get permission to hold you for longer. One final question, and if you're telling the truth it may well be my last. Did you get a look at the man in a hurry? Could you describe him?'

Miller breathed out noisily through his nose. 'Not really. I only saw him from the back. A dark jacket and trousers and I think he was medium height, maybe a bit less. He wore a hat of some sort, with a brim, and I think I saw a bit of grey hair flapping around.'

'Right, Mr Miller. You have my word there'll be no more questions without your solicitor being present.'

Once on their own, Channon looked at Bowles. 'What do you think of all that?'

At one time Bowles would have replied automatically, 'A pack of lies' or 'A load of tripe.' Now he was more careful. 'Could be the truth, sir. As a matter of fact old Deacon wears a hat with a brim.'

'And it was Deacon who helped sort out Mrs Trudgeon, wasn't it? We'll find out how he did it, and then pay him a little visit, but first we'll go through his statement and that of his friend – what's his name?'

'Baldwin – Will Baldwin.'

'Does it occur to you, sergeant, that this is the second time we've had a suspect who has suddenly transformed himself into a witness?'

'Yes, it occurs,' nodded Bowles. 'It also occurs that the other one turned up dead.'

'Get me those statements,' said Channon heavily. 'Then get Yates on the phone at the incident room. I need him to go up to Blue Leaze to find out how Sam Deacon was able to get Samantha's mother back into reality.'

'Why Yates, sir?'

'He's good with people – sensitive. He won't upset them.'

'And I might?'

'It's a possibility. You have your good points, Bowles, but tact isn't one of them. I'd go myself but I've got to have some time for thought before we take action.'

The Binghams were handing in the keys of Starfish Cottage. 'I'd have liked to stay on just for the thrill of it,' admitted Jane, 'but Kenny's put his foot down. He says enough's enough. He says it hasn't been a proper holiday with the police here every five minutes – he couldn't relax, and he says it gives him the creeps to go on the beach. The cottage, though – it's lovely, even if...' She took a breath and stopped.

Even if the owner's been arrested, finished Sally silently. Aloud she said, 'I understand how he feels, and I'm really sorry, so to try and make up for everything here – I'm refunding your rent.'

'Oh, I say!' Jane Bingham was highly pleased.

'Maybe we'll see you next year,' said Sally, willing her to go.

'Maybe you will,' said the other woman dubiously, '–if you're still here.'

Sally felt slightly better as their car disappeared from view. There was something unnerving, she told herself, about a woman who found murder 'thrilling'. Her parting remark, though ... *would* they still be here in twelve months' time? As a family? She simply couldn't look that far ahead. Her mind was blank and her heart was cold when she tried to envisage a future with Rob.

Thoughts of any future at all would have to wait, though; the next thing was to go and find out what was happening to him. She would warn the children not to leave the house on their own. Rob wasn't a murderer, he couldn't be – but somebody else certainly was.

Chapter Twenty

As Sally headed for Curdower she was confronted by Malachi and his mother walking down the lane. Reluctantly she stopped the car and wound down the window.

Zennie seemed put out. 'We're just on our way to see you,' she said accusingly. 'We set off early on purpose so you wouldn't be out.'

Sally could have groaned, both for herself and for this white-faced woman and her son. 'I'm sorry, Zennie,' she said wearily, 'but I'm just off to Truro. Did you want to talk?'

Zennie shook her head and absently laid a hand on Malachi's shoulder. 'I can talk to you better than anybody else,' she admitted, 'but it's a fact I don't feel much like it right now. I just – I just want to tell you to your face that I shouldn't'a said anything bad about your Luke. He wouldn't'a hurt Georgie, I know that. We both know it, don't we, Malachi?'

Malachi didn't reply. He was trying to control his mouth, which wanted to smile, because he mustn't smile when his dad had been murdered. He was glad his mum had said that about Luke, and he was glad – amazed, in fact – that when she was falling asleep she'd cuddled him, just as if she really liked him.

But Ben's mum was saying something. 'Thanks, Zennie, but you don't have to apologize for anything at a time like this. Listen – have you got somebody to stay with you yet?'

Zennie tossed back the wild mass of her hair. 'We don't want nobody. All we want is for Channon to get whoever done it to Georgie. Here – you're off early to Truro, aren't you? It's not Luke, is it? Has Channon got him in?'

Sally sighed. 'No, Luke's more or less in the clear. He's questioning Rob now.'

'Huh, going through the family, is he? Has Rob been there all night, then? Did they *arrest* him?'

'Yes, I'm afraid they did.' Sally found she didn't mind admitting it, not to Zennie anyway, whose troubles were even worse than her own.

The younger woman was stunned. She couldn't believe that Rob Baxter, brainy and capable and kind, could have killed her little husband. He'd *known* Georgie, chatted to him many a time. He'd asked him once what he thought about chopping down the overgrown shrubs at the front of the cottages, and when they first arrived at the roundhouse he'd given Georgie a few days' work on the garden. On an incredulous outflow of breath she asked, 'They didn't arrest him for – for Georgie?'

'No – they're questioning him about Samantha.'

The amber eyes stared intently into hers, then Zennie leaned in through the car window and kissed her on the cheek. 'You're my only friend,' she said simply, 'here or anywhere, an' I'm sorry, really sorry, but you know they've got to question folk. Channon'll find out soon enough that your Rob couldn't'a killed Samantha. She was a little madam, anyway. Led men on, she did.'

Only if they were willing, thought Sally bitterly, and in any case, Zennie was a fine one to talk. 'Look,' she said, 'I'll have to go now. I'll see you later.' She left mother and son standing side by side and in her rear view mirror they looked small, insignificant, dwarfed by the tall bright hedgerow. But what was she thinking of, she couldn't leave them there! Hurriedly she reversed the car and leaned out again. 'Sorry, I wasn't thinking. I'll give you a lift home.'

'You can give us a lift all the way to Truro if Channon'll be there,' retorted Zennie. 'I want to know what he's found out, an' why he's questioning the wrong man. He must'a thought I'd sit at home all quiet an' patient till he decided to call on me. Well, he was wrong.' She bundled Malachi into the car and together the three of them headed for the Truro road.

Yates was reporting in from his visit to Blue Leaze. 'Mrs Trudgeon was too upset to talk, sir, so I got the full tale from her husband. It seems Sam Deacon used to watch Samantha as a little girl–' He broke off and lifted both hands palms upwards at Channon's cold stare and raised eyebrows. 'I don't know about *that*, sir. Jim Trudgeon's never given it a thought as far as I could see, Deacon brought his condolences and gave them a blow-up of a photograph he'd taken years ago when Samantha was about six. Really good sir, professional standard, in a gold frame and that. Trudgeon had to take me up to his wife in her bed to see it, because she wouldn't let it go – the picture, I mean. Clutching it, she was.'

The distress of seeing the bereaved mother echoed in Yates's voice. 'Take your time,' advised Channon patiently. This was a good lad: reliable, unbiased and a sensitive inter-viewer – one people confided in. He deserved to do well in the force.

'Apparently Deacon didn't say much,' continued the DC. 'Just a few words of sympathy, then he handed over the picture and cleared off. That was when Mrs Trudg-eon broke down for the first time since it happened. I see it as being simply a compas-sionate gesture on Deacon's part, sir, but I did take Don Blamey with me, as he's a Curdower man, and he's told me a bit about the old fella's past. He says he's put it in a report, but nobody took it up because it's just a bit of background, that's all. Don's outside now if you want him.'

Channon's mind was ticking over like a well-tuned engine: assessing, considering, rejecting... 'Get him in!' he ordered briskly.

By contrast his tone with the stolid Blamey was gentle. 'Don, I hear you can fill me in a bit on Sam Deacon's early life. His statement was fine and so was Will Baldwin's, but we're checking on everybody who knew Samantha and George. Tell me, was Deacon well regarded hereabouts in his younger days?'

'Well liked, sir, but according to my mum he was a bit of a Romeo,' admitted Blamey reluctantly. 'She says he was always one for the girls – it was his friend Will who was the quiet one. She says Sam's name was linked with Maureen Blankett's in their youth. The parents were all for it because both sides were after more land – they could see their grandchildren owning half the Roseland, and didn't mind admitting it. When young Maureen finished with Sam he got engaged to a girl the other side of St Mawes, but that didn't last and he really played the field, until in the end he married a woman from up Taunton way.'

Channon was intrigued to hear that the weatherbeaten Lady Bountiful had once had a love life. He recalled her wry, almost affectionate tone when speaking of Deacon, and decided that he must have been a real charmer in his youth, whether she'd given him the brush-off or not. 'Deacon's marriage,' he said now, 'how long did it last, do you know?'

'Till his early fifties, I think.'

'Do we know why it broke up?'

'Once a Romeo, always a Romeo, I suppose,' said Blamey, and then the loyalty of a local man surfaced. 'Sir – as far as I know there's never been anything against old Sam, apart from the fiasco of that indecent exposure thing. Certainly never so much as a hint of what some folk might be thinking about him and Samantha as a little girl. We know he was a fancy dresser – a bit on the arty side, you might say – there was his interest in photography and my mum says at one time he had a go at spinning and weaving his own wool, not to mention being in an amateur concert party. Apart from all that he was a good farmer. Not exactly a traditionalist, but certainly not into organic stuff like Jim Trudgeon. He simply worked his farm, but like many another in recent years he couldn't make it pay.'

Channon held up a hand. 'Right, that's a help, I'll have a word with him myself. You can both go back to Curdower now, but tell Inspector Meade I say he's to keep you where I can get hold of you if I need you. Things are moving and I want to sort out a few loose ends.'

And how, he thought as the two men left. Where to start was the question. Miller, Baxter and now Deacon – they couldn't all be guilty but so far there wasn't a scrap of

335

forensic on any of them. The motive for Samantha was surely tied up with a relationship, and Baxter was suspect number one for that, what with the sex and the e-mail and the fact that he'd been on the cliff top. But if Miller was to be believed the chap on the slipway came a close second, and that put Deacon in the picture, unless Miller was lying to save himself. He was devious enough.

And the motive for Georgie ... it had to be that he knew something, or he'd seen something, or he was going to spill the beans about something. Even so there was a kind of devilish bravado in making his dead body into a scarecrow – and in Trudgeon's field, at that. Sick, it was – very sick.

Going back to Samantha ... evidently she'd liked older men. That thirty-year-old farmer when she was just sixteen, and Rob Baxter in his mid-forties... Would she have liked one even older? Older than her own father? One who used to watch her as a child?

The door opened and a tight-lipped Bowles walked in. 'What about Miller?' he demanded. 'His time limit's up and he's being awkward as hell.'

Channon gave a hard little smile. 'Is – he – really? Well, sergeant, I've applied to the powers-that-be for an extension and they're ringing me back in a minute to confirm that it's all signed and sealed. Miller says he's worried about being late arriving home so you'd better suggest he telephones his wife and tells her he's a witness in the murder enquiry that's filling the papers. I'm sure the only reason he hasn't demanded a legal rep before now is because he thinks she might find out about his little secret. Now, anything else?'

'Yes, Mrs Baxter's arrived – she wants to speak to you before she sees her husband and she's brought Gribble's wife as well – and the boy.'

Channon sighed. He had put off seeing Zennie Gribble and he wasn't proud of it. As for her dragging the child around with her ... he tried not to think of Malachi's wary dark eyes and unsteady mouth. Poor little lad. 'Find somebody good with children to keep an eye on Malachi while I talk to his mother,' he said, 'and after that I'll see Mrs Baxter.'

Who'd have the job?

Everything was still black, Zennie told herself, but now there were streaks of red, as well. Red for danger, red for anger: the danger that somebody else might be murdered and the anger she felt with Channon, even though he was being nice to her, offering the best chair in his office, asking how she was feeling.

'I'm feeling bad,' she told him bluntly, 'bad an' mad. I thought you'd'a been to tell me what's happening, but you haven't been near.'

'You did say you didn't want anybody,' Channon reminded her awkwardly, 'but I would have called in later today, anyway, just to put you in the picture.'

'*In* the picture? I'm so far *outa* the picture I don't even know how me husband was murdered – what do you say to that?'

Channon wriggled his shoulders and it came to him that though she looked ill, in some odd way she was more striking without the heavy make-up than with it. 'You didn't ask me how he died, so I didn't tell you,' he said simply. 'I saw no point in upsetting you even more.'

Her natural belligerence was increasing. 'It's a poor do if I can't be upset when me husband's been murdered, Mr Channon. I want to know! How was he killed?'

'Georgie was strangled,' he said.

Zennie wet her lips. 'Well then, there must be clues – fingermarks an' such.'

'We've got all that in hand.'

'So was he dumped somewhere, or what?'

'His body was left where it would be found.'

'Well, where?'

'In Trudgeon's top field.'

Another link with Samantha, she thought

338

tightly. 'It poured with rain early morning. Was he left lying in the wet?'

'Uh – not exactly lying – more propped up. Look, Mrs Gribble, in murder cases we don't usually say too much about the actual manner of death until we've charged the perpetrator – that's the murderer.'

Zennie rolled her eyes. 'I might not be educated,' she said, 'but I do watch the telly. I know what perpetrator means, an' I can tell you this, you'd better get the right perpetrator – an' I don't see the right one being Rob Baxter. He got on all right with Georgie. He didn't like me much, I always knew that, but he chatted to my Georgie. I think he had a soft spot for him.'

Channon nodded. 'I'll bear that in mind. Now, while you're here, could you see Sergeant Bowles to confirm Georgie's work times and where he went each day? That might be helpful.'

'An' it would shut me up an' make me feel useful,' she said mockingly. 'You haven't a clue who did it, have you?'

'We have several clues, but we're still working on them.' He got to his feet and stood in front of her, the streaky hair flopping on his forehead, the dark eyes intent. 'You'll have to trust me, Zennie. I'm doing my best, and so is half the Devon and Cornwall force. Will you? Will you trust me?'

It went against all she'd ever known to

trust a policeman. She opened her mouth to refuse, but there was something about him, something she couldn't have explained, unless it was that he seemed to mean every word he said. She gave a sigh that seemed to come from the very soles of her feet. 'I'll trust you,' she agreed, 'but you'd better not let me down.'

Then it was Sally's turn, and when she walked in Channon told himself that if Zennie Gribble had looked ill, this one looked close to collapse. Keep it cool, keep it brief, he warned himself, don't get involved. 'Please sit down,' he said. 'I'm afraid I haven't much time to spare, Mrs Baxter.'

'I can imagine,' she said. 'Just two things, really. The first is that I seem to recall a lack of response on my part when you tried to be kind to me last night, and I apologize.' He stared at her, but she continued without pause, 'The other thing is – are you still questioning my husband?'

'Not at present,' he told her, 'but we can't possibly release him just yet. He's still under suspicion, so we must investigate every conceivable angle.'

'Mr Channon,' she said, leaning forward, 'is my husband your only suspect?'

He shook his head. 'I can't tell you that,' he said gently. 'I'm not allowed to discuss the case, particularly with a suspect's next-of-kin. Do you remember what I said about my being careful not to charge the wrong person?'

'Yes, I remember.'

'Good. And do you believe that I'm doing my best to ensure that justice is done and the letter of the law adhered to?'

'Are the two synonymous?'

'They are when I'm in charge,' he told her.

With an odd air of finality she rose from her chair and offered him her hand, and he knew what she was saying as clearly as if she'd spelled it out for him. He'd had to ask Zennie Gribble to trust him, but with this woman trust was already there. Would it still be there if he had to charge her husband with murder – with two murders? He doubted it.

Ceremoniously they shook hands like two business acquaintances. 'You're free to go to your husband, Mrs Baxter.'

She hesitated. 'Do you know how he is?'

'I haven't seen him this morning, but the custody sergeant reports that he's very low, so we're keeping a close watch on him.' He wanted to ask how she was feeling, how the family were coping, but all he said was: 'If you ask at the desk somebody will take you to him.' And once again she simply bent her head and walked away.

Rob was in a cell and the uniformed constable who had ushered her in was by the door, staring into space. Unreality swirled around her as it had done for hours that seemed like days, weeks, years. 'I've brought you some clean clothes and stuff for a shower and shave,' she said, dumping a plastic bag on the bed.

The vivid eyes behind the glasses were rimmed with red and blinking rapidly. 'I love you,' he said stiffly, nodding his head at her. 'Sally – I love you.'

She didn't answer. It wasn't real that this was the man she'd shared her life with. She'd thought she'd known him – she *had* known him, known his body, at least, if not his mind. She couldn't stay in the same room – she couldn't. 'Has anything else happened that I need to know?' she asked.

He shook his head. 'Sally – did you sleep?'

'Of course I didn't,' she said shortly.

'How are the children?'

'Much the same. Home from school, of course.'

'Sally, they've let me make a couple of phone calls, but you'll have to do the rest. I should be checking the markets by now.'

When she looked at him blankly he said, 'It's what puts food on the table. Please, Sal.'

'Give me the names and numbers,' she said evenly. 'I'll tell them you're helping the police with their enquiries and that you'll be in touch as soon as you can.'

'That's no good, you'll have to say–'

'That or nothing,' she said. 'Take your pick.'

'This is my work, woman! It's what paid for your bloody Aga!'

'I don't give a damn about my Aga,' she said, and knew that it was true.

Grimly he handed her a list of names and telephone numbers. 'Sally – what about us?'

'Us? You mean the family?'

'Yes – no – I mean you and me.'

'I don't know,' she said, 'I simply don't know. Get your solicitor to ring me when there's any news.' She folded up the list and put it in her pocket. Then without another word she left the cell.

Channon was on edge. He felt he wasn't at the heart of things in Truro and said to Bowles, 'Let's get back to Curdower.'

'What, you want a briefing?'

'No, not just yet. I want to be where the action is.'

'But surely it's here, in the interview room?'

'Possibly, but in any case we have to go and see Deacon. Not that he's going to run off, is he?'

'You mean you're leaving him for a bit?'

'Maybe, maybe. We'll let Miller and Baxter stew for an hour or two, as well. Let's go.'

'Oh, there was a message from Eddie Platt

while you were with Mrs Baxter. The sea-weed pods in the Discovery. Nothing conclusive as to which beach they're from.'

Channon grunted. 'If they'd been from Curdower it wouldn't have proved anything.' Bowles opened his mouth to reply but Channon waved a hand. 'Don't talk. I want to think,' he said.

Ben was fed up with being told comforting little lies about his dad. In fact, he suspected that his mum had issued one of her orders, such as: 'Don't tell Ben anything – I don't want him worried!' Couldn't she see that it was more worrying to imagine something horrible than to know what was actually happening?

He'd decided to demand the truth, but he wasn't sure who to demand it from, his sister or his brother. Normally there would have been no contest, because it had always been easier to talk to Luke than to Tessa, but right now his brother's mouth was set in a tightly folded line. He might as well have had a notice plastered to his forehead: 'I am giving nothing away so don't bother to ask.'

The three of them were at the kitchen table, supposedly having a coffee and something to eat, though nobody was drinking, nobody was eating. Ben himself couldn't have eaten – he felt too sick. In desperation he forced himself to speak to them both.

'Can't either of you make a guess at why they've kept Dad in Truro all night?'

Tessa's reply infuriated him. She simply said: 'Ben, why don't you go and have a lie-down? Mum said a sleep would do you good after a restless night.'

He turned on her. 'I'm *not* lying down – I'm not a baby! I just think you two might have talked things over with me – explained things.'

Tessa gave her plait an angry tug and directed a glare at Luke. 'In order to explain something you have to know the facts, and I don't. I don't know *what's* going on. All I can say is I think it likely that Mum will bring Dad back with her.'

Luke chewed his lip and for once remained silent. He was confused; he told himself that his brain had gone into reverse. The previous night he'd gone to bed vowing to stay awake all night to think things through, but the relief of not having to keep it all secret from his mum any longer had shot him into a bottomless pit of sleep, and when he awoke he felt like he'd done when he had glandular fever – light-headed and lethargic. He was still amazed by his mum's reaction. He'd expected her to be heartbroken, her eyes red with weeping, but instead she was dry-eyed and strong, showing only two emotions: one was anger, the other anxiety in case Tessa and Ben found out.

He wished it had never entered his head that Samantha was keen on his dad. He wished – how he wished he'd never seen them together in the computer room. Now, stung with guilt at his neglect of Ben, he looked across the table at his brother's set face and said quietly, 'Look, I think it'll be all right in the end.'

Stonily, Ben stared back. 'All right for the Trudgeons and the Gribbles?' He jumped up, his voice rising unsteadily. 'And if you won't tell me anything I'm going to my room!' With that he ran from the kitchen.

'Sod it and shit!' hissed Luke viciously, looking after him.

Tessa said coldly, 'I don't know what you're swearing about. You're the one who's in Mum's confidence. You're the one who knows it all.'

'I wish I didn't,' he retorted angrily. 'I wish I'd never known a thing. I wish she'd never talked to me, I wish – uh, that is, nothing, really.' He gave a weak little laugh. 'What *am* I going on about?'

'You wish *who* had never talked to you?' pounced Tessa. 'Mum? No, you don't mean Mum, do you? I do believe you mean Samantha. Why should she talk to you? What *about*, for goodness' sake?'

'Nothing,' said Luke flatly, and took a gulp of coffee.

Tessa drew circles on the table with the tip

of her finger. 'Somebody at school once told me that Sammy T. had a thing for the science teacher when she was in Year 11. He's left now, but she really fancied him, even though he was married and quite old – at least forty. Luke – had she got a crush on Dad?'

Luke's natural intelligence deserted him. He saw a way out and he grabbed it. 'Yes,' he muttered, 'she fancied him.'

'And that's it? That's the big secret? She was an idiot! As if Dad would take any notice of a pupil – even one as pretty as her.'

'Mm – as if,' echoed Luke.

But Tessa was strung up, her instincts at full stretch. 'Just a minute – the police think he killed her, don't they – Mum told me that much. They wouldn't think that just because she had a crush on him, would they? They wouldn't have arrested him just for that? Do they think he was – you know – messing about with her?'

Luke found it impossible to avert his eyes from Tessa's compelling gaze. 'They might,' he said carefully.

To his horror she let out a wail. It sounded like a child who had fallen and banged her head. 'They're mad!' she howled. 'Channon's a fool! My dad would never have touched Samantha Trudgeon. Everybody knew she was mad for it. My *daddy!* As if he *would!*'

'As if he would,' mocked Luke, anger rising. What about their mother, he thought

347

furiously, what about the family? Weeks of tension and worry erupted in a torrent of rage so intense his vision blurred. Blind rage, he thought in confused understanding – this was why they called it blind rage.

'Your daddy was shagging Samantha Trudgeon!' he told her brutally. 'Your precious daddy was having it away with the sex-pot of the year. She said as much in the e-mail she sent him and she asked him to meet her on the cliff path that night. One of Channon's men went through her files and recovered it. That's why they've arrested him, why they think he killed her, and *that*, Tessa, is what I've been trying not to tell you! *Now* are you satisfied?' To his shame and despair a sob tore from his chest and almost choked him. 'Oh God,' he whispered, 'I promised. I promised Mum I wouldn't say a word. Tess – Tess, I'm sorry.'

This, thought Tessa in stunned amazement, was what her mother had tried to protect her from; what Luke had been concealing when Channon questioned him. He'd been shielding not just their dad but all the family.

'Tess,' he said again, 'I'm sorry.'

'Don't be,' she answered, 'don't be sorry you've told me. Let me think for a minute.' She shook her head as if to get her thoughts in some sort of order. At last, as if making a great discovery, she declared, 'Samantha was the same age as you.'

'I know.'

Her lower lip trembled and she couldn't keep it still. 'He didn't kill her–'

'I know.'

'–but he's destroyed the family.'

'I know,' he agreed for the third time.

Past differences wiped away, the clash of their personalities dismissed, brother and sister held each other close as Tessa tried to adjust to what she'd learned. After a minute, still dry-eyed, she leaned away and looked into his face. 'You tried, Luke,' she said, 'you tried.'

Chapter Twenty-One

As usual the incident room smelled of stale food and cigarette smoke, so Channon headed for his office on the village green. Following him, John Meade handed over some notes, saying, 'Here, Bill – we've listed points of interest from the statements. Nothing much, I'd say, except a half-hearted back-up of Miller being at the Rosabelle when George was killed. We can't use it because the witness is vague on times – maybe deliberately vague. As for the checks on Samantha's previous boyfriends – they all have alibis for Friday night. Oh – and a printout of interviews with everybody who employed George, currently and in the past.'

Channon folded the notes and put them in his pocket. 'Anything of interest in them?'

'Just one small discrepancy. When he still had his own farm Will Baldwin used to give Gribble a few days' work now and again. He mentioned that George had a mind of his own, which is a bit at odds with what all the others say.'

'What exactly did Baldwin mean?'

'Well, you'll read it for yourself, but it seems George didn't always do as he was told with the pigs.'

Channon considered that. He already knew that Georgie had a tough streak – he'd shown it when he let Zennie find out what he'd done with Samantha... 'We've got to go to Pengally to talk to Deacon,' he said, 'and if Baldwin isn't there we'll call on him at home.'

Meade nodded. 'Another thing, Bill. Steve Soker asked for a quick word with you before you go out again. He's still working on Samantha's computer – spending a hell of a lot of man-hours on it, actually.'

Channon nodded impatiently. 'All right, I'll see him, but he'll have to be quick.' When Soker appeared he said, 'Well, Steve, found any more e-mails?'

'I'm still in her system, sir, but all I've

found is that she has the MAFF website bookmarked sometime on Friday. Like a lot of her stuff it's been deleted and emptied from the mail-trash. It was probably school work, because she was taking Food Sciences, wasn't she?'

Channon gazed at the sunlit trees outside the window. MAFF, the Ministry of Agriculture, Fisheries and Food, could be helpful to such a student. 'Did she usually keep her school work secret?'

'No – at least, not her course work and homework. The e-mail to Baxter was different, of course. I think she enjoyed a bit of cloak and dagger stuff simply to show her expertise and liven things up a bit.'

'So what did she want with MAFF?'

'I don't know yet. Inspector Meade put me on something else this morning. Sir – should I follow it up?'

What could they lose? 'Stay with it,' ordered Channon. 'If you can, find out what time on Friday she accessed the site and what she was after. Then let me know on my mobile, even if you don't think it's important.'

Highly pleased, Soker managed not to smile. 'I'll do that, sir,' he said soberly.

'She knows,' was Luke's greeting. 'Tessa guessed about Dad and I confirmed it. I'm sorry, Mum.'

Sally sank down in the chair next to the Aga. This was all she needed, but she couldn't have Luke blaming himself. 'It's done,' she said painfully, 'if she knows, she knows. Poor Tessa – she was always her daddy's girl.'

'Not any longer,' said Luke grimly.

'What about Ben? Don't tell me he knows as well?'

'No, but he's all uptight about being kept in the dark. Can you talk to him and put his mind at rest?'

'I'll try,' she said, 'I'll try.'

'Mum, what's Dad going to do if they let him go?'

'How do you mean?'

'Will he come home?'

'I suppose so, unless I refuse to have him. Even so, the house is in both our names.'

Eyes cold, Luke faced her. 'I'm sorry, Mum, but if he's going to be here, I'm leaving. I can't stay in the same house.'

Let it all come, thought Sally, throw the lot at me, what does it matter? 'They haven't released him yet,' she said, 'but I can imagine how you're feeling. We'll talk it over but first I'm going up to see Tessa and Ben – and then, I'm sorry, but I think I'll have to go for a lie-down.'

She found Tessa in bed turned to the wall. 'Tess,' she said, 'is there anything else you want to ask me?'

'How long have you known about him and Samantha?' It was more an accusation than a question.

'Since last night, when the police came to see him.'

'Oh. You didn't suspect before then?'

'No, love. After Samantha was killed I knew something was wrong, but I had no idea what it was.'

'Mum – she was the same age as Luke.'

'I know, love.'

'Are you going to forgive him?'

God, this wasn't true – discussing it with Tessa. She was only fifteen. Bitterness and betrayal ripped through her. At that instant she remembered Rob's clean hot body in her arms as they made love. Sex had been the mainstay of their marriage – it had confirmed their love, their togetherness, it had – but Tessa was waiting. 'He's bitterly ashamed,' Sally told her, 'and he loves you all as much as he ever did. We'll get through this eventually – it's too soon to decide anything at all just yet. I'm going to talk to Ben now, and then I'll try to get some sleep.'

At that Tessa sat up. 'Mum, about earlier on, when I was – you know – a bit annoyed with you.'

'Yes?'

'I'm sorry. I do see now why you didn't want to tell me.' With that said her daughter's tears came: hard, dry sobs that seemed to hurt as they left her throat.

'Come here, love,' Sally murmured, 'come here, my pet.' She sat and rocked Tessa in her arms as if she were a toddler. 'Cry, love,' she urged, and thought, Cry for us both, because I can't raise a tear. As if in obedience to the thought, Tessa clutched at her mother and sobbed her heart out.

For once, it was easier dealing with Ben. 'Why've you told them to keep me in the dark?' he asked resentfully.

'Because none of us knew for certain what was going to happen. They arrested Dad on suspicion of murder, though I'm not sure if they meant Samantha or Mr Gribble. Mr Channon's a good man, so he'll soon find out Dad hasn't done it and send him home.'

Ben stared at her intently. 'Is that all?'

'Yes,' she lied firmly. 'That's all. It's awful, Ben, it's ghastly, but I think he'll be released very soon.'

'But why has he been so bad-tempered and everything? He was horrible as soon as he knew we'd found the body – before he even knew who it was.'

Too exhausted to do anything else, she lied again. 'I don't know, but perhaps he'll tell us when he comes home. Ben, I haven't slept for ages, so I'm going to bed for a while. Maybe Malachi could come down later on to play. Would you like that?'

'I don't know,' he said dubiously. 'Perhaps

he'll be crying and carrying on because of his dad.'

'Perhaps he will,' she agreed. 'Maybe Luke will have a game of pool with you or something.' If she didn't lie down soon she would fall down, she told herself. She kissed Ben and without another word went to bed.

Bowles sniggered through clenched teeth. 'See what I mean about an out-of-work actor?'

Channon saw. Deacon's wide-brimmed hat and velvet jacket were certainly way out for a Cornish farmer and the purple neck-cloth was tied like a cravat. He only needed a cigarette holder to be straight out of a Noel Coward play. 'The sidekick's here as well,' muttered Bowles when Baldwin's tall spare form emerged from the barn.

Channon introduced himself. 'I just want a word about the statements you both gave to the sergeant here. Could we go indoors for a moment?'

With relief he saw that the kitchen was clean and tidy when he'd half expected squalor, and at Deacon's suggestion the four of them sat at the scrubbed table. 'Now,' he said, 'as your statements coincide I think we can all chat together. First, perhaps you'd confirm the time you both got back here after the darts match on Friday night.'

Deacon turned to his friend. 'Twenty past

eleven, wasn't it, Will, give or take five minutes?'

'Yes,' agreed Baldwin mildly. 'Like I said in my statement.'

'And after you dropped Mr Deacon you went straight home?'

'Yes. Perhaps twenty-five to twelve when I got there, maybe a bit later.'

'Your home is just outside Curdower village?'

'That's right.'

'Did you go out again?'

'No,' said Baldwin calmly, 'I went to my bed.'

'And what about you, Mr Deacon? Did you stay here when Mr Baldwin dropped you off?'

The dark eyes were all at once wary. 'I told your sergeant I'd had a few at the Martennis, so I wasn't likely to go anywhere else, was I? I have to be up at five.'

'Yes or no,' said Channon shortly. 'Did you leave here after Mr Baldwin had gone home?'

'No.'

'Thank you. Now, I hear you visited the Trudgeons last evening and gave them a picture of Samantha when she was little.'

'That's correct.'

'Did you take many pictures of her?'

Dull red blotches appeared on the leathery neck above the cravat. 'No,' said

Deacon, 'just every now and again. She was such a lively little soul, but I didn't see all that much of her, even though our land adjoins. And for the record, inspector, my desires have never run to children – not in the way you might be thinking.'

'No,' agreed Channon blandly. 'Apparently you were quite a ladies' man in your youth.'

What was the point of all this, thought Bowles wearily. Couldn't they simply pin the old fool down about being on the slipway? There were times when Channon needed a rocket up his backside. 'What has that to do with anything?' asked the farmer.

'I don't know – yet,' answered Channon, suddenly grim, 'but we're working on a double murder, so you can either answer my questions here, informally, or at the station in Truro. Is it right that at one time there was a possibility of your farm and Blankett's being joined through matrimony?'

Deacon tucked in the corner of his mouth. 'Maureen been telling all, has she? I don't know what it has to do with you, but yes, fifty years ago it was more than a possibility, but it didn't happen, did it?'

'Why not?'

'Pride and ambition proved stronger than mutual attraction. Maureen was different – that's all I'll say.'

Channon hesitated. The past is a foreign

country, or whatever the quote was. Before now, though, he had found that the past, even the distant past, could influence the present to a surprising degree. He had studied maps of the farms and wondered if Maureen Blankett had baulked at accepting a man who would bring less land than she would to the union. He thought of the way she'd avoided saying anything derogatory about Deacon. Had she regretted throwing him over all those years ago? She'd stayed unmarried, hadn't she, though as an heiress she must have had other offers.

Maureen was different... Did he mean she'd been cold and unresponsive, or that her farm came before everything and everybody? Channon forced his mind into the present and turned to the other man. 'Mr Baldwin, in your statement about Mr Gribble you said he had a mind of his own. That's rather at variance with what most people have said about him. Can you tell me what you meant?'

Baldwin gave the odd little smile that had so irritated Bowles several days earlier. It was mocking, almost sly, as if the brain inside that balding old head was more alert than that of any policeman. 'George was obliging,' he said now. 'He would agree to everything – even do a bit of grovelling if it came to it, but he had his own ideas on certain things. At the same time he was working for me he was helping Jim Trudgeon change over to organic, and – well – he thought Trudgeon's pigs were better treated than mine.'

'And were they?'

'George thought so, but it was me who was making a profit and Jim who was struggling. It'd be different now, of course; he's gone through his bad times and he's in the process of being proved right.'

'So it was merely a difference of opinion about the livestock?'

'That's all,' agreed Baldwin, 'and anyway, it's all in the past. What's more,' he added deliberately, 'I bore him no grudge, and neither did Sam here. George was a good worker – wiry, you know. Just a bit low on brains and initiative, that's all.'

'And you've both confirmed that you didn't see him last evening, here or anywhere else?'

The two men didn't even glance at each other. 'That's right,' they said, almost in unison.

Channon rose from the table. 'One last point, Mr Deacon – is there anyone here who could vouch for you not leaving the farm after eleven twenty on Friday night?'

'No, there is not,' said Deacon, tossing his head. 'I live on my own. Will helps me a lot and I pay casual hands by the day.'

With a word of thanks Channon left the

two friends and once outside said to Bowles, 'It's no use rolling your eyes! We've nothing whatsoever on him except Miller's word that he saw a man in a hat on the slipway. If we'd got evidence – forensic or even another witness – it'd be different. Now, drop me off at Blue Leaze, will you? I want to put something into practice before we tackle Miller and Baxter again.'

Bowles shot him a look. He'd heard on the grapevine that Channon sometimes went walkabout in the throes of a case. Blue Leaze? Was he checking on Deacon's visit? 'How will you get back to Curdower?' he asked.

'I'll ring in when I'm ready,' said Channon, 'so stand by. And do nothing with Baxter and Miller in the meantime.'

'Where's the DCI?' asked Meade when Bowles came back on his own.

'Up at Blue Leaze wearing his deerstalker,' answered Bowles sourly. 'He left his pipe behind, though.'

Meade looked at the younger man with disfavour. 'The DCI's a fine detective,' he said coldly, 'and it'll be time for sarky remarks from you when you've equalled his record. Until then, less mouth!'

Bowles dipped his head in mock submission and went to see if anything new had come in.

Malachi was kicking a ball around in the kitchen. He wanted to go outside with it but he didn't like to ask his mum. One half of him wanted to stay close to her, the other half felt scared when he looked at her white face. Now she wasn't wearing make-up it was as if she was hiding behind a white paper mask with holes for the eyes.

In the red and gold room next door Zennie had been recalling what she and Channon had said to each other, but now she turned her mind to Sally Baxter. She was what some people would call a good woman, thought Zennie; she liked her, but there was something very strange about the way she was acting since Rob was arrested. She didn't seem upset, she wasn't crying, she was simply angry... The thud of the ball against the wall cut in on her thoughts.

'Stop it,' she commanded from the door. 'That noise is doing me head in. You can't go out to play yet – I don't need to tell you why not. You can either watch telly or do something important, like your reading for school.' Her eyes were drawn to the picture on the wall behind him. It was one she'd bought in a junk shop months ago – a horse-drawn gypsy caravan, brightly painted with a curving roof and a girl sitting at the back, swinging her legs.

'Malachi,' she said thoughtfully, 'how

would you feel about going away from here?'

He let out a sound that was both a groan and a whimper. 'Not to my real dad!' he said in horror. 'Not to him! I like my Gribble dad best.'

For almost a minute Zennie stared at him, while he tried hard not to snuffle. 'You'll never go to *him*,' she said at last. 'I'd never let you go to *him*. You're mine, not his. You're – you're my son.'

Two fat tears slid down Malachi's cheeks. He knew better than to hug her or even acknowledge what she'd said, but his heart was racing with joy. 'What did you mean about going away?' he asked casually.

The caravan was behind him: colourful, tempting, beckoning to the open road. Did people go around in caravans any more? Travellers, they called them now; they lived in lorries and clapped-out old vans. But she'd better not put ideas in his head. 'One day we'll go away from here,' she said, 'just you an' me – the two of us.' Then the golden eyes glittered. 'But not till Channon's got whoever done it to your dad!'

Malachi nodded. One day, he thought, things might be all right. One day he'd join the police and spend all his time catching murderers. No – he'd be an MP and make a law that they all had to be hanged, or better still, frizzled to death in the electric chair.

Feeling somewhat better after that decision he took out his reading book. He'd have to be a good reader to get into Parliament.

'The relief of it,' Jim Trudgeon was saying for the third time. 'Ellie's beside herself with grief and I'm relieved!'

The farmer had seen Channon arrive and hurried to meet him, hoping for news, but now the two men were sitting quietly outside the barn, talking about Ellie's belated acceptance of her daughter's death. 'That picture – it's so lovely,' said Trudgeon, shaking his head.

Channon thought of his own son and was swept by fellow feeling. 'As a matter of fact,' he said quietly, 'we've just been having a word with Mr Deacon over at Pengally. He seems to have been fond of Samantha. Did he see much of her?'

'Far from it. We'd never been all that friendly but it was a lot worse in the days when I was making the change to organic. It's hard, you know, the transition; there's years with next to no income until you can meet the conditions of the Soil Association, and what with all the other farmers complaining that I was letting pests and diseases infest the land and encouraging wild life to run riot, we weren't on good terms with any of 'em, let alone Sam Deacon.'

'You didn't speak?'

'Oh, we'd pass the time of day if we saw each other through a hedge or over a wall, but that was about it. Samantha would wave to him and she referred to him as Mr Sam, but she never really knew him. I was amazed when he said he'd taken photographs of her.'

Another theory down the drain, thought Channon. Then he said out loud, 'There's another point, Mr Trudgeon. We know how Samantha spent Friday evening, but we're not quite so well informed about the time between her leaving the school bus and being picked up for the disco at seven o'clock. For my own satisfaction I'd like to follow the path she took as she walked home across the fields. Would it upset you to talk about that for a minute?'

Jim Trudgeon dipped his head and looked at the detective from under his brows. 'Upset me? What does that matter? You can say what you like and do what you like. You can stand on your head or swing through the trees like Tarzan if only you get who did it. As for tracing her steps, you're a long way from where she started out.'

'I know that. I thought I'd walk it in reverse – the same as anyone who might have met her, or maybe watched her as she walked home.'

The farmer's lips tightened, but all he said was: 'If you come with me I'll take you to the highest point on Blue Leaze and show you the way she'd have come. She knows – she knew, I mean – all the rights of way and the short cuts.'

They walked together until from the top of a rise Channon could see the fields dipping and climbing and then falling away to the distant sea. Trudgeon stretched out an arm to encompass the scene and echoed the detective's thoughts. 'It doesn't seem possible, does it, that anything so ugly could have happened in the midst of all this? Now look down to your right, there, Mr Channon. Can you just see the top of a red van? That's on the road the bus would have taken. Samantha would have gone through that tall hedge there and across Blankett's land for about a third of a mile, down the dip to that stream – you see it winding – then up the path there between the crops and the sloping pasture.'

'Where to then?'

'I reckon she'd have cut across that big curving field – you see that grove of trees and the roof of that little white barn? She'd have skirted the trees and gone down on Pengally land for a couple of hundred yards, then back on to Blankett's until she climbed to the hedge here and on to Blue Leaze land through this stile.'

Had Miller been inside the barn? Had somebody watched Samantha from in there? Channon felt his breathing quicken as instinct and intuition stirred. Not before time, either, he told himself. 'Thanks,' he said, 'that's clear enough. I'll be off, then.'

'Shall I come with you?' offered Trudgeon, desperate to help.

'No,' said Channon firmly. 'I just want to clear my mind a bit, that's all. I'll be in touch.' He climbed over the stile and the farmer went back to his work.

Channon trod the ground slowly, deliberately, half his mind in the present, registering each stile and each clump of grass; the other half enmeshed in memory, recalling facial expressions and turns of phrase.

What, asked his more practical side, did he hope to find in this idyllic landscape? Instinct and intuition replied that this was where it had all happened: George had worked out here on the farms; Samantha had known these fields, she lived here, walked here, she'd talked to George here. They were connected, they must be, and not only by what had happened near the Martennis that night. George had been working at Blue Leaze that afternoon. They'd spoken when Samantha went out to see to her hens...

Chisel-like, Channon's memory sculpted pictures of George answering questions. The little man's eyes had been wide, guileless ... too guileless? 'She saw to her fowl like she always did. We talked about her dad getting this award. Proud of it, she was, him being accredited and that.' Had they talked of anything else? Anything that he hadn't mentioned? George had given the impression of being naive, of co-operating with the police, but it was becoming more and more clear that there was a stronger side to him than the one he showed to the world.

Channon walked on, following Samantha's route in reverse. He climbed a stile and saw that he was now on Pengally land. Winter wheat was growing here but the field didn't have such a manicured look as Blankett's and the hedges were in need of tidying. His steps slowed as he noticed a figure beneath an overhanging tree at the far side of the field, a figure in a wide-brimmed hat. Deacon was watching him. Fair enough, it would do no harm for the farmer to know that he, Channon, was still around. On second thoughts, there was one more thing he could ask him, and with a wave he headed for the small, flamboyant figure.

A minute later, deep in thought again, he was treading through bluebells towards the little white barn. It was well maintained (of *course*, he thought), with a metal B emblazoned above the door. Inside it was clean-swept, empty but for a couple of bales of straw beneath a narrow window. He looked out to see the indentations of the public footpath approaching the shed. Had a tramp slept the afternoon away here and seen her coming? Had somebody *hidden* in here and then confronted her? Had she seen Miller here?

Channon sat on a bale thinking about what Samantha might have seen and who she might have met on her walk home. It was silent except for the whisper of a breeze that carried the scent of the bluebells, fresh and green and faintly acid... Conscious that he was in the intuitive state that sometimes led to a breakthrough, Channon stood up and went slowly on his way.

On the path where Miller had passed Samantha and was later seen by Maureen Blankett, he observed her winter wheat and found himself wondering what other crops she grew on her immense stretches of arable land. He spotted two of her men repairing a fence at the far side of the sloping pasture; below them lay the big farmhouse, breathing prosperity and basking in the sun. He kept away from it, having no desire to be given the third degree about how the case was going.

As he approached the final stile he answered the ring of his mobile to find Soker on the line. 'Sir? I've been on to the webmaster at MAFF and he's been pretty helpful. He's got Samantha's enquiry logged and he knows which areas of the site were looked at.'

Staring unseeingly over the stile, Channon listened. 'Well, well, well,' he said, and a minute later, intently, 'well, well, *well!* What time, Soker? What time did she access the website?'

'Four thirty, sir. About an hour and a half before she sent Baxter's e-mail. I hope it's OK, sir, but I've spoken to her chemistry teacher. He said Samantha might well have talked to MAFF. She'd recently finished a special project for her A level course. She told him she chose it because of her dad being into natural farming. He's really cut up about her, sir; he says she was his star pupil. She used to baby-sit for him and his wife.'

'Right, Soker, that's brilliant – thanks a lot. Leave it for now and make yourself available in case Inspector Meade wants you.'

Minutes later, the sun on his face, grey-streaked hair damp against his forehead, Channon emerged from the sunlit field to the shadowed green tunnel of the lane. It seemed an age since he stood on this very spot talking to the chief SOCO in the downpour, yet here beneath his feet were the runnels of earth, now dried, that had been washed down from the fields within hours of George being killed. When had the killer struck? Thirty-six, thirty-eight hours ago?

He recalled Maureen Blankett asking him in out of the rain. She'd offered him tea and they'd had to take off their wet clothes. Then, over the teacups he'd noticed the wry, almost affectionate way she spoke of Sam Deacon. They had chatted together with the lamps lit; a cosy, calm little interlude in his busy day, with the rain battering against the windows as they talked.

Rain ... waterproofs ... clever blue eyes under a black sou'wester. He stood in the lane and once again opened his mind to intuition. After a minute he sat down in the hedge and took out his mobile. 'John? Send Bowles up here to Blankett's, will you, and listen, here's what I want you to do...' After a minute Channon took from his pocket the bundle of interview notes and slowly began to read.

Chapter Twenty-Two

With his customary squeal of brakes Bowles stopped the car, staring in disbelief at the DCI sitting in the hedge like a farm labourer having a break. 'Back to Curdower?' he asked uncertainly.

'Not yet,' answered Channon grimly. 'I want you to stand by while I ruffle a few feathers. I've been too gentle with everybody on this case.' Bowles opened his mouth to agree but Channon's set expression kept him from speaking. Intrigued, he followed the other man past the flower-beds towards the white farmhouse.

'Good morning!' Looking sparklingly clean and efficient in navy trousers and a white shirt Maureen Blankett was coming across the yard holding a clipboard.

Channon nodded affably. 'You've met Sergeant Bowles, I think, Miss Blankett? We'd like a brief word.'

'Of course. How are your investigations going?'

'Slowly,' replied Channon, 'but we're hoping for a breakthrough. Vital information has emerged in the last few hours.'

Bowles kept a straight face. Lying was part of the new tough approach, was it? 'Miss Blankett,' continued the DCI, 'you recall that I said I might walk the route taken by Samantha on the day she was killed?'

'Yes, of course I do. Please feel free to follow the path if that's what you're after.'

'I'm not after it – I've done it. On my way I called at the little white barn where your land joins Pengally and Blue Leaze.'

'Oh? It's hardly a barn as such – I use it more as a storage shed for the odd consignment of cattle-feed supplement and so forth. Is the place significant?'

'Only in that Samantha must have passed it. I wondered if somebody could have been in there watching as she approached. There are several sets of old tyre marks, but I'm thinking more of passing vagrants. Have you ever had anybody like that up there?'

Maureen Blankett at once became deeply attentive. 'We have had the occasional vagrant,' she admitted. 'It isn't always locked because there's nothing of real value there and sometimes a stockman will need to get in. As for tyre marks, they'll be from delivery vans. There's access from the lane so that supplies can be dropped off without having to use the farm's main entrance; access to Sam Deacon's land as well, for that matter.'

'Miss Blankett, I wonder if we could go somewhere private? We have several more questions.'

She looked put out, as if her hospitality was in doubt. 'I'm so sorry, I thought you merely wanted a brief word. I've told you before, Mr Channon, if there's anything I can do, anything at all ... but come into the house. Perhaps you'd both like coffee?'

Channon declined the coffee but accepted a chair, while Bowles hovered curiously, his notebook at the ready. 'I know you've already been asked if you saw anything of George

Gribble the evening before last,' began Channon. 'Obviously he'd been near here as his bike was in your hedge.'

'My man spotted it, as I told you, but *I* didn't see George. Why would he come here late in the evening?'

Channon lifted a finger. 'I didn't specify "late" in the evening. I merely asked if you'd seen him.'

That brought forth a chilly stare. 'I said "late" because it's common talk that he was seen heading away from the village after nine o'clock.'

'Oh, of course. Now let me see... I have an outline of the statement you gave yesterday as one of George's employers. You say he was always agreeable and obliging. Do you still hold to that?'

She frowned in perplexity. 'Of course I hold to it or I wouldn't have said it. What do you mean?'

'He was never awkward or uncooperative? Either recently or in the past?'

There was a silence. 'We might have had a slight difference of opinion at some time, but if so I can't recall it. This is my farm. I give the orders. What I say goes.'

'Absolutely, but I've been told that on at least one occasion you went almost berserk when you thought George was costing you money.'

'Berserk?' She repeated the word as if

she'd never heard it before. 'George always cost me money, Mr Channon, because I paid him a wage – a better wage than he was likely to get on any other farm. Have you been told *that?*'

'Yes, as a matter of fact, I have.'

'I'm glad to hear it. I'm a businesswoman, chief inspector, and quite simply I don't like waste or inefficiency.'

Channon was unperturbed. 'To go back to Friday evening. Can you tell me what you were doing between eleven o'clock and eleven thirty?'

'I'd have been in bed, I suppose. I'm usually asleep by eleven, but I can't be sure to five or ten minutes. What *is* this, Mr Channon? You must be getting desperate.'

'No, not desperate, just a little closer to the truth. Is there anybody who can vouch for you being here at that particular time?'

The skin of Maureen Blankett's temples took on a faint blue tinge, but she gave a rueful laugh. 'Goodness, I feel like a character in a detective novel! No, there's nobody to vouch for me, as you put it. I'm alone here at night. My housekeeper comes in at eight and leaves again at about four. Your men have already questioned the rest of my workers.'

'Yes, apparently they were all elsewhere when Samantha crossed your land.'

'They must have been, because none of

them saw her.'

Channon's voice was now velvet soft. 'She wouldn't have returned in the late afternoon, would she, Miss Blankett? She wouldn't have come back here for any reason after your housekeeper had gone home?'

He almost missed the sudden stretching of her mouth, but one of her canine teeth remained outside her lower lip, like a little fang. It gave her a slightly ludicrous air. 'You mean on Friday? To see me? What on earth for?'

'We know she made no phone calls after she got home, but she did chat to George Gribble sometime after four thirty. I wondered if after that she decided to talk to you about something she'd seen in your barn.'

For long seconds the farmer didn't move, then she leaned forward with interest, one hand cupping her chin. 'Such as what?'

Channon felt a sinking sensation beneath his ribs. He was making a fool of himself; acting on impulse, on his blasted intuition, but it was too late now to retract. Behind her he could see Bowles, wide-eyed and sceptical.

'Such as what?' she repeated.

Channon took a deep breath. 'Such as a toxic pesticide, Miss Blankett? A banned pesticide?'

She gaped at him. 'In my storage barn? On my land? Are you serious? Yes, I do believe you are.' The bright eyes narrowed. 'How dare you? How *dare* you say such a thing? Blanketts have farmed this land for four hundred years.'

'Yes, and you're the first woman to run the farm in her own right.'

Her mouth framed one syllable while her eyes stayed cold and watchful. 'So?'

'So I think Samantha saw something suspicious in your barn – possibly something just delivered. We have reports of an unmarked grey van in the vicinity not long after she left the school bus – she might even have seen it unloading – and when she got home she accessed the MAFF website. She was checking, Miss Blankett, on banned pesticides – a subject on which she had some knowledge. Later she sent an e-mail to somebody who shared her interest in the environment, saying she needed his advice urgently.'

Maureen Blankett swallowed with difficulty, as if her throat was sore. 'Give me one good reason,' she said coolly, 'why I should use a banned pesticide?'

'The first that springs to mind is money. I think that a firm producing, say, a variation on a certain pesticide that was banned or about to be banned, would pay a sizeable fee to have a reputable farmer conduct trials for them. Most farmers in this area have had a bad time recently, they're hard up – yes, maybe even you, in spite of appearances to the contrary. Many farmers have permanent overdrafts, but sometimes the banks dig their heels in, don't they? I assure you we can and we will check your finances, Miss Blankett.

'I think that because of your unique position in the community you wouldn't want it to be known that you of all people were battling with bankruptcy, and so some extra cash would help keep you solvent and protect the family name. But if somebody, even a young girl still at school, should reveal that you were using a banned pesticide you could be prosecuted, couldn't you, and that would drag the name of Blankett through even deeper mire than financial ruin. Now tell me, am I getting close?'

She almost snorted in disgust. 'I've never heard such drivel in my life! And in any case, what has all this to do with Gribble?'

Channon leaned forward and fixed her with his dark gaze. 'On Saturday evening George told his wife he was going up to the farms because he knew where to get some money. There are only three farms on this side of Curdower where he was well known – Pengally, Blue Leaze and here. He wouldn't have expected to be given work at that time in the evening, so I think he came here to try a spot of amateur blackmail.'

'Why here?' she pounced. 'How do you

know he didn't go to Pengally? He could have seen Deacon on the cliff path, he could have seen him killing Samantha. Now that *would* have been a reason for blackmail!'

It was 'Deacon' now, Channon noted, not 'Sam'. 'But what on earth makes you think that Sam Deacon was on the cliff path, Miss Blankett? Or is it that you'd wanted other people to think that he was? No, as I see it Samantha told George what she'd seen; maybe she asked him if he knew anything about it. I certainly think she told him that she was coming over here to talk to you, and he kept the knowledge to himself in case it should come in useful. Then next day, when Samantha had been killed and he himself had been taken in and questioned, he thought about it and decided to go for the blackmail. On you, Miss Blankett.'

Wild, wild supposition, Channon told himself, yet his instincts insisted it was true. This was a battle of wits with a clever old woman, and if he wasn't careful he would lose it. He would have to rattle her so that she dropped her guard.

'And you have proof of all this?' she was asking derisively. 'That spineless little nincompoop coming here to blackmail me? *Me?* You should be writing detective fiction, not trying to solve real life crime. You'll be saying next that I killed him to keep him quiet.'

'Maybe you did – in this very room.' He looked around at the evidence of long-established wealth and privilege. 'Maybe you stabbed him as he was sitting in this very chair.'

'He wasn't sta–'

Channon bent his head to hide triumph. He was right!

'Uh – surely he wasn't stabbed, was he?' she asked hurriedly. 'I thought he was killed outside, in Trudgeon's field.'

'He was killed and *then* taken to the field. In your wheelbarrow.'

She shrugged. 'I told you it was missing, didn't I?'

This was cat and mouse, thought Bowles. Was Channon going to pin her down or wasn't he? The sound of car doors slamming made him look outside, to see five men and a woman, all in uniform, getting out of two police cars.

Channon got to his feet and announced briskly, 'We are about to search your premises, both this house and the farm buildings.'

Bloody hell, thought Bowles, he could move when he felt like it. Maureen Blankett was on her feet, a lock of grey hair falling over one eye. 'Do you think I'm a fool? Where's your search warrant?'

Channon almost smiled. 'Madam, the Criminal Law Act allows us to search the premises of anyone about to be arrested, without the necessity for a warrant.'

'Arrested?' she echoed. 'On what grounds?'

'The murders of Samantha Trudgeon and George Gribble,' replied Channon calmly. To Bowles he said, 'Sergeant, go ahead.'

Bowles tried to look unruffled, though in fact he was seething with resentment at being kept in the dark. Even so, it gave him a kick to let the familiar words of the caution roll off his tongue...

Minutes later two uniformed men were going methodically over the farmhouse and three more were searching the outbuildings; the housekeeper was with several farm-workers in a silent, apprehensive group in the garden and Maureen Blankett was sitting stiffly in her chair, watched over by the policewoman.

Bowles was with Channon in the hall. 'I didn't keep all this to myself deliberately, sergeant,' muttered Channon awkwardly, 'it simply erupted in the last twenty minutes.'

To his own surprise Bowles merely said, 'You're the boss.' His doubts, though, wouldn't be silenced. 'You've said we've no evidence on Deacon, so what the hell have we got on Blankett?'

'Not much,' admitted Channon, 'but even she will have had her work cut out to dispose of a consignment of banned pesti-cide without anybody getting to know about it. Then there's forensic – they can go over this house for traces of George; they might find the ligature used to garrotte him. They might find the knife she used on Samantha.'

It was so weak, so tenuous, that Bowles almost laughed out loud. 'What about Deacon in the hat?' he demanded.

'I think it was Blankett, not Deacon,' Channon told him. 'Only minutes ago in the lane outside I remembered she'd been wearing a black sou'wester when it was pouring with rain yesterday. You might say her wearing it again so soon after that night was a reckless thing to do, but she *was* reckless; there's been a sick kind of bravado in everything she's done. I think she believed she was bright enough to outwit us all. And another thing, after I'd been to Blue Leaze I saw Sam Deacon out in his field and persuaded him to tell me a bit more about the past – I just had a feeling about it.

'He said he'd never admitted it to anybody, not even Will Baldwin, because he'd loved her and wanted to protect her from humiliation, but the truth was that he was the one who broke the engagement. He simply couldn't stand her obsessive pride – he said it frightened him. She's clever; she'd convinced me that she still had a fondness for him, but I think that in fact she's harboured a grudge against him for years. When she felt compelled to commit murder she simply couldn't resist a quick attempt at incriminating him by wearing the hat in case she was seen. In the same way she had seized the chance, when it came, to drop hints to me about him watching Samantha as a child.'

'But had she the strength, the physical strength to kill two people?'

'I think so. She once told me that she never asked any worker to do anything she couldn't do herself. She's wiry and very fit and, most important of all, she had surprise on her side.'

'But she had to lug George's body around, and as for Samantha ... three different attempts before one worked. It must have been strenuous, to say the least, and how did Blankett know where to find her at that hour?'

'I'm hoping we'll get the answer to that when we question her. I suspect she trailed Samantha after the disco but couldn't get to her. In the end she killed her only minutes before Baxter and Miller came on the scene. Miller did catch sight of her, don't forget, though he took her for a man.'

Mentally, Bowles relinquished Miller as a suspect. Seconds later he jettisoned Baxter, but he had one last reservation. 'It was all a bit – a bit audacious, wasn't it? A bit hit-and-miss for an organized old bird like her?'

'As she saw it, there was too much at stake

to mess about, so she went for it. Perhaps taking risks is in her blood – her precious ancestors weren't averse to it, after all.'

'Huh?'

'The Normans, Bowles. William the Conqueror and his men.'

'Oh,' said Bowles in disgust, 'that lot!'

'Sir!' A uniformed constable called from the door. 'Sir – there's a room behind one of the barns, but it's padlocked!'

'Use the cutters!' ordered Channon, following him.

Inside the windowless room were six ten-kilo sacks: innocent, innocuous, unmarked except for a black label on each bearing a chemical formula in very small print. 'Don't touch!' warned Channon. 'Bring Miss Blankett here.'

When she arrived Maureen Blankett no longer looked sparklingly clean and efficient. She looked grey and faded and very old. She glanced bleakly at the sacks and then turned her gaze on Channon. 'I underestimated you,' she said faintly, as if she could hardly believe her own lapse of judgement. Then she wafted a hand in the direction of the workers waiting in the garden. 'They know nothing. They're used to me giving orders that they don't always understand or agree with. They were never exposed to anything toxic. I did it all myself.'

'I'll bear that in mind,' Channon said

gravely. To Bowles he said briskly, 'Take her in!'

'So your guesses were all correct, chief inspector!' Maureen Blankett glanced at the tape, as if to make sure her words of praise were being recorded for posterity. Once in the incident room in Truro she had regained her composure and appeared faintly amused by all the meticulous questioning.

'They weren't guesses, they were deductions,' said Channon, who was in no mood to receive compliments from a woman who had committed two savage murders. Already she had refused a legal representative and he was beginning to suspect she was angling for a plea of unsound mind.

'Wasn't it a somewhat drastic way of raising money?' he asked quietly. 'Using toxic pesticide that might have damaged not only the environment, but you as well?'

'Huh!' She waved a hand dismissively. 'I've used them for years, chief inspector, until the interfering busybodies frightened everybody to death. Why do you think the manufacturers approached me? Because they knew me – I was one of their biggest customers. How do you think I came to have the best yield of crops in the county?'

'Are you blaming your financial difficulties on not being able to use pesticides?' he asked in amazement.

'Not altogether. I lost money – a lot of money – in the fiasco over BSE. What a fuss about nothing! Do the public really believe that other countries never cut corners on animal feed? Not that I did cut corners, not knowingly. I was let down by the feed producers. That said, the fact remains that raising beef cattle is a business. Treat animals like people and you'll never make a penny out of them. Jim Trudgeon will find that out sooner or later.

'You'll see – the people of this country will get tired of paying top price for this so-called organic stuff. When the novelty wears off they'll be after their cut-price meat and eggs and vegetables, but by then a lot of farmers will have gone to the wall. I didn't intend going to the wall – that's the difference between the lesser fry and me. My bank manager had turned awkward – no doubt under orders from somebody who hasn't the faintest idea of what farming is all about. I was facing ruin – complete ruin. That's why I had no option but to silence that interfering young woman so that I could conduct my trials and get paid for it – well paid.' Maureen Blankett gave a rueful little smile. 'But for you, Mr Channon, I'd soon have been solvent again.'

At the DCI's side Bowles was baffled by her attitude. In his experience killers didn't just sit there and admit to everything as if they were proud of it. He asked in puzzlement, 'Did you really believe you could get away with it?'

She shrugged. 'I'm used to taking my decisions quickly. I simply didn't consider failure.'

The sergeant chewed his lip. 'It was all a bit hit-and-miss, though, wasn't it?'

'It was impromptu,' she corrected, 'it was daring. There wasn't the time for detailed planning. I'd seen Samantha walking home along the path and I knew she would pass the barn, but the delivery wasn't due until four thirty. Then within minutes I spotted the top of the van as it turned out of the lane and knew it must have delivered its load. At once I took a tractor and moved the sacks, so that if she'd spotted them it would simply have been her word against mine. I was too late, as I soon found out.'

'But how did you know she wouldn't spill the beans to somebody else after you'd talked?'

'I didn't, I simply tried to persuade her otherwise. I told her that if she kept quiet about it until her father returned we would talk about it with him and at the same time discuss something very important that he'd mentioned to me a few days earlier.' Maureen Blankett's lips twisted in scorn. 'It was almost as if he'd guessed that I was desperate for money, because he'd asked to buy some of my land – Blankett land. What a fool! Naturally, Samantha thought that I was going to relent and let him have it. So I took the chance, sergeant, I seized the day!'

Channon cut short the self-congratulation. 'You've told us how you trailed Samantha,' he said carefully, 'and how George was sitting waiting for a glass of sherry when you throttled him, but tell me, was there any attempt on your part to discredit Mr Deacon?'

'Yes,' she said, shrugging, 'but only as a side issue. Sam Deacon was an amorous fool who prevented me from becoming the biggest landowner in the Roseland and I've never forgiven him for it. *He* broke off our engagement – imagine it! I made the decision to silence Samantha and as I left the house to find her I caught sight of the hat. I turned down the brim and wore it throughout.'

'One last point. Why, *why* the scarecrow?'

The blue eyes became cold as steel. 'That slow-witted little lecher tried to threaten me. *Me!* The scarecrow was appropriate, that's all.'

'Lecher?' repeated Bowles.

'Yes, lecher. I've told you I was trailing Samantha and I heard young Baxter protesting to her about her relationship with his father. Oh yes, there were two eavesdroppers on that little conversation, it was like a theatrical farce. Then I watched her go indoors and saw which light came on as she got to her room. I waited until the light went off and was about to go in and silence her for good when she came out again. When I saw what she allowed Gribble to do to her, I was repelled. It seems to me the whole country – the whole world is obsessed with sex and he was no exception. He was a lecherous dimwit and she was a promiscuous, clever, but fatally over-confident young woman. They threatened my position, both of them.'

'The scarecrow,' Channon reminded her.

'I'm coming to that. I'd often seen Trudgeon's turnip-headed object flapping around while his much-vaunted crops were being eaten by birds and pests and vermin. It simply struck me as fitting to put Gribble there instead – one useless dummy replaced by another. Heavy rain was forecast; it was ten thirty at night and everywhere was deserted. Moving weights around is no problem to me; it's merely a question of distribution and leverage. I've practised it for years, and in any case I'm as strong as any man.'

Channon fought down disbelief at her total lack of remorse. He couldn't wait to get away from her and stood up, ready to switch off the recorder. 'In a few minutes you will be given a copy of the charges against you, Miss Blankett. You will read them and sign them. We will oppose bail. In view of your full confession, the charges will lead inevitably to conviction. Is that quite clear?'

He watched as the crisp, confident woman was replaced, maybe for ever, by the grey old lady who had surveyed her bags of pesticide. Even the eyes became dull. She didn't speak – it was as if she couldn't think of suitable words. She simply nodded and lowered her head as the two detectives left the room.

Chapter Twenty-Three

'We'll provide transport to Truro station, Mr Miller,' said Channon.

The man leaving the cell stared at the DCI and the custody sergeant behind him. 'I'm supposed to be grateful for that, am I?'

Channon shook his head wearily as they all walked to the desk to pick up Miller's belongings. 'We've only done what's required of us, what's expected. If you'd been more forthcoming it might have speeded things up a bit, because your information did help. As it is, you're free to go as from now. There's a car waiting.'

'So who've you charged? The big fair fella

with glasses?'

'I'm not at liberty to say,' answered Channon. 'Goodbye, Mr Miller.'

The pale green eyes were swivelling from side to side, looking for Bowles in order to deliver a last cutting gibe, but the sergeant was keeping well out of the way as his number one suspect was released from custody.

With Miller gone Channon took in a long deep breath and sank into a nearby chair. Now for Baxter, he thought. The custody sergeant was waiting to go back to the cells with him, but Channon raised a delaying hand and wiggled his fingers. Some perverse impulse was urging him to inflict a few more minutes of custody on Sally Baxter's husband. 'Give me a little while, sergeant,' he said. He'd expected to feel good, euphoric, but there was none of the elation that usually came with the solving of a case. He wanted to ring Sally Baxter to tell her that her husband was being released; the temptation to do it was so strong he could almost taste it.

No – he would treat her no differently than any other wife of a suspect. He would tell Baxter he was free to go and he could tell his wife himself. Nodding an unwilling acceptance of the decision he got to his feet and was confronted by Bowles, who was shuffling his feet uncomfortably. 'Sir, before you get embroiled with Papa Baxter I'd like to – well – what I mean is…'

Channon ran a hand through his hair. 'Something on your mind, sergeant?'

Bowles told himself there was a first time for everything, even this. 'Yes. I just want to say, congratulations.'

'Well, thank you, Bowles, and thanks for all your help. Has John Meade sent everybody home?'

'Yes, they've all been thanked and they're highly delighted. The other thing I want to say is – I know you and I haven't always looked at things from the same angle, but when your next big case comes up I'd appreciate it if you asked for me.'

Channon almost smiled. 'Maybe we have something in common after all, Bowles?'

'Maybe we do,' agreed the sergeant.

'Come on then, we'll go and let Baxter off the hook.' At that moment the main doors opened and Sally Baxter rushed in. 'Mrs Baxter!' exclaimed Channon, 'we're just about to release your husband.'

'He's still here, then? Can I see him?'

'Of course you can, but first perhaps I should give him the news officially?'

'Right,' she said. 'Thank you.'

Then for what he told himself was the very last time on this case, Channon followed instinct rather than protocol. 'Sergeant,' he said quietly, 'would you excuse us for a moment?'

Bowles looked from one to the other, re-frained from raising his eyebrows, muttered something under his breath and strolled away.

With relief Sally watched him go. She didn't like him, but she supposed that didn't mean he wasn't good at his job. Around them was the noise and bustle of the station, but Channon himself was very still, very quiet.

'Zennie and Malachi have just told us that you've arrested somebody, Mr Channon. She says it's the talk of the village. Is it true?'

'Yes,' he said, 'we've actually charged somebody, though I can't confirm who it is at this stage. Brief details will be on the news bulletins on TV and radio. Mrs Baxter, I want to say I'm very pleased that it's not your husband.'

'You asked me to trust you,' she whis-pered, 'and I did.'

'I know,' he said. 'Thank you.' He held out his hand. 'I'll say goodbye, then.'

Sally told herself that all they ever seemed to do when they met was shake hands and thank each other. His grip was firm and warm and comforting; she didn't want to relinquish it but she edged her hand from his. 'I'll wait here until you've told him, shall I? There's just one more thing. You – you might be wondering what's going to happen now with the family?'

'Yes,' he answered gently, 'I'm wondering.'

'The thing is, I can't forgive Rob for not supporting Luke,' she said painfully, 'for not even trying to protect him. I might have tried to cope with the other thing – Samantha – but I can't accept the way he's let down our son. I have no idea how we'll work it out or what we'll do, I only know I don't want to live with him any more.' There, it was said – all she had to do now was tell Rob himself. She felt hot and slightly sick and wondered if she was mad, babbling about her personal affairs to Channon.

For the last time she looked into his eyes. No, she wasn't mad. He'd wanted to know. He cared.

'Thank you for telling me,' he said quietly. 'Goodbye, Mrs Baxter.'

She didn't reply. She simply leaned against the wall and watched him go.

They faced each other: Rob blinking uncertainly and gnawing his lips, Sally completely exhausted. She was stunned by the change in him; he seemed to have lost weight in a matter of hours. The red-rimmed eyes avoided hers. 'Good news,' he said politely, 'I mean about them catching the murderer. Do you know who it is?'

'Everybody's saying it's Maureen Blankett.'

He showed no surprise, no reaction. She

couldn't tell if it had even registered. All at once he groaned, 'Sally, what are we going to do?'

'You mean about the future? Our future?'

'I want everything to be like it used to be,' he said desperately. 'I've told you I'm sorry and I meant it. Some sort of madness came over me with Samantha.'

'She was the same age as Luke. What were you trying to prove? That you were still young and virile? That you could out-perform the teenage boys? "Talk about the difference between the man and the boys," that was what she said, wasn't it? The difference? Of *course* there was a difference. You were experienced, you'd had years of practice – *on me* – and maybe on a string of other girls that I knew nothing about.'

'No, she was the only one.' Shaking his head, he leaned forward with his hands flat on the table.

Sally looked down at them, the big, clean, competent hands that she'd always loved. Those hands had stroked her, caressed her, touched her secret, most intimate places. She looked at his mouth, at the lips that had kissed hers with wild, sweet passion, that had kissed her breasts, her whole body. Loss and regret swept through her – regret for what used to be between them, for what he had so readily tossed aside.

In the silence it came to her that she felt

bereaved, because surely bereavement was pain and loss and a kind of abandonment. Why, why had she ever thought, why had she ever told Channon that she might have been able to cope with it? She would tell Rob this instant what she'd decided and then she would go.

Before she could speak he asked, 'Do Tessa and Ben know about me and Samantha?'

She shook her head. 'Only Tessa.'

'Did you tell her?'

'Of course I didn't. She was questioning Luke. She'd worked out that the police thought you'd had a relationship with Samantha. She said they were fools to think that her daddy would do such a thing. Luke lost his cool and told her the truth. For the record I've assured her that you're sorry and that you love her as much as you ever did.'

'I can't face them,' he said flatly.

'You faced Luke easily enough,' she pointed out. 'He told me what you said to him.'

'That was before you knew – when I was still petrified you'd find out.'

'It wasn't before he'd been questioned by Channon. It wasn't before he'd kept it secret for ages so I wouldn't be hurt. God above, he's not eighteen yet but he comes out of it with more credit than you do! I don't want you to come back with me, Rob. I can't live with you any longer, and even if I could,

Luke says he'll leave home if you're going to be there. He'll have to be at home to take his A levels, so I suggest you move out.'

'For good?'

'I don't know,' she said wearily, 'I simply don't know. We'll have to see the summer through at the roundhouse, what with the three of them at school and the cottages being let.'

'I'll move out,' he agreed, and she thought she could hear relief there. Relief at not having to face his children? Relief at being away from recrimination? 'I won't come back for my things just yet,' he said. 'I'll get my computers and stuff from the police and stay in a hotel until I can find a place to rent. We'll take it from there, shall we?'

Evidently this was no surprise to him, no shock – he'd thought it through and prepared himself. 'Yes,' she agreed, 'we'll tell the children it's a temporary measure. We'll tell everybody it's temporary.'

'Will it be, Sal? Will it be temporary?'

'I don't know,' she said. 'Let's take it a day at a time.' A day, a week, a month, a year … a lot could happen in a year, she thought.

They parted without touching, without even looking at each other. There was nothing left for Sally to do except walk out of the station and go to her car. She felt drained and empty as she drove towards Curdower and when she reached the first house she told herself that it would never be the same village again. Blue Leaze and the Trudgeons would never be the same again without Samantha, Zennie and Malachi would never be the same again without Georgie, though it seemed that strange, beautiful Zennie might possibly become closer to her son.

And what of Maureen Blankett, the cause of all this upheaval? Was she even now being analysed in some psychiatric hospital? Was she sitting in a cell in Truro, reflecting on what she'd done, justifying it to herself? Was she still proud of a family name that would soon be synonymous with murder?

Sally drove down the lane to Curdower beach and the roundhouse thinking that she didn't know the answer to any of those questions. She didn't know what she was going to tell Ben, she simply didn't know. All she did know was that her children were safe. They were safe and their father still loved them. That would have to be enough for now.

The publishers hope that this book has given you enjoyable reading. Large Print Books are especially designed to be as easy to see and hold as possible. If you wish a complete list of our books please ask at your local library or write directly to:

Magna Large Print Books
Magna House, Long Preston,
Skipton, North Yorkshire.
BD23 4ND